RANDY DIRTY WIVES

TAD HOLINGHURST

Safe Sex is essential: your very life may depend on it. Please remember that some of the sexual practices that are featured in this work of fiction (written in an era that pre-dates lethal STDs) are dangerous and they are not recommended or in any way endorsed by the publishers; by the same token, we do not condone any form of non-consensual sex for any reason: it is reprehensible and illegal and should never become a part of a person's real life: rather it should remain firmly in the realm of sexual fantasy.

Ranchers' Dirty Wives
Past Venus Press
London 2005

Past Venus Press
is an imprint of
THE *Erotic* Print Society
EPS, 1st Floor, 17 Harwood Road,
LONDON SW6 4QP

Tel (UK only): 0871 7110 134
Email: eros@eroticprints.org
Web: www.eroticprints.org

© 2005 MacHo Ltd, London UK

ISBN : 1-904989-07-1

Printed and bound in Spain by BookPrint S.L., Barcelona

No part of this publication may be reproduced by any means without the express written permission of the Publishers. The moral right of the author of the text and the artists has been asserted.

While every effort has been made by PVP to contact copyright holders it may not have been possible to get in touch with certain publishers or authors of former editions of some of the titles published in this series.

RANCHERS' DIRTY WIVES

TAD HOLINGHURST

*E*PS

Prelude

The elegant young woman lay diagonally across the black satin sheets of the big bed, naked as the day she was born, her gorgeous auburn hair spread around her head like a flaming halo. But Vivienne Lanier was feeling anything but saintly. She raised herself and, leaning on her elbows, hands folded under her chin, looked up at the dark haired man as he pulled on his boots, getting ready to go. It was always this way: they would have sex and then he would leave. She gave him a cool, appraising look. He wasn't going to win any handsome prizes, true: slender and wiry, with a weaselly, ratty kind of face and that stupid little moustache that she'd told him a hundred times to shave off. Damn! Just my luck to find one who got whooped with the ugly stick, she thought. But Rex Reed was going places; he would be rich one day, very rich. And she was going to be his side then and share in his… success. Her plans most definitely included a rich husband and never having to work another day in her life – even if most of her 'work' was on her back these days. Viv knew that Rex would be a hard man to lasso – "Every man is born free and equal. If he gets married, hell that's his fault,"

Rex was fond of saying, with a nasty grin. Viv would have her work cut out for her, that was for sure.

But it wasn't only Rex's looks or ambition that bothered Viv: there was something dangerous about the guy: those hypnotic eyes, the sharp features that matched his natty attire. Ever since his employers had been killed nearly a year ago when their truck had overturned, under peculiar circumstances, in a small creek on the north range of the *Lazy Q*, Viv had had a niggling doubt as to Rex's involvement. The sheriff had guessed some sort of foul play, but as Rex really had no obvious motive, he was never a true suspect, and besides, it was the sort of accident that couldn't really be proved one way or another. Rex had seemed genuinely upset about the deaths of the Sanchez father and son who had treated him so well for the five years he had worked for them. Alice McCluskie, old man Sanchez's daughter, had unexpectedly inherited the ranch and she wasn't real interested in running the show. She had her own problems. Viv wondered idly what Rex had in mind for the heiress to the *Lazy Q*.

But just for now it seemed that even running the biggest ranch for miles around wasn't enough to keep her ruthless lover happy, even though he had been given a free hand by Alice, who just wanted the income from the yearly sale of cattle. He was an excellent ranch manager; the hands looked up to him and he was popular enough, even though he ran a tight operation.

These days Rex was obsessed by acquiring still more land to make the *Lazy Q* even bigger, to make the part he played in the county even more powerful than it already was. To this end, he had already hinted at dark plan in which she would have a starring role. It wouldn't be the first time that he'd used her body to get his own way. The county sheriff, the mayor and the local senator had all enjoyed Viv's physical charms with varying degrees of intimacy. What difference would one more make, she thought bitterly.

She scrambled off the bed to light the cigar that Rex had just stuck in the corner of his mouth. He drew hard, creating clouds of pungent smoke, blowing a stream in her face; Viv pretended to love it, although she couldn't help coughing a little.

"Bye honey, you be sure and keep that bed all nice and warm for me."

"Bye, darlin'," she cooed. "You know you can always get down and cool the seat of your saddle here…"

He laughed, a deep, rich laugh for so slim a man, jammed the pale Stetson on his head and left for his office.

PART I

Chapter 1

"Let her go!" Danny yelled.

His elder brothers opened the chute, and the colt under Danny bolted into the corral. A grin split Hank's broad, handsome face and Seth squinted through the swirling dust as the bronco bucked furiously. The twenty-year-old rider clutched the reins with one hand, his other waving jerkily in the air. He bounced in the saddle.

"Danny! Oh my God, you'll get hurt! Stop it!"

Seth shifted his gaze to his brother's new bride who was screaming and jumping up and down in alarm. Beneath her fancy Western shirt, Billy Jo's breasts bobbed erotically, sending ripples through the shimmering, cream-colored satin. Her corn-coloured hair glistened in the bright sunshine as she tossed her head. Lust uncoiled like a snake in Seth's loins.

"Hang on, Danny boy!" Hank shouted. "You've almost got her made!"

Seth kept watching Billy Jo. He didn't see his kid brother glance around in search of his bride's admiring eyes. Seth also missed the bronco's vicious buck which sent Danny hurtling from the saddle.

When Billy Jo let out a shriek and began scrambling up the heavy rail fence into the corral, the rangy twenty-six-year-old glanced briefly at his brother who lay writhing in the dust, then returned his attention to Billy Jo. He mentally stripped the tight pants from her full, seductive bottom as she went over the top rail and dropped to the dusty floor of the corral.

"Look out for that bastard horse!" Hank, who was ahead of her, yelled. He delayed giving aid to his brother long enough to grasp Billy Jo's arm, jerking her out of the berserk horse's path.

"Oh, see about Danny!" Billy Jo wailed urgently. "Is he badly hurt?"

"Hell no!" Hank snorted. "He just got bruised some."

He moved to his brother's side and squatted. The handsome dark-haired youth lay grimacing in pain, clutching a leg that was stiffly extended.

"You all right?" Hank asked.

"I think my leg's busted!" Danny moaned. "It hurts like hell!"

"Oh, no! My poor baby," murmured Billy Jo as she leaned over her fallen husband.

Seth ambled up behind the curvaceous blonde. Her pants were so tight that the

Ranchers' Dirty Wives ★ 11

crotch seam and leg elastics of her panties made imprints in the thin cloth. Seth imagined wedging his stiff prick into the softness of her upturned ass.

"Help me carry him to the house," blond-haired Hank said to his dark, wiry brother.

"Let him lie," Seth replied. "In case something's busted, he shouldn't be moved."

"Well, we can't just leave him here!" Billy Jo protested.

"Get that horse back in the stable," Seth snapped at Hank. "I'll call Doc Carpenter."

Danny was whimpering and screwing up his face as he gingerly touched his stiff leg.

"Oh, darling... darling..." Billy Jo sobbed, caressing his dust-streaked, sweating cheeks.

"That'll teach the little shit to show off!" Seth snorted to Hank as he ambled toward the corral fence.

"You know, you can be God damned mean sometimes," his robust younger brother replied. But there was a twinkle of grudging admiration in Hank's eyes. He turned to capture the horse that had trotted to the opposite side of the enclosure.

"They're getting someone to help you, honey," Billy Jo said as she continued soothing her injured husband. "Just try to lie easy."

"Did you... see me up there?" Danny asked, bright pride flashing in his pain-racked eyes for a second. "I was... really riding that sonofabitch. I would've broken him too... if I just hadn't... looked around."

"Don't try to talk," Billy Jo implored, clutching her young husband's head to her firmly resilient breasts. "Everything will be all right. Oh, how long will it take that doctor to get here?"

* * *

As the ambulance pulled away from the white frame house at *Los Altos* Ranch and headed down the long driveway to the road, Billy Jo turned disconsolately toward the porch.

"He'll be okay," Gus McCluskie said, slipping his arm around her slender waist. "My sons are made of rugged stuff, all of 'em."

The pretty blonde smiled bravely at her new father-in-law. She had liked old Gus from the first, more than Danny's brothers. He had all of her young husband's charm, though she sensed a lonliness and suffering that she put down to his separation with Alice, his younger wife. Seth was the strong silent type, not unfriendly, but definitely not a natural conversationalist either. Hank was more friendly, but a little immature. He was always flirting or making suggestive remarks that sounded a little silly to Billy Jo. Danny was so unlike either of them.

The big silver-haired man clomped heavily onto the porch and opened the creaking screen door. He held it, giving Billy Jo a reassuring, crinkly-eyed smile as she preceded him into the house. Seth and Hank followed their father.

"I wonder if Danny will have to stay in the hospital," Billy Jo said as she settled into a chair in the living room.

"That depends on the X-rays, I reckon," Gus replied. "One thing's for sure – he's going to be laid up for a spell."

"That'll be kind of hard on you, huh Billy Jo?" Hank asked. "I mean, you two being newlyweds and all." He couldn't suppress a slight smirk.

"Dry up!" Gus snapped. Billy Jo merely raised her eyebrows and gave him a long-suffering look. "You and Seth hightail it outa here and go tend to your chores."

"We ain't got nothing to do right now," Hank said.

"Come on, you heard the old man," Seth put in, heading for the door.

"Yeah, but…"

Seth gave his younger brother a poke in the ribs. Hank glanced at Billy Jo, then turned and followed Seth out of the house.

"Don't take this too hard, honey," Gus advised as he pulled out his pipe and began filling it. "Accidents happen. It may not amount to much of anything at all."

"I hope it doesn't. I don't know why the doctor wouldn't let me ride into town with them."

"Cause there's nothing you could do." Gus lit his pipe and expelled a cloud of smoke, bluish in the broad shafts of sunlight that penetrated the room. "We'll be hearing pretty soon. Let me go tell Rosita to listen out for the phone."

As the elder McCluskie left the room to seek the pretty young Mexican housekeeper, Billy Jo lapsed into a reverie which carried her back exactly one week to her wedding night. Though she and Danny had engaged in intercourse daily since then, it was the first night that stuck in Billy Jo's mind.

* * *

Billy Jo Fell had been born the wrong side of the tracks. Abandoned by her feckless parents when she was no more than a baby, she had been in and out of institutions – some good, some bad – nearly all of her short life. Inevitably she had learned all about sex early on, learned to enjoy it, too, and discover a sensual nature in herself that she could only control with some difficulty. But what Billy Jo had always longed for what she had never had: the security of a big family, a simple country home, far away from the grime and squalor of big city living. Sort of like 'The Waltons', only with more sex. Much more sex. So when she took a job as shop girl in Mulberry, the small town close to the McCluskie's ranch *Los Altos*, and Danny, the second youngest and best looking of the four McCluskie boys, walked into the shop one day and fell for her irresistible charm and beauty, it looked as though all of her dreams were being fulfilled at once. In fact, life on a ranch with a big adoptive family was more than she had ever dreamt of, and she had accepted Danny's proposal that they get married as soon as possible with something close to ecstatic joy.

During the first day of their honeymoon, Billy Jo suffered growing apprehension. Would Danny, whom she guessed was something of an innocent country boy, become disillusioned if he suspected her lurid past? The bedroom light in the honeymoon suite of *Mon Plaisir*, the 'luxury hotel' in Branson, was finally turned out and Danny approached the bed. Billy Jo had made up her mind. She would play the innocent young virgin to the hilt. She chuckled inwardly at the inappropriate pun. But it was the only way she could think of not to spoil her husband's almost certainly over-idealistic view of her.

Besides, she really did want their love to be pure and... special. Not like the last

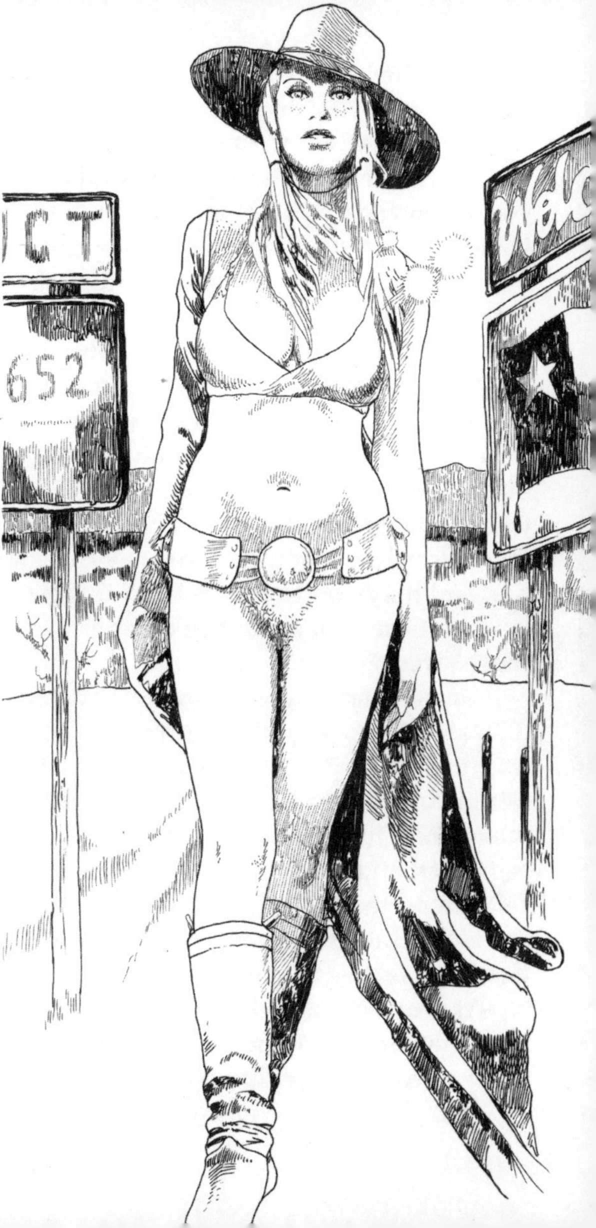
CT
652

time she had sex. Oh god, she had needed it so bad. Jake and his four hippy friends had 'shared' her when the other girls in the little commune had left for a couple of days. Billy Jo had never known that such bad, bad sex could be so very, very good. She had taken everyone's cock in her mouth, her ass, her cunt at least once in those few days. She had tried and, for the most part, loved, every single permutation of sexual intercourse that was possible with five horny men. And then it became just too much. That old sense of self-disgust, of longing to reclaim her self-respect came flooding back. It was time to get her few belongings together, catch the Greyhound bus and move on to another town. That little home on the range still beckoned to her, now more strongly than ever.

As she waited alone in bed, she wondered if Danny's cock would turn out to be as impressive as it had seemed when she had felt his urgent swelling through his tight jeans while they had kissed and petted. She loved big cocks and, as far as she had been able to tell, his certainly fit the bill. A little tense and anxious, Billy Jo waited to find out whether her hope or her fear would be fulfilled.

As soon as Danny had removed his robe he slid into bed beside her. Billy Jo was secretly amused to discover that he was naked.

"Oh Danny... wh-where are your

pajamas?" she asked tremulously.

"I don't have any," her bridegroom responded with a chuckle. "And you don't need this thing, either."

Passing his hand quickly across the front of Billy Jo's nightgown and thrilling her as he rolled her full, firm breasts, Danny immediately began sliding the nightie off her smooth shoulders.

"No!" she exclaimed, clutching the diaphanous fabric.

"What do you mean 'no'? Honey, we're going to make love. We can't do that with no nightgown in the way."

"Danny, I'm so afraid!" she blurted.

His hands withdrew and he gazed intently at her shadowy face. "Afraid? Of what?"

"Of... of you... of your thing... of... sex!"

"Aaaw, baby! There's nothing to be afraid of." He snuggled into her neck and resumed stroking her titties through the sheer nightgown. "I'm the same guy you've been dating all these weeks."

"Yes, but... we've never been like this before, without our clothes on and – "

Billy Jo stopped talking and sucked in her breath. Danny had shifted his lower body against her, and she felt the thrilling hardness of his penis. It was like a huge club lying across her thigh. Billy Jo heaved an inward sigh of relief.

Ranchers' Dirty Wives ★ 19

"What's the matter?" Danny asked as he cuddled her.

"Your... your thing!"

He chuckled softly against her ear. "You mean this?" He flexed his erection against her thigh.

"Danny!"

"It's pretty hard, ain't it?" His voice had grown husky. "That's cause I want you so."

"Oh... but it's so... big! It'll hurt me!" Billy Jo said.

"Maybe a little bit, the first time. But you'll get over that right away. Come on... let me feel you up. Then you'll want to screw just as much as I do."

"Danny, don't talk dirty!"

"It ain't dirty to say screw," the youth replied indignantly. "What do you want me to call it? There's a worse word I could've used."

"Daniel McCluskie, don't you *dare!*"

Danny sat up, the covers skidding to his waist. He stared down at his lovely, shivering bride. "Now look – we're married, honey. I let you put me off all the time we was goin' together, but now things are different. I'm your husband, and I've got a right to make love to you. I realize how girls are... when they're cherry and all – they've got to be treated gentle. Well, I'm goin' to treat you just as nice as I can. But we're goin' to make it, Billy Jo, so there's no sense our bein' silly about it."

Billy Jo realised that she was already very aroused. The wetness had started to seep out of her cunt and soon she was going to blow her 'cover' of an innocent, apprehensive newlywed. She began to struggle against him as if she wanted to get out of bed altogether.

Hurt and angered, the young bridegroom responded in just the way that Billy Jo had hoped he would. Forcibly pressing her against the mattress, he scrambled atop her. As if panic-stricken, Billy Jo attempted to claw or slap him, but Danny managed to catch her wrists and pin them against the bed.

Glaring down, breathing hard, his dark chestnut hair hanging across his face, the man Billy Jo had fallen in love with seemed to have turned into a monster. He let go of one of her arms long enough to grasp the top of her nightgown. Yanking viciously, he split the filmy garment down the front. As Billy Jo squealed and writhed, the torn edges of fine cotton flew away from her heaving chest. Her bobbing, round tits were exposed, her large coral nipples sticking up stiffly.

"Baby... aaw, baby!" Danny groaned, pressing his open mouth to one of the creamy pink-tipped mounds.

Billy Jo gasped as her husband's tongue swabbed moistly across her sensitive nipple.

He caught the thrusting bud between his lips and tugged at the firm, rubbery protrusion, stretching her pliant breast upward. His lips slid against the pebbled flesh of her areola and onto the silken surrounding skin. Then, pulling as much of her titty into his mouth as he could hold, he bathed her erect, tingling nipple in his saliva as his tongue repeatedly stroked the small knot of erectile tissue, gliding and twirling.

Billy Jo's senses reeled. Now her cunt was not only wet, but there was an almost overwhelming desire for it to be filled by her eager husband's long, hard cock. She felt electric shivers of lust that coursed from the hairy gash between her legs to the twin peaks of exquisite sensation that were her breasts, currently the objects of so much attention. She panted, her firm young breast flesh quivering against her husband's mouth. He wrapped a hand around her other breast and squeezed. Her nipple tingled excitingly against his palm. She was acutely aware of Danny's deliciously thick, hard rod sandwiched between their bellies.

Danny lifted his head and gave her a warm smile. "I'm sorry about tearing your nightie," he said. "But we've got to do this right." His eyes stroked down to her breasts. "You're so pretty. Gosh, honey, I love you!"

He sealed his lips to hers. Danny's

churning tongue filled her mouth, caressing her tongue and the silken inner walls of her cheeks. His hand surrounded a breast and squeezed rhythmically, making the sensitive flesh throb.

Billy Jo was hard pressed to maintain her act. It had been simply upstaged by a surge of passion stronger than anything she had ever imagined. As Danny pulled up her nightgown, his cock trailing a thick, clear pre-ejaculate liquid over her bare stomach, she felt her nerves drew taut. Her eyes stared up at him in the dimness, wide with lust and wonder. It felt almost as if she really were about to be deflowered for the very first time.

Danny rolled off her, and Billy Jo relaxed slightly. But when his hand glided down across her smooth, shivery belly and onto the hairy, puffed softness between her legs, she gasped in response. Danny smiled, though there was a tension in his features as he fingered her swollen sex petals apart and probed a questing finger into her moist, slippery cleft.

"Heck, you're ready, sweetheart," her bridegroom said exultantly. "You want it. You really *want* it!"

"No! Oh, I don't know *what* I want!" she said, as if she were confused.

"I do. You want what I've got for you. Feel it."

Danny grasped her hand and carried it to his quivering, upthrust prick. Billy Jo's fingers curled appreciatively around the thick, warm column. She was amazed by its bonelike hardness, and her lust suddenly surged to even greater heights.

"You'll hurt me with that!" she exclaimed, trying to keep the excitement out of her voice. "Danny…"

"Come on," he said thickly. "It's time."

Danny slid between her full, firm thighs, pressing them wide apart. The tip of his penis probed for the opening in Billy Jo's soft, wet cunt. She held her breath. Her heart was thumping like a kettle drum. In a few seconds, she would be a virgin no more, she almost convinced herself.

Danny pushed in.

She bit her lip to stifle the shriek that welled up in her throat at the imaginary pain of her hymen being ripped to shreds. Her eyes glazed with real tears. While the pain might have been feigned, the emotions she felt were real and deep.

Although the pain of defloration may have been imagined, Billy Jo certainly felt a shocking sense of fullness.

"It's in!" Danny exclaimed, breathing hard. "Baby, it's in you!"

Billy Jo gave what she hoped was a moan of discomfort.

Danny started pulling and thrusting… jabbing… burrowing… wedging his hard cock deeper and deeper into Billy Jo's reluctantly yielding slit. The sensations that she felt were amazing. There was only pleasure. How could she pretend otherwise? How long would she have to keep up this charade? She wanted to let out a great whoop of joy, but she was still holding her breath, letting only enough air in and out to keep her lungs functioning.

But as Danny's massive rigidity tore ever more deeply into her belly, bringing yet more pleasurable sensations, Billy Jo began gradually to relax. The slight discomfort at the mouth of her vagina, though aggravated by the friction of his shaft, was the sort that she had only previously experienced with really big cocks. With relaxation Billy Jo allowed herself her first voluptuous response to the cock stroking inside her, going so deep. She writhed and let out a little moan of lust. She resumed active breathing, though her breaths were heavy and uneven.

"Unnh... oh... oh God, that's good!" Danny panted.

"Yes... yesss." She closed her eyes and twisted her lips. Almost of their own accord, her hips started moving with his.

The sheathing snugness of his bride's tight pussy, now bobbing jerkily around his fast-stroking shaft, gave Danny such intense stimulation that, despite valiant efforts not to succumb to his natural desires, he couldn't

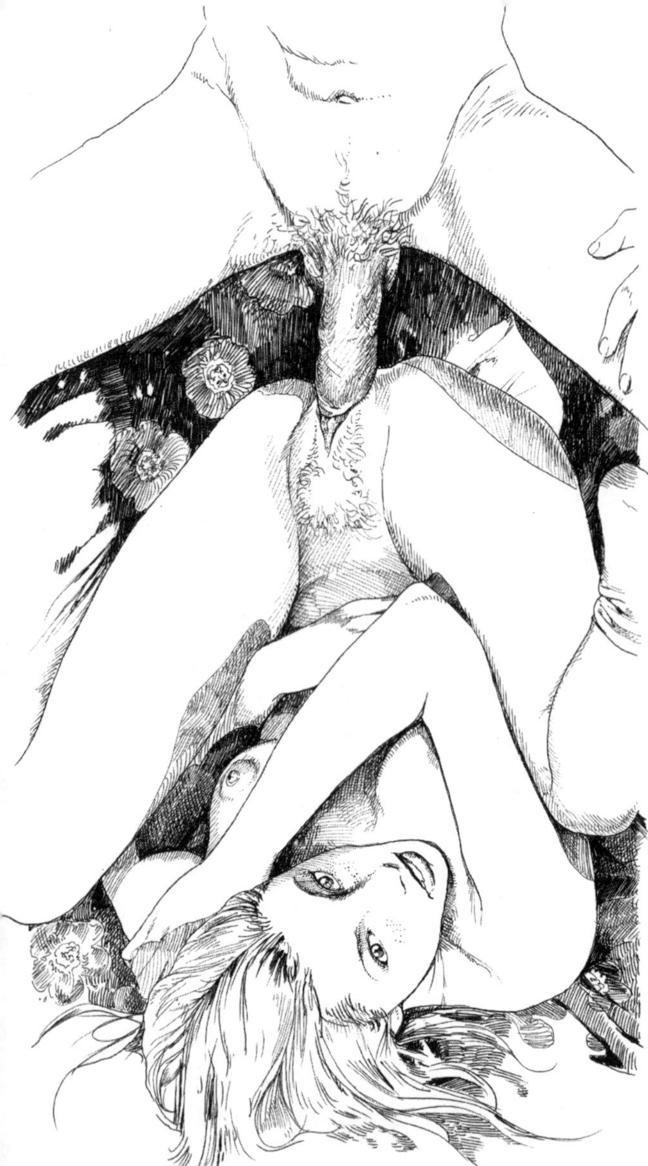

hold off the orgasm which was welling up in him. He groaned in despair as his whole body stiffened, and his prick rammed deep inside her. She gasped, then mewed with pleasure as she imagined she could feel her husband's warm seminal spurts, accompanied by a spastic twitching of his embedded rod.

Danny sighed and lurched forward.

Billy Jo lay motionless beneath him except for the rise and fall of her cushioning breasts. She felt as if she were on a carnival ride that had slowed in preparation for a new burst of frenzied motion. But the burst didn't come. Billy Jo found herself experiencing a vague and unfulfilled sense of excitement.

Danny's cock was softening and shrinking inside her. He was getting heavy, but that didn't bother Billy Jo. She was far more worried that Danny might turn out to be more of a sprinter than a long distance runner. The young bride had encountered premature ejaculators before, and although she felt sorry for their plight, she needed more from her man. She wanted their sex life to be perfect.

Danny pushed back, his soft penis slurping out of her. He grinned boyishly. "Pretty good, huh?"

A little gush of semen streamed out of her wide-stretched cunt and made a sticky pool between her thighs before soaking into the sheet.

"I... I guess so," Billy Jo said.

"Baby, you're wonderful," Danny purred, snuggling down against her, wrapping her in his strong arms. "I love you!"

"And I love you, too, darling," Billy Jo replied a little mechanically.

It was all going to be fine, she reassured herself. These things can be quite easily cured.

In less than a minute Danny fell asleep, his arms still draped around her, his head resting against her neck. Billy Jo eased herself clear of him and lay staring at the dim ceiling. Finally she too dropped off...

* * *

"Fuck with me, baby!" Danny was saying excitedly. "Ooh, man! God damn! Oh, that's wild!"

The room was still dark, and Danny was atop her. He lay sprawled between her thighs, supporting his torso on straight arms planted next to her shoulders, and he was pistoning his hard cock inside her at a frenzied rate. Billy Jo's thick blond hair tossed about the pillow. Her full tits shook. Her belly was thrusting upward to absorb her husband's rapid, pounding strokes.

The whole thing seemed to have happened of its own accord, and Billy Jo hadn't become aware of what she was doing until she was in the midst of it.

"That's good... oh, it's good!" she panted. "I love it!"

"Yeah!" Danny said huskily. "Yeah! Oooh, God *damn!*"

His prick was a wondrous thing – thrusting, gliding, pumping, filling her with the throbbing power of his love. Billy Jo was reaching for him eagerly, absorbing with her warm, wet pussy his every jarring plunge. She thrilled as his inrushing prick expanded the elastic sheath of her vagina, warming her insides. She felt his big balls flop sensuously against her tingling anus.

The carnival ride was really swinging now – wheeling, dipping, climbing.

This was more like it, she grinned to herself: primitive, good old hard sex. And this time her stallion was staying the course... Her orgasm was building, slowly, surely and then...

"Oh god, darling Danny, yes, *yes*..."

Fireworks seemed to go off all around her and inside her. Her cunt exploded in a starburst of acute, blissful sensations that rippled outwards to every extremity of her body.

"Oooh God, Danny! Wow! Oh... Unnh!" Billy Jo cried, "I'm *coming*... oh yes, I'm coming *nowwwwwww!*"

She bucked and quivered with the force of

her rapturous orgasm, letting Danny feel her vaginal tunnel spasmodically squeeze his big cock as it began to spit its second deposit of thick, viscous sperm deep inside her.

The thrusting stopped, and there was a pooling of warmth in Billy Jo's belly.

She clutched her strong young husband's hard lean body with her legs as well as her arms and they rocked from side to side, moaning and panting from the bliss that had come to them in the middle of this, their wedding night...

It was all going to be wonderful, just wonderful, she thought happily to herself.

* * *

"Billy Jo, the doc just called."

Snapping from her reverie, the girl jumped to her feet and asked Gus, "What did he say? How's Danny?"

"Now, take it easy." Gus made a patting motion in the air.

His elder sons stood behind him, Hank with a funny little grin on his face, Seth as grim as ever.

"Danny's coming home," Gus said.

"Then he's all right!" Billy Jo exclaimed. "Oh, thank God!"

"He's gonna be all right," her father-in-law corrected. "He's got a busted hip. But he don't need to stay in the hospital. Doc's going to rig up some traction for him in the spare room upstairs. I figured it was better that way, so you could be near him and take care of him."

Billy Jo sank into her chair. "How long will he be laid up?"

"Doc ain't sure," Gus said. "Maybe a month."

"Tough break, Billy Jo," Hank said.

She turned dazed eyes on the heavyset young man who stood with his legs planted apart. He was swaying slightly forward and back, his tight jeans outlining the bulge of his privates. Embarrassed, Billy Jo quickly lifted her line of vision. Hank wore a faintly discernible smirk.

Billy Jo looked at Seth. He was staring at her, his dark eyes as inscrutable as ever. A little hungry, maybe, she thought. He said nothing. But then he hardly ever did.

Chapter 2

Billy Jo stepped out to the porch. She rubbed the back of her hand across her perspiring forehead and stood quietly, gazing out across the rolling rangeland. In the distance, purple mountains blended with the sky. A brilliant sun bathed the landscape, keeping the temperature in the nineties – warm for Texas hill country, especially in late September.

Doc Carpenter had left a few minutes ago. Billy Jo had helped him set up the contraption of ropes and pulleys necessary to support Danny's cast, after which she had remained in her husband's room and had tried to make him as comfortable as possible. Danny was pretty good-humoured about the whole thing. But Billy Jo felt terribly depressed.

The screen door creaked behind her, and she turned around. Hank stepped onto the porch.

He grinned. "Danny's a lucky devil. He's sure got a pretty nurse to take care of him."

Billy Jo turned back toward the landscape and didn't reply. She wasn't in the mood for a flirtatious exchange. Danny's robust brother moved up beside her. She wished he would go away. She didn't feel like talking with anyone.

"Sure hot, ain't it?" Hank asked.

"Yes."

"This kind of weather gets me to thinkin' about lying under a nice cool shade tree with a pretty gal. Know what I mean?"

Hank slid a hand lightly across the small of Billy Jo's back and took hold of her side, spanning the ridge of her panty elastic beneath her light dress. She tensed as he fingered the elastic.

"Somebody like you," Hank went on, his voice lower and a little huskier as he spoke from right above her ear. "Yes sir, Danny's a lucky guy."

Billy Jo gave Hank a scornful glance. "How can you say Danny's lucky when he's in that awful cast?"

"Well, he won't have no work to do for a while. But me and Seth will have to work twice as hard."

Why don't you get to it, then? Billy Jo felt like replying. But she remained silent.

After a few moments, she shrugged away from Hank's casual embrace and walked to the end of the porch. He watched her lovely bottom move and jiggle under her cotton skirt. His loins ached with the wish to pull her skirt up and strip down her silken pants, part those full ass cheeks and...

Fuck Danny! he thought. How come a wet-nosed kid like him rates a beautiful chick like her? It ain't right. Now he's going to be lyin' up there in that room for a month, while Seth and me work our butts off. And he'll have this luscious babe waitin' on him hand and foot. He won't be able to screw her, though. No, sir! Not while he's in that cast. Hank smiled to himself. That's going to be rough on them both. Unless I miss my guess, this little filly may be as friendly as fire ants, but she likes her fuckin'. God damn, would I

Ranchers' Dirty Wives ★ 33

love to give her the feel of my cock!

"What're you standin' there for?" Seth barked at his brother as he stepped onto the porch. "We've got to fix that fence up at the draw."

"Hell, don't you think I know it?" Hank growled. His voice brightened somewhat as he added, "See you later, Billy Jo."

"Sure, Hank," she said without looking around.

"What a piece!" Seth said under his breath as the brothers walked off towards the barn.

"Man, you ain't kiddin'! How come *we* never saw her in town? How come Danny always smells out the best stuff?"

"I saw her clerkin' in Connelly's store. She'd never hardly look at me, though."

"That's what I mean. Danny's always had a way with 'em, ever since he started sproutin' hair on his nuts."

"I'm goin' to have her," Seth vowed.

Hank looked at him. "Why, you sound like you mean it, big brother!"

"Damned right I do!"

"The old man would tar us if he caught us messin' around with Danny's wife."

"How old are you, Hank?"

"Why, twenty-four. You know that."

"And I'm twenty-six," Seth said. "We don't have to take no shit from the old man no more."

"Come on now," Hank derided. "*You're* the one who always hops to every time he yells."

"Cause he's usually right," Hank's slim elder brother replied. "But when it comes to tail, a man's gotta make his own decisions."

"Yeah, but Seth, she's our sister-in-law…"

"It's better if you lay off Billy Jo anyhow," Seth said as they entered the barn. "That way I'll have a clear field for myself."

"Think you can really make her?"

"Hell, I *know* I can!" the sharp-featured rancher said with a rare, wolfish grin.

* * *

On the porch, Billy Jo started to think about Hank's arm around her waist and the way he had talked to her. She knew what he wanted and she knew that she should have given him the brush-off more promptly, but nevertheless, she had responded to his touch. It's just that sex is so important for me, she decided. Danny and I have only been married a week, and now – oh God, why did that accident have to happen just as we were discovering each other?

Billy Jo had just made her young husband comfortable, helping him with the bedpan, and then emptying it. She nearly giggled at his self-conscious embarrassment, but she took care not show her amusement and hurt his male pride.

At night the big Texas sky was like a black velvet pincushion full of pinheads that glittered like diamonds. The air was warm and a light breeze carried with it all the mysterious scents of the Hill Country flora.

Rounding the corner of the house, she stopped on the small patch of lawn. It looked inviting. She squatted and felt the grass. There was no dew, so she sat down, tucking her skirt underneath her bare thighs.

The breeze felt good. From out on the range, she could hear the faint and intermittent lowing of the cattle.

"Feel like company?" a male voice inquired.

Billy Jo jumped and looked up. "Oh, you startled me, Seth!"

He lowered himself to the grass beside her. "Sorry. I figured maybe you'd like to talk." Seth flicked his cigarette in a glowing arc across the lawn.

This was new, thought Billy Jo. Seth had hardly said a dozen words to her since she and Danny had arrived at the ranch the night before.

The fact was that she felt like talking. She smiled at Seth's dusky profile beside her. "It's beautiful here at night."

"I like the quiet," he said. "I spent a week in Austin once. I could hardly sleep for all the cars and sirens."

Billy Jo planted her arms in the grass and leaned back. Her full, firm breasts were thrown into startling prominence.

"Oh, I don't know, cities have their good points too," she said. "I lived in Dallas for a while. That was kind of exciting."

"Dallas is okay – if you have money to burn."

"Is money important to you?" Billy Jo glanced at Seth and caught him ogling her breasts. When she turned towards him, he looked quickly away.

"I like it right here," he told her. "I'm gonna run this spread some day."

"You and Hank and Danny, hm?"

"Ah, they'll probably take off."

"Danny says he wants to be a rancher all his life."

"What does he know? He's still just a kid."

"He's two years older than I am."

"But you're a girl. Girls mature younger."

There was silence for a while as Seth and Billy Jo entertained their separate thoughts.

"How come you married such a young guy?" he asked.

She gave a little laugh. "I'm in love with Danny. Anyway, he's the right age for me."

"You sure about that?"

Seth looked at her closely, his eyes hard and sharp. Billy Jo felt uneasy. She wanted to get up and return to the house, but she didn't wish to offend Seth.

"I'm sure that I love Danny. Of course I am," she said.

Seth felt frustrated. His verbal gambit hadn't gotten him anywhere. That was how it usually was when he was with a girl. He could never seem to get around them by talking, and he didn't have those boyish good looks that they all seemed to like.

But he had what they needed, and he knew how to give it to them. Billy Jo would like it, he was sure, once he put it into her. He'd never had any complaint from a girl whose resistance he had been able to break down.

Suddenly his hard, lean body crashed against Billy Jo, his strong arms twisting her to face him. She gasped, but couldn't get out a cry before Seth's firm lips pressed hers, spreading her mouth open. His tongue crowded in.

Billy Jo was surprised and not a little shocked. As Danny's brother, Seth had no right to behave this way.

She began to fight, writhing in his determined embrace, trying to slide her mouth away from his. But Seth was pressing her backward to the ground, and her attempts to wriggle free only caused her breasts to wobble and rub against him, exciting him all the more.

Billy Jo's brain reeled. Her brother-in-law's thrusting tongue, stroking hers as it churned in her mouth, gave her the kind of excitement which only Danny had been able to arouse in her before. Seth pinned her against the hard, ground, and there seemed nothing she could do to restrain him. One arm was free, and she beat at his back and side, but she knew the blows were having no effect. Seth was sprawled across her other arm and her legs, holding them down. She breathed gaspingly through her nose as the French kiss continued, causing her blood to race.

Seth slid a hand up her front to grasp a breast from underneath. He squeezed the large, pliant mound through her brassiere. A strong new thrill coursed through Billy Jo.

Oh, this is so *bad!* she thought. I really can't let him do it!

Seth's hot breath was bursting against her cheek as he ground his open mouth on hers, hurting her lips with the brutal pressure. His wet, meaty tongue was flapping against her tongue and the walls of her mouth. Billy Jo tried to move her jaws to bite him, but the force of his kiss prevented that.

His hand, which now covered her tit, was squeezing the warm, soft melon spasmodically, causing her nipple to swell against the cup of her bra.

Billy Jo felt a flare of warmth in her loins. She was thrown by what was happening, but it seemed that her body couldn't help responding to it – almost as if she were with Danny. She was utterly confused.

Seth's hand glided down across her belly, blazing a trail of hot sensation. He pawed at her pubic mound through her clothing, and Billy Jo quaked deep inside. Desperately, she twisted onto her hip so he could no longer touch her most intimate area. Seth's hand skidded over her thigh and across the hem of her skirt, onto her bare skin.

Billy Jo's thigh tingled where he touched her. Gasping through her nose and making anguished sounds in her throat, the distraught girl raised her knee in an effort to dislodge his hand. But that hand glided up the back of her smooth thigh, underneath her skirt, and grasped a buttock through the clinging silk of her panties. He squeezed the lusciously resilient mound, his fingertips pressing her panty fabric into the crack between her buttocks.

Humiliated and thrilled by the shockingly intimate contact, Billy Jo writhed, shaking her buttock in Seth's gasp. He pressed closer to her, and she felt his cock. Hard as an iron bar, it seemed about to burst through the coarse fabric of his jeans.

Giving a frenzied twist, Billy Jo finally dislodged her mouth from Seth's. She gasped and was about to scream, but then she realized it would cause a fuss. Danny would find out. Maybe he wouldn't understand.

"Stop it!" she hissed at Seth, breathing hard and straining against him in an effort to break his hold.

He answered with a passionate groan against her sweet, soft neck, and his lascivious fingers clawed at the elastic top of her panties, grasping the thin band and pulling it down at the back.

Cool air touched the girl's exposed buttocks, followed by Seth's work-roughened hand as he stroked across her rear crack, spanning both satiny cheeks and squeezing them together.

"Oh, God!" Billy Jo exclaimed as her hips heaved spastically, her mound grinding against Seth's hard-on.

He caught her mouth again, once more filling it with his tongue. She couldn't think. The strength seemed to be draining from her body. Her loins had turned into an inferno.

Seth pulled her panties down, slithering the elastic and cotton along her hot thighs. He left the briefs wound like a silken rope around her knees and pressed her onto her back. Billy Jo gasped as her bare ass sank into the thick, tickling lawn. Seth placed his hand on her hairy mound, and the strongest blast yet went through her.

But her mind kept shrieking against the

outrage. Her sense of indignation was joined by real anger. She had never believed a man could rape her; she would always be able to keep her legs together and fight him off, she had assumed. But she was no longer certain of her ability to resist. Something was working inside her to make her give in, even though she was beginning to loathe Seth.

He jammed his hand down between her thighs, forcing them as far apart as the panties around her knees would permit. He stroked her soft, hairy cunt. Blast after blast of hot excitement coursed through her.

"No, Seth! Oh, no you musn't..." she moaned weakly as Seth sat up and gazed in the sparse light at the beauty of her lower region.

Butter-colored curls formed a thick, bushy triangle above her closed thighs. Her soft, rounded belly was thrillingly white, punctuated by the cute depression of her navel. Seth bent and kissed the pliant flesh just below her belly button.

Billy Jo writhed against the grass, unconsciously shaking her tummy against Seth's face.

"Let's get your panties off," he growled as he raised his head.

He took hold of the dainty pink undergarment with both hands and hauled it up her legs as he lifted them in the air. He took the panties off Billy Jo's feet, working the elastic over her shoes.

Seth knelt beside her and looked down, grinning tensely. His black hair fell across his forehead. "You want it now, don't you?" he said.

"No! Oh God, no! I do *not!*"

"Little liar!" he laughed as he clawed at the front of his pants, opening his fly.

Billy Jo could have jumped up and run back to the house, she realized. Still she didn't move. She stared at her rangy brother-in-law through wide eyes.

He dug a hand into his open fly. His fist came out, clutching a prick that was thicker and longer than Danny's. Its bare rosy head was huge. The sight of it both thrilled and appalled his young sister-in-law as he started to scramble between Billy Jo's legs, his erect cock swaying.

At that moment Billy Jo's angry indignation welled up, overcoming the erotic lethargy that had gripped her. She quickly pulled her legs back and rolled away from the crouching man.

"Hey, wait a minute!" Seth exclaimed. "Where are you going?"

Billy Jo was on her feet and running toward the house. Her thighs slithered moistly together, unhampered by the presence of panties. Her buttocks felt shockingly naked against her flimsy, dancing skirt.

Seth didn't run after her. He knew that

Ranchers' Dirty Wives ★ 43

would only cause a scene.

"Sonofabitch!" he snarled, slamming his balled fist against the ground.

His penis slumped.

Billy Jo's panties, a soft puff of pink, caught his eye. He picked them off the lawn and held them up, using both hands to stretch the elastic and shake them into shape.

He pressed them to his face and inhaled their intimate scent, rubbing the sleek silk against his nose and mouth. Then he jammed the panties into a pocket of his jeans, tucked his penis in, and closed his fly.

She won't tell anybody what happened, he thought as he got up. She liked it, and in the back of her head she's hoping it will happen again. It will! And I'll get her next time!

The frustrated young cowboy went off in search of Rosita. The lively young Mexican housemaid was always eager to earn a few dollars extra by giving him a hand-job, a tit-job or a blowjob. Sometimes, if she was in a particularly good, horny spirits, she would even take it up the ass. But this young senorita was reserving her pussy for her wedding night. That part of her anatomy was definitely off-limits, and pussy was what he craved right now.

* * *

The TV in the living room was on. Gus and Hank were laughing over a comedy show. They didn't glance at Billy Jo as she hurried to the stairs.

She went directly to her room – the room she had shared with Danny last night but which she would occupy alone until he recovered. After closing the door carefully, the tense and quivering girl approached the dresser mirror.

Her thick blond hair, long and flowing, was now in wild disarray and had bits of grass in it. Still trembling, she picked up a comb and, with violent strokes, began to restore it to its normal immaculate state. She stopped and stared into her reflected eyes, trying to read what was in them, trying to understand why she had responded to Seth as she had.

What sort of person *are* you? she asked her image.

There was no answer.

After Billy Jo had calmed herself and was sure that her appearance gave no hint of what had happened, she walked down the hall to Danny's room.

He smiled warmly at her as she entered. "Hi, baby. Come on over here."

Billy Jo returned his smile. "Feeling all right?"

"As good as a guy can, I guess, when he's flat on his back with one leg in the air. Where you been?" He took her hand.

"Uh... outside. I went out to look at the stars."

"Hey, no fair! You ain't supposed to look at the stars unless I'm with you. That goes for the moon, too."

"Fool!" she said, laughing softly. For some reason she didn't understand, her eyes misted over.

Danny moved his hand to her leg. Before Billy Jo could stop him, he reached under the hem of her skirt and stroked up her silken thigh to her buttock.

His eyes widened. "Where's your panties?"

Billy Jo turned red. "Oh, I... uh... took them off. It was so warm."

"Well listen, young lady," Danny said as he patted her rounded, quivery buttocks, "don't go runnin' around here with no pants on, understand? I've got two horny brothers, and my old man ain't exactly senile yet."

"Danny! I'm surprised at you!" Billy Jo shrugged away, pushing his arm down.

His eyes narrowed. "Feel me," he said softly.

"What?"

"Feel my dick."

"Danny!"

"Oh, for God's sake!" He grasped her hand and carried it to the crotch of his pajamas where a single sheet covered him.

Billy Jo's eyes widened. "Why, Danny!

You... you're hard!"

"Hell, yes! You see what one feel of your ass can do?"

"Shame on you for talking like that!" she said, smiling broadly and jerking her hand away.

"Baby, when are you gonna get it through your sweet head that we're married? We can say anythin' to one another, and it ain't bad."

"Well, certain words are..." She looked down demurely.

"Excitin'! That's what they are. Come on, honey – take your clothes off."

Billy Jo stared at her earnest young husband. "But we can't... do anything."

"We can't fuck, if that's what you mean," he said, his eyes twinkling. "But there's somethin' else you can do – that is, if you love me enough."

"You know I love you," Billy Jo murmured.

"Then take off your clothes." His voice had grown husky.

Billy Jo had a shrewd idea of what he had in mind, and she wanted to please him. It seemed particularly important after what had happened outside.

She stepped back and turned away from the bed. She reached behind her neck, lowered the zipper on her dress partway, then reached up from below and pulled it the rest of the way down. She shrugged the dress off

Ranchers' Dirty Wives ★ 47

her shoulders and let it drop.

She was naked, except for a bra. Danny gazed at her beautifully pert bottom, the cheeks so pink, smooth and perfectly contoured. His cock throbbed harder.

Billy Jo tingled as she reached for the clasp of her bra and opened it. It gave her a strange, exhibitionist thrill to appear before her husband in the nude, and the erotic tension that had occurred on the lawn with Seth still lingered.

She turned to face Danny, deliciously conscious of her young husband's eyes devouring her triangular blonde tuft and the full, proud mounds on her chest. In response to this scrutiny, her pink nipples stood up, aimed at the junction of wall and ceiling.

"My God, but you're beautiful!" Danny said reverently, passionately.

Billy Jo smiled and approached the bed, blushing a little. She gave a shiver of self-conscious delight and her tits jiggled softly in response.

Danny twisted slightly and reached out with both arms. He slid one hand down her slender, graceful back while the other glided up a thigh. They met at her bottom, each cupping a rounded, fleshy buttock. He wiggled Billy Jo's ass as he pulled her closer to him.

Knowing what he wanted, she leaned

forward. Her generous breasts hung above his face like exotic fruit, ripe on the bough. Danny's mouth opened, and he let out a little groan as he caught a succulent pink nipple on his moist tongue and drew it into his mouth. Billy Jo closed her eyes and wiggled her shoulders slightly as he sucked her tit, the full breast wobbling against his face.

With a soft little slurp, Danny let go of her wet, tingling nipple, and she shifted, sliding the other tit between his moist, loving lips. He sucked the nipple deep into the hot cavern of his mouth.

She could feel Danny's fingertips entering the cleft of her buttocks, one hand stroking downward until he was touching the hair-bordered, slippery folds of her vulva. The middle finger of his other hand tickled the hot, depression between her buttocks until it arrived at the puckered dimple of her anus. Billy Jo was in heaven.

Danny let her well-kissed boobs bobble away. "Take hold of my cock," he growled softly.

"Oh, *Danny... !*"

"Please."

Taut with excitement, Billy Jo pushed the sheet away and snaked her hand through the fly of his pajamas. She grasped her husband's warm, upthrust column and brought it out.

His prick was so stiff! And the head was

rosy and plump. But Danny's organ wasn't as long as Seth's, Billy Jo realized again. She was ashamed of herself for making the comparison and let go of his cock.

"Don't drop it like it was a hot poker," he said.

"It is hot."

"I know it. It's hot for you. Play with it, honey."

"H-how do you mean?"

"Don't you know how a guy likes to be played with?" Danny's eyes twinkled warmly as he looked up at her.

"You *know* I never saw another man... this way," Billy Jo lied convincingly.

"Put your hand around it," Danny instructed huskily. "Pump it up and down."

Billy Jo blinked at him. "What'll that do?"

"It'll make me shoot. That is, if you do it right."

"Do you... want to come? I mean, like this?"

"I'd rather come inside you, baby. You know that. But if we can't fuck, this is the next best thing." He hesitated and looked at her searchingly. "Or almost."

God, if only she would suck me off! he thought. He'd had a girl do that for him once at the cathouse in town. His brothers had taken him there when he was just sixteen. The girl he was with had seemed to get a kick out of the fact that he was a virgin. She had said, "I want to eat this sweet thing before you ever stick it in anyone else." And she had sucked it until he had come, spurting into her throat like a Texas gusher. After that they had screwed. But the sucking had remained one of his fondest memories.

Danny assumed no decent girl would do such a thing, and he therefore hadn't asked any of the girls he had dated. He wouldn't think of asking Billy Jo.

But God, if she only would! he thought. It would thrill him so much.

The question had crossed his mind as to why a decent girl wouldn't do as much for love as a whore would do for money. Anyway, the whore hadn't done it just for money. She had done it because she wanted to. But he supposed that's what had made her a whore – wanting to do things like that.

Blissfully unaware of her husband's musings, Billy Jo stared at her husband's upthrust cock. She sure would love to suck it, she thought. It seemed such a shame not to, somehow, suck it and pump it until the warm come shot into her warm, enveloping mouth. But she knew she had to try to retain her image of a young innocent bride. Besides, she wondered how Danny's penis would look when it spurted. How high would he shoot, and could she really please him that way?

Ranchers' Dirty Wives ★ 51

Finally she wrapped her hand around the shank of his organ.

"Hey, that feels great!" Danny said. "Your fingers are so soft and cool."

"Just... what do I do?" Billy Jo asked innocently.

"Stroke your hand up and down – slow, but steady."

"Like this?" Billy Jo began pumping his cock expertly.

"Yeah! That's good! Oh baby, that feels wild, why – you're a natural!"

Billy Jo felt rather frustrated, milking Danny's stiff dick. She would so much rather be sucking it. But the fact that he was obviously enjoying it gave her pleasure.

"Harder now!" Danny groaned. "Faster!"

He grasped her swaying, quivering tits, clutching both of them and squeezing. After a little while, he glided one hand to her ass while he brushed the other back and forth across the hard, pink tips of her titties, shaking the luscious boobs. His middle finger wormed into Billy Jo's hairy softness. The lips of her pussy were excitingly wet.

She felt aroused by what she was doing: the act was kind of exciting. But although she was giving Danny such pleasure, inwardly, her frustration was building up.

"Oh, God!" Danny cried. "JEE – zusss! Oh wow, that's good! Baby... angel...

sweetheart!"

She pumped his stiff cock faster. Her hand flew up and down on the hard, throbbing column. Clear fluid had seeped out of the gaping little piss hole at the end of his prick and had washed over the bulging rosy head, making it gleam and feel slick between his glans and her fingers.

"Baby, I'm gonna – Oh! Aaaaaagh!"

Danny's hips had lurched, and he had felt a blinding pain. The doctor had warned him against moving that way.

"Sto... stop," he said. He lay panting.

"What's the matter?" Billy Jo asked, slackening her grip on his prick. She was afraid she had done something wrong.

"I moved and... hurt myself," he said, speaking with obvious difficulty.

"Oh, darling!" she exclaimed. She let go of his penis.

"It's all right now," he said. "I'll be careful not to move. You can start again."

"Are you sure it's okay?"

"Yeah... yeah. I've gotta get my rocks off!"

The whole thing began to seem a little sad and one-sided to Billy Jo. But she shouldn't blame Danny, she realized. He couldn't do anything for her as long as he was in the cast.

The naked bride resumed stroking his prick. Danny didn't say anything for awhile. He just

Ranchers' Dirty Wives ★ 53

stared at her and breathed heavily. Finally, though, he began to let out little cries. He grasped one of her breasts and squeezed it.

Billy Jo's back was stiff from bending forward for so long, and her arm ached from pumping. She was beginning to hope he would finish soon.

Suddenly Danny gasped, let out a strangling moan, and his cock erupted. A jet of thick, milky fluid spurted up about three feet in the air, then another and another. Billy Jo stopped stroking him as the thick blobs landed on his pajamas and on her hand. They felt like warm cream.

"Ooooh..." Danny sighed. He seemed to relax, but his penis remained hard.

Billy Jo gave it a couple of final strokes. A thick glob of pearly semen oozed out of the piss hole and down over the head. She licked her lips and found the temptation to bend down and lick it off almost irresistible.

"Is that... all you want me to...?" Billy Jo asked hesitantly.

"Yes." Danny's hands had fallen away from her.

She let go of his cock and backed up. She felt rather foolish. Her body throbbed with sexual tension. She watched Danny's penis as it turned soft and small: and with it, she thought, any chance of my fun...

"Thanks, baby," he said, warmly smiling

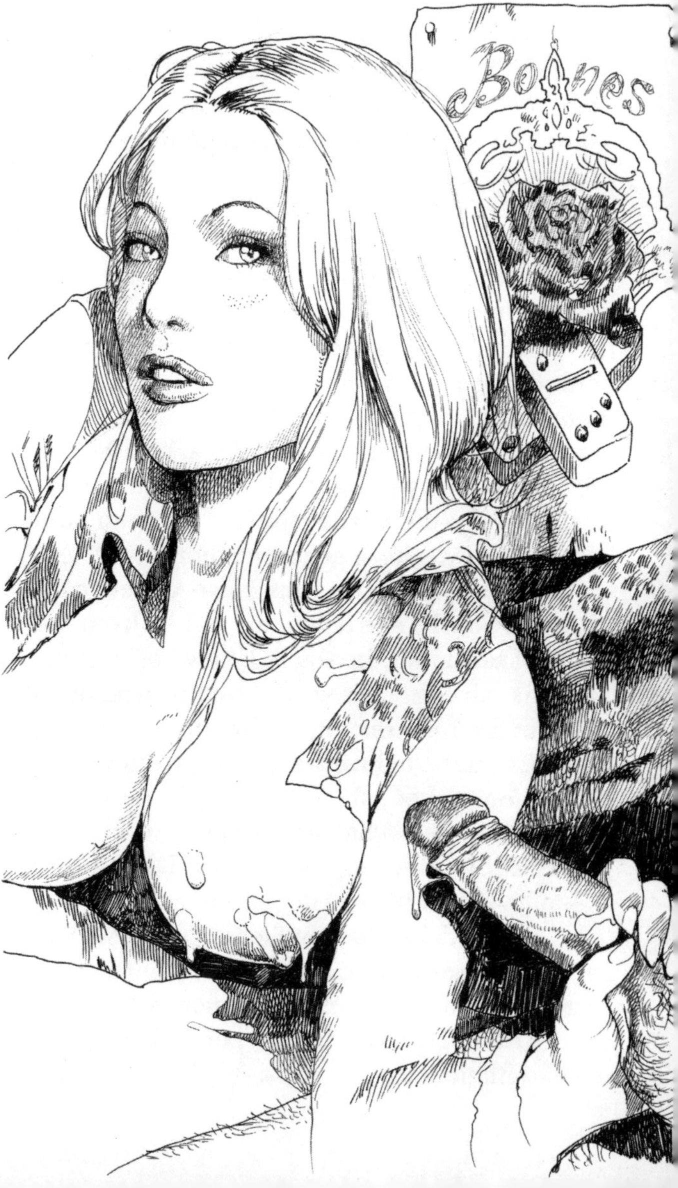

up at her.

"That's... kind of messy, isn't it?" she said, looking at the semen which lay in a couple of small pools on his pajamas. It was soaking into the cloth.

"It's all right," he said. "You can get me some fresh pajamas tomorrow."

He was breathing slowly, eyes heavy, as if he were about to fall asleep.

Billy Jo looked at her hand which gleamed with his cum. Its funky smell was a pure aphrodisiac to her.

"Do you want me to go?" she asked Danny.

"Whatever you want." His eyes fell closed.

Billy Jo drew the sheet over him and turned away. She glanced at him as she put on her bra. Danny's eyes were closed now. Surreptitiously, she licked his semen from the back of her hand, its thick, gooey consistency and its strange, alien flavour provoking a current of raw sexual desire that ended in another cunt-tingling blast of frustration.

He's satisfied, she thought. *His* needs are catered for. But what about *me?*

Billy Jo put on her dress. Danny still hadn't opened his eyes.

"Good night, darling," she said, trying to make her tone warm, though she didn't exactly feel warm toward him at the moment.

"'Night, baby," he responded vaguely, already half asleep.

Billy Jo turned out the light and left the room.

Chapter 3

When Billy Jo arrived downstairs in the morning, Gus and his sons were already at breakfast. Rosita was serving and she gave Billy Jo a cheerful smile.

Gus got to his feet. "Sorry to start without you, Billy Jo, but we figured maybe you'd feel like sleepin' late. No use you gettin' up with the rooster just cause we have to."

"That's OK, Gus," Billy Jo said, returning her father in law's smile. She took her place at the table.

"Mornin', Billy Jo," Hank said from across the way.

"Good morning."

She glanced shyly at Seth. His eyes were directed at his plate as he speared a forkful of steak and egg.

"So I'm goin' in to the county seat and have a talk with Bill Merret," Gus said to his sons, obviously continuing a conversation which had been in progress. "Maybe there's somethin' he can do."

"Not likely," Seth replied, chewing. "Bill just sends out the tax bills. He don't make appraisals. We should've yelled when our appraisal was set up last spring."

"I didn't check it, cause I didn't figure it would take a big jump," Gus said defensively.

"That happened 'cause Reed pulled some strings and got his appraisal cut. There's bin talk of that in town. With him ownin' half the land in the county, everybody else just naturally has to pay more."

"It ain't right!" Hank said vehemently.

"Danged right it ain't," his father agreed, his brow darkening. "I've known Bill a long time. Maybe I can get him to give us a break."

"Dad, you're grabbin' at straws," Seth said. "We're just gonna to have to pay the increase somehow."

"With cattle prices the way they are, it'll bust us," Gus complained.

A smiling Rosita brought a large glass of orange juice and a huge mug of steaming, strong coffee for Billy Jo, who thanked her with a *'muchas gracias'*. She took a sip of juice as she thought about what she had just heard.

Danny had told her of the trouble his family was having with a ranch manager named Reed. The *Lazy Q* holdings completely surrounded *Los Altos*, and he was pressuring the McCluskies to sell out. In recent weeks there had been a number of strange happenings on *Los Altos* territory – stock had been rustled, fences broken, and the access road had been flooded by water spilling over from the land Reed managed. Apparently getting the McCluskies' taxes increased while the *Lazy Q*'s were lowered was the latest of Rex Reed's tactics.

Gus finished his coffee and stood. "Excuse me, Billy Jo, but I've got to be goin'. It's better'n an hour's drive to the county seat, and I want to be there when Bill opens his office. How's Danny this mornin'? Did you look in on him?"

"Yes," Billy Jo replied. "He's getting along all right."

She glanced guiltily at Seth and caught him watching her. He quickly averted his eyes and stood.

"Come on, Hank," he said.

"Be with you in a minute," the younger man responded. He grinned across the table at Billy Jo.

Her breakfast arrived. It consisted of a generous serving of steak and eggs, with a stack of hotcakes on the side. Billy Jo had never eaten so much in the morning in her life.

Hank kept his blue eyes on her as he sipped coffee. "How about lettin' me show you around the ranch today?" he suggested.

"Danny didn't get a chance to do that before he was hurt."

"Thank you, but I'll have to stay here at the house," the young woman replied. "Danny needs looking after."

"Rosita can tend to him."

"I'd rather look out for him myself."

"If I was the one that was hurt, would you be lookin' out for me?" Hank asked, his eyes shining.

"I'm married to Danny," Billy Jo replied coolly.

"But now it's almost like being single again, ain't it?"

Billy Jo coloured and looked down.

"Well, let me know if you change your mind about ridin' across the ranch," Hank said as he got up. "There's some mighty pretty scenery around the back line."

"Thanks, Hank. I'll let you know."

Billy Jo watched the husky young man leave the dining room. As she finished her breakfast, she was alone with her thoughts. They turned first to Danny, than to Seth.

I was foolish to let Seth go as far with me as he did, Billy Jo thought. Even Danny never got under my dress. Before I was married, it was different, but now I've got to play it pure and innocent; there'll be plenty of time for playing around later.

She wondered what had happened to her

panties – whether Seth had kept them. What if he showed them to Hank or somebody else?

Billy Jo smiled to herself. So what if he did? She would run rings around him, make him look the fool. Seth wasn't the sharpest knife in the drawer, but he sure had a nice cock...

She visualized Seth's stiffly erect penis as she had seen it last night on the lawn.

No! she told herself sternly. I can't think about that. Danny's my husband, and I love him. Anyway, I mustn't have another man stick his cock into me – I'd enjoy it way too much. And if one of Danny's brothers were to do it, it would be a double thrill – I'd go totally crazy.

Even so, she hoped Seth wasn't saving her panties in order to show them to someone. Whoever saw them would think he had fucked her. He might even say that he had.

Billy Jo felt more and more horny. She couldn't finish her breakfast, though the food was delicious.

She left the table and thought about returning upstairs to be with Danny. But she felt she couldn't face him right then. She decided to step outside and get some fresh air.

The day was already warm. A bright sun was blazing in a virtually cloudless sky. Billy Jo stood in the shade of a large tree and breathed in the subtle, invigorating scent of the prairie.

"So you decided to come out after all," Hank said as he emerged from a little building next to the house.

"Just for a minute," Billy Jo replied.

Hank grinned as he walked up to her, moving with a cowboy swagger which Billy Jo found a little comical. "I had to adjust the pump," he said. "Have you seen it?"

"No."

"I'd better show you how to turn it on and off. We only run it a few minutes a day, to fill the water tank for the house. It's going now."

Billy Jo followed the robust young man to the open door of the shack. He stepped aside and let her enter first. Inside an electric motor was whirring. A pipe extended from the motor down a dark shaft.

"That's our well," Hank said. "Take a look down there."

Leaning against the protective railing, Billy Jo bent forward. Suddenly she felt a hand at the back of her thighs. She straightened quickly, but not before the hand had scooted all the way up under her skirt and was pressing her panty-clad bottom.

"Hey! Cut that out!" she exclaimed indignantly, whirling to face Hank.

Keeping his hand where it was, he used

his other arm to draw Billy Jo into a snug embrace. Her breasts crushed against his chest. Almost before the startled girl knew what was happening, Hank was pressing his mouth to hers. His lips were thick and moist. He didn't try to use his tongue, but he kissed Billy Jo with ardent force as his hand squeezed and jiggled her asscheeks.

Clenching her fists, she beat at Hank's strong, thick body. She tried to squirm away from him, but the effort proved futile. Her belly merely rubbed against his belt buckle.

Billy Jo felt Hank's cock come alive against her. The organ turned hard and pushed upward.

Billy Jo was outraged. Twisting her mouth against Hank's, she bit his lip. He quickly backed up and let go of her.

"Why you danged little savage! Who stuck a burr under your saddle?" he said, touching his lip, then looking at his hand to see if Billy Jo had drawn blood. She hadn't.

She was breathing hard and staring at him with angry condemnation in her eyes. "You had no right to do that!" she exclaimed. "If Danny knew about it, he'd beat you up."

"What're you givin' me?" Hank retorted scornfully. "He couldn't beat up nobody. Shit, he can't even get outa bed! Anyhow, you don't need to act so high 'n mighty. Seth showed me the panties he took off you last night."

Billy Jo gasped. Her face turned red. She was about to turn and run from the pump house, but she decided she couldn't leave without correcting the wrong impression Hank had obviously gained.

"I didn't let Seth take my panties off," Billy Jo said, blushing furiously. "He... he just grabbed them. I couldn't stop him."

"Oh, sure!" Hank laughed derisively. "Listen, no gal gets her pants pulled off unless she wants it to happen – or unless the guy's holdin' a knife or a gun on her. Seth didn't do that, I'll bet."

"No, but he took advantage of me!" Billy Jo maintained, her cheeks continuing to glow and her eyes flashing angrily.

"He claims he screwed you. Is that right?"

"Certainly not!" Billy Jo's cheeks were hotter than ever. "What dirty boys you are – you and your brother both. You should be ashamed of yourselves!"

Hank's answer was a laugh. "Well, if old Seth didn't fuck you, he came mighty close to it. How come you let him go that far and wouldn't let me?"

Billy Jo backed up. Her eyes were wild with anger. "I'm going to tell your father on you!"

"Yeah? And have him tell Danny?" Hank moved close to her, crowding her against the wall. "If you was goin' to tell Pop anything, you'd have done it last night or sure as hell this mornin'. You don't want no fuss, baby. Now be nice, huh?"

Hank's ham-like hand covered Billy Jo's left breast, and he rolled the resilient orb through her blouse and brassiere. She gasped and her brain turned giddy. She wanted to scream, but she was afraid of what would happen if anyone were to come and catch Hank and her together. Anyway, old Gus had left the ranch. Only Seth and Rosita were about.

"Please stop it!" Billy Jo exclaimed, squirming against Hank and pushing at his arm.

He kissed her again, this time spreading her lips wide and jamming his thick tongue against hers. Her back was pressed to the wall. Hank's large, firm belly was snugly against her, and his cock had hardened again.

The nipple of Billy Jo's stimulated left breast had stiffened and was tingling against her bra cup. Moisture was leaking from the glands in her pussy.

She didn't believe Hank could actually screw her in the pump house, since the small enclosure was crowded with machinery and there was no place to lie down. Nevertheless she was a little apprehensive.

What bothered Billy Jo more than anything else was her response to Hank's coarse actions. She knew, suddenly, that she wanted him. But she also knew that just couldn't be so. She would ruin her chances for a happy new life if she became the sexual plaything of Danny's older brothers before they had even established a sexual relationship of their own.

Realizing as well as Billy Jo that he could make no further progress with her in the cramped pump house, Hank finally released her and stepped back. Her gaze instinctively dropped to the front of his Levi's which were badly out of shape. Now she wanted him even more. Her cheeks glowed hotter as she felt the lust consuming her.

Hank grinned sadistically as he studied her. "I'm gonna let you go this time," he said, teasingly. "That'll give you a chance to think things over. We could have a lot of fun, if you'd just quit being so darned snooty. Hellfire, Danny wouldn't have to know... or Seth, for that matter. I ain't the kind that brags."

Billy Jo didn't believe him. He would brag as much as Seth, if not more. She had the feeling that there was some sort of contest between the two brothers to see which one of them could break her down. Part of her was flattered.

Her cheeks still glowing, Billy Jo slid along the wall and hurried out of the pump house. She heard Hank's soft, mocking laughter. But he didn't follow her out right away.

She was about to enter the house when she noticed a car coming up the driveway. It was a new, sporty model. The sun glinted off its chrome trim.

Billy Jo waited, thinking she might have to greet the visitor even though she still felt flustered from Hank's pawing. Just then he emerged from the pump house and stopped, watching the car approach.

Billy Jo proceeded into the house. In front of a mirror in the deserted living room, she checked herself to make sure there was no telltale sign of her encounter with Hank. She took several deep breaths to calm herself, then looked in the mirror to carefully arrange her hair so that it was as neat and tidy as always.

When Billy Jo felt she was ready to face her husband, she went upstairs. But in the back of her mind, guilt nagged.

It was your fault as much as theirs, she thought concerning Seth and Hank. You didn't have to let them go so far. You could have fought them off.

As she reached Danny's room she wondered if she shouldn't tell him what was going on with his brothers – before it all got out of hand. No. She could handle it; after all, those boys were nothing she couldn't control... She put on a cheerful smile and opened the door.

Chapter 4

"Well, hi there!" Hank said with a grin as he swaggered up to the flashy car which had stopped in front of the ranch house.

The driver and sole occupant was a young woman with bright auburn hair done in a fancy coiffure. She wore dark glasses. Her pink lips glistened.

When Hank reached the side of the car, his gaze dipped into the luscious white cleavage revealed by her low cut blouse.

"Is this the McCluskie place?" the girl inquired, her voice carefully modulated to achieve a sexy effect.

The small hairs on Hank's neck prickled. "That's right." He kept grinning. "Who'd you want to see?"

She removed her glasses. Her eyes were a limpid aquamarine. "You're not Seth McCluskie, are you?" Her lips curved invitingly.

"No, I ain't. That's my brother." Hank was visually caressing the lissome lengths of the girl's sleekly stockinged legs. The hem of her miniskirt was almost lap-high.

"Is he around?" the redhead asked.

"Yeah. He's out at the barn, most likely."

"I wonder if you'd be good enough to call him."

"Sure. Uh, who shall I say wants him?"

"My name's Viv Lanier. I'm from San Antonio."

"Sure. Well, just a minute, Miss Lanier." Hank flashed another smile. "Don't go away now."

She laughed throatily and turned off the car's engine.

Hank hurried to the barn. He found Seth throwing hay down from the mow.

"Where the fuck have you been?" the older brother snapped. "Do you expect me to do every God damned thing around this place?"

"Keep your pants on. There's somebody out here to see you."

"Yeah?"

"A babe!" Hank's eyes glinted. "Man, wait until you get a look at her."

"Who is she?" Seth started down the ladder.

"Her name's Viv Lanier. She said she's from Reno, that's all."

Reaching the ground floor of the barn, Seth faced his brother. "And she asked for me?"

"Yep."

Seth headed out of the barn. Hank started

to accompany him.

Seth stopped. "I'm the one she asked for. Knock down some more of that hay, why don't you? 'Bout time you realised no one ever drowned in sweat."

"Aw, for Christ's sake!" Hank grumbled, but he turned to the task.

As Seth approached the car he saw the reason for Hank's excitement.

"Seth McCluskie?" the girl asked.

"Yeah." He squinted at her.

"Oh, this is going to be fun!" She smiled enticingly. "I'm a freelance writer, Mr. McCluskie. Uh, can I call you Seth?"

"Sure." His dark eyes stroked the tops of her thrusting tits.

"Hank, call me Viv... please. I made some inquiries around here and they told me you were the man to see about running a cattle ranch. I mean, I don't want to run one." She laughed softly. "I just want to write about it. I need some background information."

"Well, this place ain't mine. It belongs to my dad."

"But you sort of run it for him, don't you?" The attractive redhead's big eyes were very wide and earnest.

"You might say that," Seth responded proudly, permitting himself a rare smile.

"Then you're just the man I want!" His hand was resting on the window ledge of the car, and Viv placed her hand atop it. "Where can we talk?"

Her warm, gentle touch sent a thrill racing through Seth's body. He feared for a moment that his cock might get hard.

"Well, uh, wherever you like, Miss... I mean, Viv. Uh, in the house?"

"You were working out in the barn just now, weren't you?"

"Yeah."

"Then let's go there. I want to see what you were doing, and you can explain it to me. All right?"

"Well, sure... if you want me to."

He backed up, and Viv opened the car door. He watched her swing her legs around, catching a quick flash of her white panty crotch before she pressed her legs together and stood.

Viv remained close beside him as they walked to the barn. He was very conscious of her warmth. It seemed amazing that she had suddenly appeared from nowhere, asking for him. Her explanation was improbable, but Seth wasn't about to question it. She was there, and he wished to enjoy her presence.

"What a beautiful big barn!" Viv said. "What all do you keep in it?"

"Hay and special feeds... and other stuff. We keep the horses in a stable that connects to it."

"Why do you call the place *Los Altos* Ranch?" Viv smiled up at him as they walked along.

"That was the name when my father took over. There are three big hills over to the west of the property. Could be why."

"How interesting! Do you have wild horses?"

"We still pick up a wild bronc every once in a while. My kid brother was trying to break one yesterday. He got throwed and busted his hip."

Viv seemed concerned. "Oh, is he all right?"

"He will be. He's flat on his back right now."

They had reached the door of the barn, and Seth stepped aside to let Viv enter first. He watched her cute rear end undulate in her short, clinging skirt.

From the mow, Hank saw them enter. Curious, he put his pitchfork aside and descended the ladder.

"Well, there ain't nothing much to see in here," Seth said quickly. "Why don't we go into the stable?"

Viv glanced from Seth to Hank, who was approaching with a big grin on his face.

"Better keep knocking down that hay," Seth said.

"Aw, there's enough down here now," Hank replied. "What can we do for you, Miss Lanier?"

"I explained to Seth that I'm a writer looking for some background information about cattle ranching."

"This here's my kid brother Hank," Seth said reluctantly.

"Yes, we met a little while ago." The redhead smiled at him warmly.

Hank took her arm. "Well, I'd be glad to show you around the place, Viv. Seth's going to be pretty busy."

"No, I ain't!" the older brother flared.

"Remember you was telling me you'd have to check the stock vaccination records? The vet's coming out in the morning, and you're the only one who can read your chicken scratches on them cards." Hank grinned mischievously. "Anyhow, Billy Jo's apt to get jealous if she sees you with another gal."

"Who's Billy Jo?" Viv asked, a little confused.

"Nobody!" Seth snapped. His expression turned vicious. "She ain't nobody. Butt out, Hank!"

"I don't want to cause any problems, Seth," the redhead said. "I imagine Hank can show me what I want to see."

The husky young man tossed Seth a triumphant look as Viv let him lead her away. Seth glared.

"I didn't realize Seth had a girl friend

Ranchers' Dirty Wives ★ 73

living here at the ranch," Viv said to Hank when they were out of his brother's hearing.

Her concern about competition struck Hank as peculiar. He had mentioned Billy Jo only to embarrass Seth. But since it seemed to matter to Viv, the younger man decided to use Billy Jo to maximum advantage.

"Yeah, Seth's pretty sweet on Billy Jo," he replied.

"You probably have almost as much to say about running the ranch as he does, don't you? I mean, even though he's older?"

"Oh, sure. I can tell you everything you need to know. I can show you a few things, too." Grinning suggestively, he gave Viv's arm a squeeze.

"That sounds interesting," she purred, letting her hip brush against him.

This is my lucky day! Hank thought. Seth can have cold-pants Billy Jo. I'm going to get me something even better!

* * *

"Wow!" Viv murmured enthusiastically as her hand boldly stroked the front of Hank's snug jeans.

They had just toured the stable and walked around to the far side of it where there was a pile of clean straw. The location was secluded – out of sight from the house and from the work area at the other side of the barn. Viv had suggested that they sit down in order to "talk more comfortably." Relaxing in the soft straw, the exciting young woman had purposely leaned against Hank. Not one to let such an opportunity slip by, Hank had embraced and kissed her. His cock had hardened, and she had felt it pressing against her thigh.

With her soft, delicate hand stroking his eager member through his pants, Hank was fired into action. He pressed the beautiful redhead onto her back in the straw and began running his hands over her body.

She writhed pleasurably, making no effort to restrain him. "Mmmm, you're so big and strong!"

Again Viv touched the front of Hank's pants, this time even more boldly. She clutched the turgid column of his penis which was straining against the coarse fabric.

Emitting a voluptuous groan, the young man pressed his fleshy face to the softly quivering tops of her titties. He licked and sucked at the pliant, perfumed flesh as his rough hand skidded up the outside of Viv's thigh. Her skirt easily slid above her hips, and Hank palmed the resilient mounds of her bottom, sheathed in white, silken briefs. Her stockings, which had self-supporting tops, ended just below her buttocks.

"Why, Hank! You're such a tiger! Mmmm... you're making me so... hot!"

Viv clawed at the fasteners on his jeans. A new surge of pleasure went through the young cowboy as she reached into his fly and caressed his bloated organ through the fabric of his jockey shorts. Finally Viv's fingers threaded through the shorts' fly and grasped his naked prick. She pulled out the virile tool.

Hank raised his head from her breasts and stared at the stimulating sight of Viv's hand wrapped around his cock, clutching it just below the bulging head. She was smiling, as if she had never before gotten hold of anything so good.

Hank pulled up her stretchy blouse, bunching it at her armpits. Her white, quivering breasts were cupped in a flimsy bra which didn't have to be unfastened. It was only necessary for Hank to stretch it and pull it up, as he had done with the blouse. Her naked titties shook free and quivered before his lustful eyes, the nipples and their areolas startlingly pink, like coral, he thought.

While Viv caressed his upthrust prick, playing it like a piccolo, Hank eagerly grasped her tits. He squeezed the smooth, pliant mounds, forcing her nipples high in the circles formed by his forefingers and thumbs. He bent and swabbed his wet tongue across the little knots of erectile flesh.

"God, we mustn't do this!" Viv exclaimed, with as much sincerity as she could muster, but doing nothing to stop him. Rather she gripped his cock hard, daring him to try to take it away.

Hank didn't think about the possibility that Seth might come looking for them. Had he thought of it, he wouldn't have cared. His only wish was to enjoy the sexy creature that lay beside him in the straw, and he didn't want that enjoyment to stop until he had entered her to his balls and worked himself to a frenzy.

After taking long, delicious sucks at her titties, he twisted to look at her lower region. Viv's white panties were stretched to near transparency over the slight curve of her belly and the abrupt little rise of her pubic mound. Curling auburn hairs showed through the sheer undergarment above the seam of its crotchband. Narrow strips of white thigh gleamed between her stocking tops and the elasticized edges of her light briefs.

Hank bent and kissed Viv's belly button, licking into the knotted hollow. She shivered responsively and tousled his thick blond hair.

The blood was pounding in his veins, and his brain swam with excitement. He nuzzled the front of Viv's silken pants, breathing in the clean, sweet scent of her. His thick hand stroked her stockinged legs. Viv lifted her knees and widened her thighs to let his hand slide down onto the warm, smooth skin of her upper thigh.

Hank's blood-engorged prick quivered with excitement. Pre-coital fluid was oozing out the hole at its tip. His balls, contracted at the base of his shaft, were churning with a need that had accumulated for nearly a week – ever since he had last given Rosita a few dollars to jerk him off.

He stroked the narrow strip of white satiny fabric that passed between Viv's legs, pressing her warm, plushy softness through the sleek material.

"Hurry!" she said. "If you're going to do it, please hurry "

Hank needed no further encouragement. He quickly pulled down Viv's panties, lifting her slender legs into the air to take the dainty undergarment off her feet. She spread her stocking-clad thighs wide apart, and the impassioned rancher gazed with delight at the luscious display of ass and pussy nestled in the soft straw.

The silken, wispy hairs that tufted Viv's mound and bordered her enticing slit were as delicately red as the hair on her head. The inner lips of her pussy, exposed by the separation of her outer labia, were lusciously crimson. The smooth, meaty folds gleamed with liquid arousal.

Hank pressed his hand against her naked cunt and thrilled to its warm, dewy softness. His middle finger wiggled into her split, gliding on an oily film as it penetrated the mouth of her vagina.

"I want your cock!" Viv exclaimed, pulling at the rampant organ. "I know it's wrong, but I can't help myself. Screw me, screw me, Hank! Come on – stick it in me!"

"You're wonderful!" he whispered. "Man, how'd I get so lucky?"

Viv smiled up at him, but her eyes were tense with sexual urgency. Her glistening lips were parted to facilitate her heavy breathing.

Hank knelt beside the luscious girl and pushed down his underwear and jeans, his stiff prick pulling in through the fly of his briefs, then bouncing out above the waistband of the retreating garment. The edges of his blue work shirt framed his sexual potency.

He lost no time in scrambling atop Viv. She eagerly extended her arms around him and raised her legs. Gripping his cock, he worked the end of it into her slit. Pushing, he experienced a magnificent sensation as his rock-hard cock glided smoothly up Viv's honeyed cunt. Her channel gripped him snugly and warmly. She smiled up, her eyes alight with passion. Her legs hooked around the backs of his thighs.

"Baby!" Hank exclaimed. He began to fuck her fiercely.

His shirttail flapped against his hairy, bobbing butt. He lowered his chest against her titties, and the rough shirt fabric scratched Viv's nipples. But if this gave her discomfort, she showed no sign of it. She moaned pleasurably and gripped the hunching cowboy with her arms and legs as his bulb-headed dong pumped up and down in her tight, velvety channel.

Neither Viv, who was looking straight up, nor Hank, whose face was buried in her sweet neck, saw a slender male figure round the corner of the stable and stop, facing them. Seth stared at the erotic spectacle in the straw and hated Hank for having cut him out with the obviously hot-assed redhead.

First Danny got himself a cute little bride, then Hank caught the only good-looking piece of tail that had ever wandered onto the ranch – and he, Seth, was left with nothing. He figured it wasn't right.

For Hank the moment was right indeed. His eager prick plunged time and again into the warm, slippery depths of Viv's pussy. He felt her voluptuous sheath grind gently and bump up to meet him. Viv let out little murmurs of delight as she clutched his back with her sharp nails and skidded her stocking-clad legs against his flexing thighs.

When she sensed Hank was nearing his climax, her heels flailed his buttocks, and she panted, "Uuh... uuh... ooh, wow... fuck me... *fuck* me... Ooooh!"

Viv's clutching vagina contracted skilfully around Hank's thrusting cock, and his overtaxed balls shot out their spurts of thick, warm cream. He groaned with bliss as his pecker jerked in Viv's hot clutches and his semen foamed in her belly.

Seth turned, quivering with frustration, his aroused prick forming a hump in the front of his pants. Retreating around the, corner of the stable, he made a silent vow to get what he needed from Billy Jo that very night. It would serve Danny right, he rationalized. The kid couldn't take care of a hot young cunt like Billy Jo, anyway. And as for her, if she hadn't told anybody what had happened last night, she wasn't going to tell at all.

She would be his for the taking, Seth believed. He only had to make the move and let her know he meant business.

Tonight was the night.

Chapter 6

Billy Jo lay in the dark, unable to sleep. She

had been tossing and turning for half an hour. Though she occupied a room which was just down the hall from that of her handsome young husband, she had never felt so lonely and forlorn. To make matters worse, she was tense with physical frustration. She kept seeing images of Seth's rigid prick. She kept feeling his hands upon her, and feeling Hank's hands, also. She recalled the thrust of Hank's excited organ as it had strained against her belly when he had embraced her.

The horny eighteen-year-old blamed herself for entertaining such thoughts, but she could no more turn them off than she could stop the moon from shining or hush the breeze that whispered across the prairie.

What would Danny think of me if he knew I had let his brothers touch and kiss me? she asked herself. And if he knew I was thinking about their bodies?

The speculation brought made her feel a little guilty. Billy Jo loved her husband – now more than ever, as she sympathized with his discomfort, lying in a lonely bed with his leg in a cast. But she needed him in a tangible way, and she couldn't have him – not for a month or more. Billy Jo didn't know how she would be able to stand it, or how she would be able to hold off Seth and Hank for that length of time. Still, she would have to do so somehow, she vowed. She would have to be true to Danny.

She stared at the moonlight flooding in through her open window. The entire room was bathed in a soft glow. Every once in awhile a steer would bawl from out on the range. From somewhere farther away, a coyote bayed at the moon.

I'm not going to sleep at all tonight, Billy Jo thought with alarm. This is awful!

Her right hand slid under the single sheet that covered her and stole down her body to her tense and smoldering loins. Through the gossamer material of her honeymoon nightie, she touched her hairy mound.

No! she thought, jerking her hand away. I shouldn't!

Billy Jo heard a click. Her eyes popped wide open, and her startled gaze swung to the door. It was opening.

Fear clutched Billy Jo's throat. She sat up, the sheet falling to her waist. She was about to scream.

Then it occurred to her that she probably hadn't closed the door carefully enough and that the breeze was opening it. She threw back the sheet, intending to climb out of bed and push the door shut.

No! Someone was there! Billy Jo held her breath and didn't move.

"Don't yell," Seth said as he entered the room. Wearing a terrycloth robe, he quietly closed the door behind him.

"What are you doing here?" Billy Jo demanded in a harsh whisper. Her heart was thudding, her throat tight.

Seth approached the bed and took off his robe. He was naked. His long cock curved forward from his heavy balls. Billy Jo stared at the shocking exposure.

"Get... out of here!" she demanded in an urgent whisper, finding it somehow difficult to speak out loud. Her heart seemed to be trying to leap from her chest.

"Take it easy," Seth warned as he sat on the edge of her bed. "If you make a fuss, I'll show Danny those pants I took off you the other night. He'll figure you was leading me on, 'specially since you never told him what happened."

"I think you're awful!" Billy Jo exclaimed. She clutched the sheet around her firm, quivering breasts.

"We'll see," Seth said laconically. He swung his legs onto the bed and clapped a hand over Billy Jo's mouth as he lay back, drawing her down beside him.

She whimpered and writhed, pushing at the intruder. But she couldn't dislodge his hold. When she felt his prick thrusting urgently against her, Billy Jo's muscles turned to jelly. She moaned.

Seth lifted his hand and quickly slid his

lips onto hers, filling her mouth with his thick, hot tongue. She gurgled as his saliva dribbled past her lips. His hand slid along the back of her thigh, pushing up her nightgown. He clutched a smooth, round bottom-cheek.

The aroused man twisted slightly to permit his straining prick to snap upward, and he sandwiched it between their bellies. His tongue stroked and circled in Billy Jo's mouth.

Her brain whirled. She retained enough presence of mind to continue trying to push Seth away, but her efforts seemed foolishly ineffectual. Billy Jo felt as if she were being sucked into some irresistible whirlpool; she found herself thinking: if Danny finds out, I can always explain my way out of trouble.

Seth pressed her onto her back and peeled her nightgown up to her armpits. As he continued to grind his hot mouth against her, he covered her breasts with his big hands and squeezed. Thrills coursed through Billy Jo, and her nipples firmed against Seth's palms. Her pussy started to dribble like a leaky faucet.

Seth finally released her mouth, and she gasped for breath. Now was her chance to scream, but she didn't want to. Her cries would bring Gus and Hank rushing in; then Danny would find out. And if Seth were to show him the panties he'd snatched from her... and so on. She almost smiled to herself as she realised that Seth had outmanoeuvred her, after all.

This realization flashed in Billy Jo's mind within a span of less than a second, while Seth rolled her breasts and dragged his penis against her as he slid down her body, preparing to suck her tits.

She knew what was going to happen, and felt powerless to stop it. She felt that it was out of her hands now, she could no longer be held responsible for what was going to happen, but then she knew that she didn't really *want* it to stop: she wanted Seth to take her.

His hot, demanding mouth on the stiffened crests of her titties sent the frustration-plagued girl into an orbit of sensual delight. Seth's rough hands, mauling her pliant tits as he sucked them, added to her excitement. She was glad he was treating her so crudely. She felt she didn't deserve tenderness, and she wanted none from him.

He moved farther down her body, letting her breasts bobble free. He licked and sucked at her navel. Billy Jo bit her lip to stifle the shriek of mingled delight and passion welling up in her. What was happening was wicked, it was wonderful – and she loved it!

Any guilt about her temporarily disabled husband was overcome by her newly awakened sexual needs, which Danny was currently unable to service.

Forgive me, darling – oh, please forgive me! she silently implored her bedridden husband as his brother lifted one of her lovely legs and slid his tongue along the inner side of it, gliding up... up... up, dangerously near the warmly throbbing organ between her thighs.

Danny had never kissed so close to her pussy. As Seth nibbled at the smooth flesh of her inner thigh, licking and sucking, Billy Jo gasped. His hand touched the hairy lips of her vulva, pressing the lush softness. He caressed up and down between her legs, manipulating her soaking wet, responsive cunt.

Billy Jo tingled. She wanted to roll her hips against Seth's stroking hand. She felt the honey dribbling warmly and thickly through her labia. She wished Seth would spread her legs wide apart.

Do it! she mouthed silently. Please... just do it!

Billy Jo twisted her neck and stared at Seth in the dim light as he planted moist, gliding kisses on her belly and thighs. He continued to stroke her hair-lined split, making her yearn for deeper contact, her flesh exulting under Seth's kisses and his caressing touch.

He leaned back and stared at her pussy. The outer lips, adorned by blond curls, failed to hide the succulent folds within. He bent, lifting her leg over his head. With her thighs spread well apart, Seth pressed his thumbs against the portals of her cunt.

Billy Jo's wet, pink pussy was unfurled before his avid eyes. The smooth coral flesh gleamed with the passionate glaze spread over it.

The aroused girl quaked as Seth's hot eyes and the cool air kissed her cunt at the same time. She couldn't help loving the feeling humiliation when a man looked at her this way. The thrills that powered through her had reached an almost orgasmic pitch.

Oh God, do something! her need screamed at Seth, while she struggled to maintain the image of the outraged, near-virginal bride.

The slim, dark-haired cowboy bent his head. Billy Jo held her breath.

She thought, surely he isn't actually going to...

"Oooooh!" she exhaled delightedly as Seth's eagerly sucking mouth smacked into the wet, warm, slippery slit of her cunt.

Billy Jo felt his mad tongue flip and glide along her honeyed folds, stropping the tip of her clitoris. She thrilled as never before, silently thanking this simple cowboy for his unexpectedly sophisticated skills as a lover.

He lifted her smooth, supple legs onto his shoulders and burrowed deeper into her juicy, musk-scented twat. Since he was no longer holding her labia apart, the slick, elastic folds clutched at his sucking lips and poking, fluttering tongue. He breathed in the clean, hot, female fragrance of her crotch. His blood pounded. His prick throbbed as it was sandwiched upward between his squirming belly and the bed.

"Oh, my!" Billy Jo exclaimed between gasps as Seth ate her ravenously. "No... no... oh, I can't stand it!"

She squirmed, twisting her flaming, wet pussy against Seth's mouth as she tossed her head from side to side. Her mane of golden hair whipped across the pale sheet. Her tits leaped and trembled.

Suddenly an orgasmic vibration shook her, and Billy Jo felt a release of tension. But as Seth kept sucking and licking at her convulsing cunt, his lascivious tongue wiggling in the pudding of wet, warm flesh, her release was cut short. Tension began to build anew.

"Oh... unnh... no... oh, darling!" Billy Jo babbled, not thinking of what she was saying or whom she was saying it to, feeling only the wondrous thrills which were both good and bad, both desirable and shocking.

Seth's tongue and lips skidded out of her vulva. He caught a mouthful of outer lip, hair and all, sucking at the gloriously meaty morsel.

Mad with passion now, he rolled Billy Jo onto her belly and buried his face in the pillowed softness of her quivering, writhing

Ranchers' Dirty Wives ★ 89

ass. Seth even kissed and slurped at her anus, and as his tongue stroked wetly up and down between her buttocks the springy mounds vibrated against his cheeks.

Billy Jo moaned against her pillow and clutched the mattress, her fingertips digging in. She had never before known such thrills. After climaxing once, she was about to come again.

But Seth stopped kissing her ass before she could reach the second pinnacle. He rolled her onto her back once more and sprawled atop her, smearing his wet mouth across her bobbling breasts, snaking his tongue around her throbbing nipples, pulling the pink projections into his mouth.

Billy Jo's hands caught in his long black hair and tousled it anxiously, finding it straighter and coarser than Danny's…

Oh God, Danny! she thought. What am I doing? This is Danny's brother, for chrissakes! I really shouldn't. Or at the very least I should put up some more resistance…

She jerked her hands away from Seth's bobbing, twisting head and exclaimed, "No! Stop! Please stop it!"

Seth's lengthy, rigid cock was whacking against her thighs and belly as he squirmed voluptuously, sucking her titties. Billy Jo knew he would pay no attention to her plea. But at least she had voiced her dissent.

Seth's lustful, thin-lipped face loomed above her, and Billy Jo held her breath, anticipating his thrust. She wasn't concerned about her ability to absorb him without pain. Her pussy had never felt so wet and open. It was practically begging for his prick.

The massive head pushed against her slit, forcing the lips inward as it penetrated the tight opening. Then, inch by cunt-stretching inch, Seth's rod sank into her, slippery crevice.

The rigid, thick invasion caused the young bride's eyes to widen. Seth's penis had looked larger than Danny's; now she knew it truly was. The thing was huge! But there was no pain – only a marvellous, voluptuous sense of fullness. Every nerve end in her vagina became delightfully titillated as the great shaft pressed deeper and deeper into her belly.

Seth's eyes were hard and his lips cruelly quirked as he gazed down at the impaled young woman. At last he had what he wanted, and it felt even better than he had expected.

"How's that feel, huh?" he rasped softly. "You don't feel like fightin' now, do you?"

"It's... it's awful!" she said, panting.

Seth gave a cynical little laugh. He wasn't stupid. He could tell by her eyes and the way she was breathing hard that she loved the feel of his dick. She wasn't moving a muscle, except within her cunt where the elastic

Ranchers' Dirty Wives ★ 91

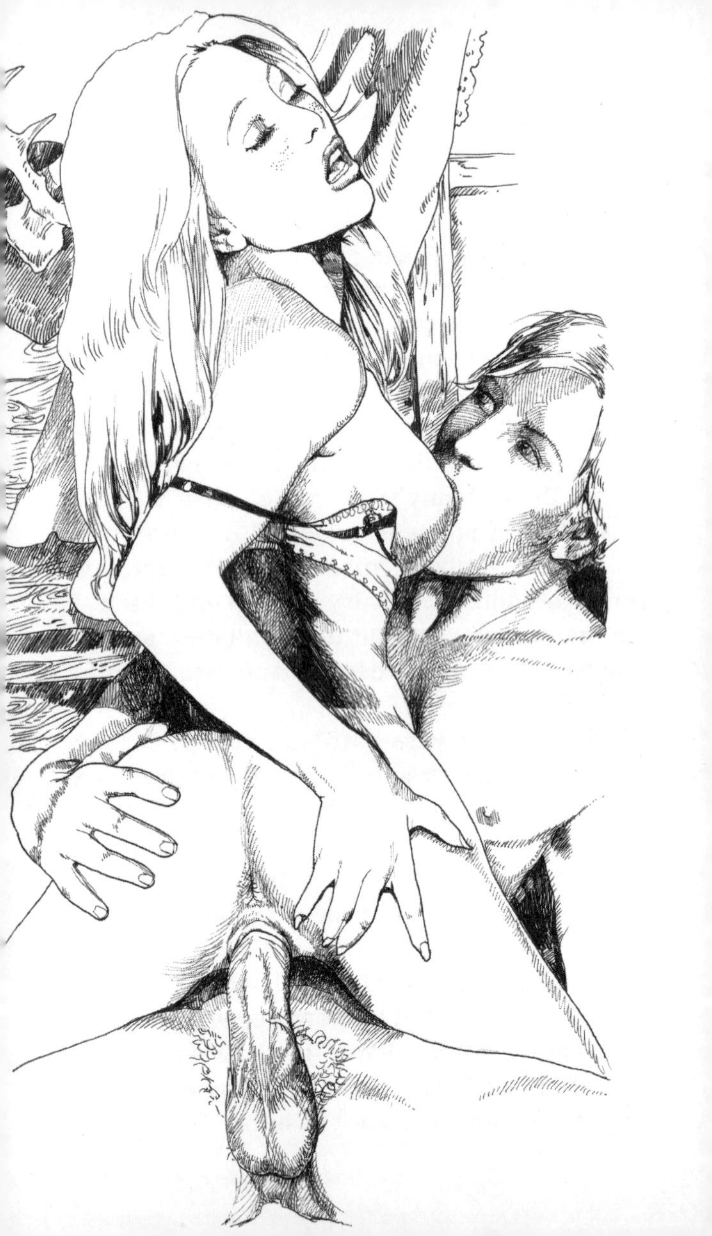

encircling membranes were making spastic little contractions.

He twisted more deeply into her, then withdrew a little, releasing Billy Jo's outer labia and allowing her hairs – which had been pulled in with his thrust – to escape. He pushed once more, drawing another cry from Billy Jo as he forged deeper yet.

How much more of him is there? she wondered wildly. She kept her eyes open wide. Her pink lips were parted in excitement.

Drinking in the sight of her passionate countenance, Seth twisted his cock to the side, forcing her tightness to yield further. He withdrew until the hard ridge of his glans was at the orifice of her channel, then jammed it into her for a third time, straight and hard.

"Ooooh... God!" Billy Jo moaned and bit her lip. That thrust had hurt a little, but it was a nice kind of hurt; Seth was forging deeper than Danny had ever gone. His thick cock seemed to be crowding her internal organs, forcing them up.

Still she feared she didn't have all of him. She hadn't yet felt his testicles against her anus.

Seth pulled and thrust again... again... again, grinding and pushing. Tears clouded Billy Jo's wide blue eyes. She kept biting her lip. As he gave a final deepening twist to his bone-hard, penetrating tool, Billy Jo felt his coarse, contracted scrotum tickling her asshole.

He was all the way into her at last. Billy Jo had never imagined that a girl could be so stuffed by a man.

"Now fuck with me!" Seth grated as he continued to lean on straight arms and gaze down at her shocked and thrilled countenance.

"Yes... yes," Billy Jo gasped, beyond the point of offering pretence, however much she might have wanted to do so.

Seth withdrew his long, hard, slippery pecker until she felt the fat head throbbing in the tight circle of her cuntal lips. Then he jammed the wicked instrument all the way in once more.

"Umph!" Billy Jo exclaimed.

He withdrew and jammed it into her again.

"Wow!"

Again.

"Man!"

Again.

"Unnh!"

"Fuck me, damn it!" Seth rasped.

"Yes... yes... oh, baby!"

Billy Jo began to move against his quickening thrusts, finding it easy to fall in with the copulative rhythm. Her buttocks bobbed against the mattress. Her thighs rubbed with seductive smoothness against

Seth's pumping flanks. Her soft little belly patted against his corded stomach as his extensive rod stroked deeply into her again and again.

Billy Jo stared up at the man whose cock was in her and marvelled over the fact that he wasn't Danny. Now that her channel had deepened and widened to accommodate the size of his extra-long, thick tool, he felt almost like Danny. If she were to close her eyes...

She did so, and found it possible to imagine it was Danny who was fucking her.

Yes... oh, yes! she thought, screwing up her face and giving herself over completely to the passion that filled her.

She tossed her hips at Seth with unrestrained ardour, encompassing his entire shaft on every plunge. His bulbous cockhead jammed against the neck of her uterus as her wet cuntlips nibbled at the base of his stalk. His big balls socked solidly into the valley of her buttocks, grazing her puckered anal sphincter. With every gliding, jarring stroke, Billy Jo's excitement grew.

She began to babble: "Danny darling... baby... oh screw me, screw me! That's so good! Oh, lover!"

"I ain't Danny!" came a guttural response. "I'm Seth! Call me Seth!"

Billy Jo refused to hear. "Danny... Danny... fuck me, Danny! Oh, *fuck* me!"

She cried, revelling in her sudden, liberating use of words that she had never spoken to her husband before, only silently thought to herself.

The young bride's hips began moving out of control – slamming rapidly upward as her cunt gulped hungrily at Seth's long, stiff cock. She bowed her back, lifting her head and shoulders; clinging to his neck. At last all her pent-up tension was coming out. She was letting it all go.

Seth fucked her fiercely, driving his hot cock with slippery speed into her rippling pussy. Billy Jo writhed, screwing upward, panting and moaning as she twisted her hips around the blissfully impaling prick.

The thrusting stopped and Seth's deeply embedded pecker jerked, the head ballooning in the pit of Billy Jo's vagina. Each burst of his hot semen, exploding into the mouth of her womb, gave Billy Jo an added shuddering response. Her orgasm grew until finally the bed all but disintegrated beneath her, and she felt as if she were floating on a cloud, utterly free of all earthly bonds.

She felt Seth relax against her with a groan of deep satisfaction, but even this didn't bring her back to reality. It wasn't until a minute or so later, when the lanky cowboy withdrew his softened penis and rolled off of her, that Billy Jo opened her eyes and thought about where she was and what she had done.

Sitting beside her, Seth grasped her chin and made her look at him. "You ain't gonna tell nobody about this, understand? You liked it as much as I did, and you're going to keep quiet."

She merely stared at him as if the awful significance of what had happened had only just permeated her mind.

Seth got off the bed, picked up his robe, and wrapped it around him.

He stood in the dimness, staring down at the well-fucked young woman. "Just keep quiet, or you'll plough up snakes. Remember that, or it'll go bad for you as well as me." He permitted himself a slight smile. "You're a damned good piece of ass. I'll be coming to see you again."

After Seth had left the room, Billy Jo lay unmoving in the silent darkness, her nightgown still rumpled around her neck, her vagina dripping with Seth's sperm.

Idly, she dipped a finger into her widely-stretched cunt and brought it, dripping, to her mouth. It couldn't have been better! she thought, triumphantly, as she savoured the mingled sex juices.

But she knew all too well that she was running a risk. Well, hell, it was worth it! For the first time since Danny's accident, her body was perfectly relaxed. All tension had melted away.

Billy Jo pushed down her nightie and pulled the sheets up to her neck. She would figure out some sort of plan tomorrow. In less than a minute, she fell asleep.

Chapter 6

It was a dream, Billy Jo thought after awakening in the morning. I dreamed the whole thing!

But the vividness of the memory made such a conclusion difficult to accept. Slowly, uncertain of what she would find, Billy Jo reached underneath the sheet that covered her and glided her hand down her body, across the ruffled hem of her nightgown and up into the soft-haired cleft between her thighs.

Her pussy remained slightly puffed, the passage easy to enter. Slipping two slender fingers inside, Billy Jo fearfully felt around. She encountered thick, gooey moisture.

Uh-oh! she thought. Seems I was a bad girl after all...

She spooned out a sample of the suspicious substance and brought it up to where she could smell it. One sniff confirmed that it was semen.

She lay back, planning her next move.

Feeling a twinge of guilt, as soon as Billy Jo had dressed and fixed her hair and makeup, she went to Danny's room. Her young husband had spent a restless night, and he was so full of complaints about his miserable condition that he hardly looked at her. Billy Jo felt relieved, but a little hurt because he wasn't taking an interest in her.

She felt like saying, hey buster! I let your brother fuck me last night! But the mere thought sent a new wave of desire flooding through her, and she turned away to hide her flushed cheeks.

When Billy Jo finally went down to breakfast, she found that the rest of the family had already eaten and gone out. She was glad of that. Rosita brought her usual enormous and delicious breakfast, which this time she wolfed down with a ravenous appetite, while the maid looked on with obvious approval.

She still needed to work out some strategy with those two horny brothers. It wasn't going to be simple, but it had to be done.

Billy Jo felt a little better after having reached this firm resolve. She finished her coffee and returned upstairs to be with Danny.

If only he weren't in that awful cast! I wouldn't have this silly situation on my hands. But, hell, I've known worse, she thought, and her full, sensuous lips curled in an impish smile.

Ranchers' Dirty Wives

* * *

At the dinner table that night, Seth kept eyeing Billy Jo. Each time she caught him looking at her, she looked away, unwilling for a silent dialogue to ensue. She glanced at Gus and found that he was also watching her. His leathery face bore a funny inquisitive look. Billy Jo suddenly felt ill at ease.

Maybe Gus knows what happened, she thought. If he does, will he tell Danny? Oh God, he better not, that's not in the script, for sure.

Hank was in his usual jovial mood, but he took no special interest in Billy Jo. He ate quickly, and then announced that he was going into town.

"On a week night?" Gus inquired with a scowl.

"Why not?" his son answered, grinning. "I won't be out too late."

"You going to see that red-headed writer?" Seth asked casually, his eyes on his plate.

"What's he talking about?" Gus asked Hank.

The husky young man looked uneasy and shuffled his feet. "It ain't nothing, Pop. Seth's just shooting off his mouth. Well, I'll see you later." He turned to leave.

"Wait a minute," Gus said. "There's somethin' I want to say while we're all here together. I've already had a talk with Danny."

"What is it?" Hank asked, obviously anxious to be on his way.

Seth looked at his father but said nothing.

"Like I told you," Gus continued, "I couldn't get no place with Bill Merret yesterday. We're stuck with them sky-high taxes. So while I was in town I, uh, dropped over to see Rex Reed at the *Lazy Q* office."

"You didn't tell us that before," Hank said.

"I know." Gus looked down. "Figured I wanted to give it some thinkin' first. But I guess... well, you boys have got a right to know."

The middle-aged man raised his eyes and looked at both his sons. "Reed upped his offer for the ranch. He's willin' to give us another million. That's above market value and... well, if you boys and Danny decide you want to sell out, I'll go along with it."

Seth squinted. "But, Dad, this place has been your whole life."

"That's just the point. I ain't got a hell of a lot of workin' years left, and it'd be wrong for me to insist on holdin' on here if you boys want to take the profit from the sale. Like I've said before, I figure you both, Danny and Matt each own twenty percent of this place, for the work you've done. I can take my twenty percent of the sale money and buy me a little spread I can handle by myself for as long as I feel like workin', then sell out and move to Florida or some place."

"Aw, c'mon Pop!" Hank said. "You're talkin' crazy!"

"Hank's right," Seth spoke up. "My future's on this ranch. We can pay the taxes somehow. Next year we'll check the appraisal when it first comes out and file a protest while there's still time."

Gus grinned. "Heck, boys! I was hopin' you'd say that. But remember," he added, his expression turning grave again, "any time y'all decide among you that you want to pull up stakes, I won't be standin' in your way."

"Sure, Pop," Hank replied. "Well, be seein' you." With a wave of his hand, he took off.

Seth got up from the table. He glanced at Billy Jo, then turned and walked into the living room, taking out his cigarettes.

"Danny's pretty worried about all this," Billy Jo told Gus. "He thinks that Reed fellow might try something else to force you out."

"Long as my boys stand with me, we can face up to whatever Reed does," Gus said. He stood and gave her a smile. "Want to watch some TV?"

"Maybe later," Billy Jo said as she stood. "I want to be with Danny for a while."

As she turned to leave, Gus took hold of her arm. In a soft, gravelly voice, close to her ear, he asked, "Is everythin' all right, Billy Jo? I mean, between you and Danny and all?"

Colour rose in her cheeks. "Of course, Gus. Why do you ask?"

"No special reason." The silver-haired man was watching her closely. "You just seemed kinda upset today. Seth or Hank ain't been givin' you a bad time, have they?"

"Why, uh, no."

"You sure?"

"Yes." Billy Jo forced a smile.

Gus let go of her arm and watched thoughtfully as she left the room. Then he took out his pipe and walked to the living room to join Seth.

* * *

That night Billy Jo placed a chair under the knob of her bedroom door. She lay awake in the darkness, wondering whether Seth would try to get in. Though the chair furnished evidence of her wish not to see him, she nevertheless felt an aroused tingle in her loins.

She kept thinking of the marvellous fucking he had given her on the preceding night – how pleasurable it had been. But it was risky – too risky for now.

Later she dreamed she was with a man who had visited her to give her the hard fucking she craved so badly. The man's face had been indistinct, as was his form except for his massively rigid penis which had stood handsomely before her, then had burrowed deep into her belly. The dream had ended before Billy Jo could achieve a release.

In the morning, thinking back over it, she wasn't sure if her dream lover had been Danny or someone else.

After tending to Danny in the morning, the frustrated young bride decided to go for a walk. With fall on the way, the weather had turned cooler, though the sky was clear. It was a perfect day for hiking.

Wearing blue denim jeans and a clinging red and white top, Billy Jo set out walking along the trail which took off from the stable area, cutting across the open rolling rangeland. Seth and Hank were working near the stable. The younger man yelled a greeting while Seth merely looked Billy Jo's way and said nothing. She gave them a wave and went on.

After topping the second rise, Billy Jo felt like taking a short rest. Green grass bordered a meandering little stream that was lined by shade-giving oaks. Billy Jo walked over to the inviting spot and sat down on the grass. The water gurgled pleasantly. Birds sang in the branches above her. The hot sun shone through the leaves and cast a lacy filigree of light on the ground.

She leaned back on her elbows and gazed at the blue sky above the horizon. At that moment, the world seemed perfect. All Billy Jo needed was to have Danny beside her at that lovely spot

I'd let him fuck me right here, the young bride thought daringly: Right out in the open, under the beautiful sky, with the birds to watch us.

The thought set Billy Jo's loins to tingling again, and she decided she had better continue her walk. She rose and brushed at the seat of her snug jeans, causing her taut, pert buttocks to quiver very slightly.

As she turned back to the trail, she heard the sound of a horse's hooves approaching. She tensed. Over the rise loomed Seth on horseback. He pulled his trotting horse to a stop and swung off.

"What are you doing here?" Billy Jo demanded, her expression turning cross.

"You heard what Dad said last night," Seth replied with a slight smirk as he moved up to her. "The ranch is twenty percent mine. So I guess I have a right to ride across it."

"That isn't what I mean. I want to know why you followed me."

"Guess," Seth said. He suddenly pulled Billy Jo into his arms.

Her full tits mashed against his manly chest, and he caught her startled, open mouth with his. She could smell an intoxicating mix of horse, leather and fresh male sweat. His tongue jammed between her lips as his lips suctioned. Billy Jo felt an immediate response that shocked and shamed her.

The other night seemed to be happening all over again. But Billy Jo had promised herself that she wouldn't give in to Seth again until she had worked things out. She began to struggle fiercely, beating at the slender cowboy and writhing in his embrace.

Finally Seth had to let her go. She backed up, breathing excitedly. Her large breasts rose and fell beneath her light blouse.

"Who are you tryin' to kid?" Seth asked with a sneer.

"I don't want you!" Billy Jo exclaimed. "What happened the other night mustn't happen again. Now if you don't ride away from here right now and leave me alone, I'll tell your father."

"He's Danny's father, too."

"I don't care! If Danny finds out, it will be just that much worse for you."

"No, baby. For you." Seth's eyes were hard and evil. "Remember, I've still got those sexy panties I took off you. How will you explain them?"

"Why, I... I'll just say you attacked me... and I couldn't stop you from taking my panties off."

"And you think Danny will believe that? Unh-uh." Seth shook his head. "He'll figure you cooperated. And he'll know I'm telling the truth when I say you took me into your bed the next night."

Billy Jo was silent. She was thinking fast as Seth spoke.

"We're all alone out here," he said, taking a step toward her. She backed up. "If you yell, nobody will hear. I won't have to work too hard to take you, 'cause you remember how good it was the other night."

Billy Jo kept backing up. When Seth made a lunge, she whirled away and began running across the grass. Her heart was pounding with a wicked excitement. She knew Seth was determined, and she knew she wouldn't be able to get away from him. But she also knew she had to try, for appearance's sake.

As they dodged among the trees, Seth in close pursuit of her, Billy Jo lost her footing and tumbled to the ground. Seth was on top of her, rolling her over on the soft grass and straddling her middle.

The horny young girl stared at him, her eyes wide. Her body throbbed with intense desire.

"I don't want to tear your clothes," Seth said, his breath heavy. "Cause after this is over, I know damned well you won't want to tell anybody."

"Seems like I don't have a choice then, does it," she retorted with spirit.

He scooted slightly forward so that he could pin her arms to the ground with his legs. She heaved and twisted beneath him, but it was no use. She couldn't throw him off or slide free.

Gazing down at her, his eyes twinkling insolently, the rangy young man proceeded to open the fly of his jeans. He reached inside, grasped his thickened penis, and drew it out. The wonderful thing curved forward from the gap in his pants.

"See what I've got for you?" He asked. "I want you to kiss it and make it stiff."

A strong thrill of pure lust went through Billy Jo. She was wrong-footed again. She hadn't imagined Seth would demand anything like that.

"No!" she exclaimed, her eyes wild with panic. This was wrong. She should suck her husband off before his brother, surely.

"You'll like it, baby. It tastes just as good as Danny's."

"But I've never..." She bit her lip, stil eyeing Seth's cock, her mouth watering.

"You mean Danny never got you to suck his?" Seth chuckled. "That shows what a dumb kid he is."

"Danny's fine and decent! He wouldn't expect me to do anything so... nasty!"

"I'll bet he's never sucked your pussy, either – like I did the other night. Remember?" Seth's prick lifted as he talked. "You liked that. And you'll like sucking my pecker, too."

"No!" Billy Jo cried.

"You see?" Seth said, looking down. "It's gotten stiff all by itself, just from me thinking about your soft, sweet lips around it. I'll bet your pussy's dribbling."

Billy Jo spat at him, writhing desperately. But she could accomplish nothing. Seth remained firmly astride her, his knees pinning her arms to the ground, his immense prick waving back and forth just inches from her face.

The musky scent of his aroused penis drifted into Billy Jo's nostrils, and she began to feel almost sick with desire.

If he doesn't push that thing against my mouth soon, she thought, I'll die!

Seth wiggled a little farther forward until his knees were planted next to Billy Jo's shoulders and the ankle portions of his boots were hooked over her wrists. His massively erect penis soared directly above her face. The young bride stared up at it and turned slightly cross-eyed.

"Now we're gonna see," Seth said huskily, "how much you like the taste of cock."

"Oh, no... no!" she hammed.

Paying no attention to Billy Jo's moaning

protests, Seth ringed his thumb and index finger around the base of his manly stalk and tilted the organ down until it rubbed across the tip of her cute, upturned nose. She gained a stronger burst of his fragrance. She also felt some moisture from his organ.

Seth waggled his stiff cock across her face, and Billy Jo tossed her head from side to side in a vain effort to avoid contact. His spongy cockhead kept colliding with her cheeks, nose, and eyelids. She held her eyes shut and her lips together.

Finally Seth gripped her head with one hand and pushed his prick firmly against her nose with the other. He held her in that humiliating position as she wailed in her throat. After a short while Billy Jo had to take a breath; the scent of Seth's penis was a pure aphrodisiac.

He swiped the bloated, rubbery bulb against her lips, and Billy Jo began to moan and whimper. She was enjoying the role of reluctant cocksucker too much to stop now. She tried to turn her head, but Seth's strong fingers were laced through her blond hair, holding her steady.

Positioning the end of his pecker at the centre of her full, pink lips, he twisted. Try as she would, Billy Jo couldn't prevent her lips from being pried apart. The spongy head of Seth's penis slid between them. But she kept her jaws firmly closed, and he was unable to get between her teeth.

Pleased for the moment with the gain he had made, the lustful cowboy swabbed his cockhead along her teeth, caressing her lips in a way that titillated Billy Jo despite her delicious humiliation. Waves of excitement were coursing through the warm-blooded girl. She felt moisture dribbling along her sexual folds.

"Okay, baby," Seth barked at last, "we've played long enough! Now you're going to suck my cock."

"Nnnnnnn!" Billy Jo said. That was the closest she could come to saying "no" without opening her mouth.

She knew that she would have to open her mouth pretty soon. Then his big, nasty cock would be inside it. Her mouth flooded with saliva in anticipation of the tasty treat. Seth continued to rub his penis back and forth between her slack, moist lips. Her labial nerve ends tingled. The urge to open her mouth grew stronger and stronger.

Finally Billy Jo gave in to it, and her jaws sprang apart. With a grunt, Seth pushed his entire large, smooth glans into her mouth. The bulbous mass depressed her tongue and skidded along the velvety track. She gulped convulsively, which forced her lips and teeth to clamp around the shaft of his organ.

The flavor of Seth's fat, juicy cock titillated her taste buds. Billy Jo revelled in the warm cockmeat's exotic flavours. There was a slight saltiness to it. He wiggled his stiff prick in her mouth while gazing down through slitted eyes, enjoying her changing expressions. As his organ pushed toward the back of her tongue, Billy Jo fought a gagging reflex. Billy Jo couldn't keep from gulping repeatedly as the slippery, bulging knob twisted in her mouth.

Seth began to stroke his stiff pecker in and out of the soft, slippery circle of her stretched lips. His glans glided forward and back on her wet, slightly abrasive tongue.

Grinning, Seth pulled the spit-slick shaft out of her mouth. Billy Jo stared up at him and said nothing. Her lips remained slightly parted. She was breathing heavily.

"Now lick it a little," Seth directed.

Without a second thought, Billy Jo stuck out her pink, slippery tongue. Seth smacked his cockhead against it. Billy Jo's tongue slowly began to circle the bulging, dripping glans. She swallowed his juice along with her own copious saliva.

She found that she had become very hot. The crotchband of her delicate panties was plastered to her moist, throbbing labia. Her nipples were painfully stiff in her bra.

Seth pushed his prick forward a little,

and Billy Jo pursed her lips around the tip of it. She sucked of her own accord, no longer willing to keep up the charade of distaste for this succulent, monster cock.

"That's the way, baby..." Seth growled. "Nice, huh?"

Before Billy Jo could answer Seth jammed his cockhead fully into her mouth once more. Her brain whirled. She sucked deliriously.

"Okay, that's enough!" Seth said, and pulled his prick out of her mouth.

"Now how about a fucking?" Seth asked as he slid backward along Billy Jo's body, his hands mauling her tits through her blouse and bra.

She was panting.

"Say, 'Yes, Seth'," he insisted as he began unbuttoning her blouse.

"Yes... yes... I mean... oh, no!"

He chuckled, opened her blouse, and palmed the loaded cups of her brassiere, rolling the firm, spongy breasts. He felt her nipples standing up hard.

Seth backed up farther, opened the top of her denim jeans and pulled them down. Underneath she wore pink bikini briefs, trimmed with white lace. He pulled the jeans off her feet, taking her shoes also.

Billy Jo kept staring at the monstrously virile organ, sticking out and upward from the fly of his pants. Her thoughts were divided

Ranchers' Dirty Wives ★ 113

between recollections of how his prick had felt and tasted in her mouth and her anticipation of how it was going to feel when he jammed it up the itching, passion-puffed crevice between her thighs. There was no point in stopping him now, Billy Jo thought; she could hardly wait for the penetration to occur.

Seth drew her to a sitting position, unhooked her bra, and took it away. Her luscious knockers stuck straight out, their erect pink tips tilted slightly upward. The mounds were gloriously full, with no hint of sag. Seth brushed a hand roughly across them, shaking the wobbly globes and sending a thrill coursing through Billy Jo. She mewled hungrily.

"You want it, don't you?" he challenged. "Here – take hold." He grasped her hand and wrapped it around his thrusting cock.

"Oh God, it's so hard and huge!"

"Tell me you want it," he demanded.

"No... yes... I mean..." She gripped his prick harder.

He grasped her tits and pressed them together. "Tell me you want to be fucked!"

"I want you to...!" She could not quite bring herself to say it. It was too humiliating.

"God damn!" Seth snarled, straddling her waist on his knees. His thrusting cock bumped across her titties.

As Billy Jo stared down, delighted and

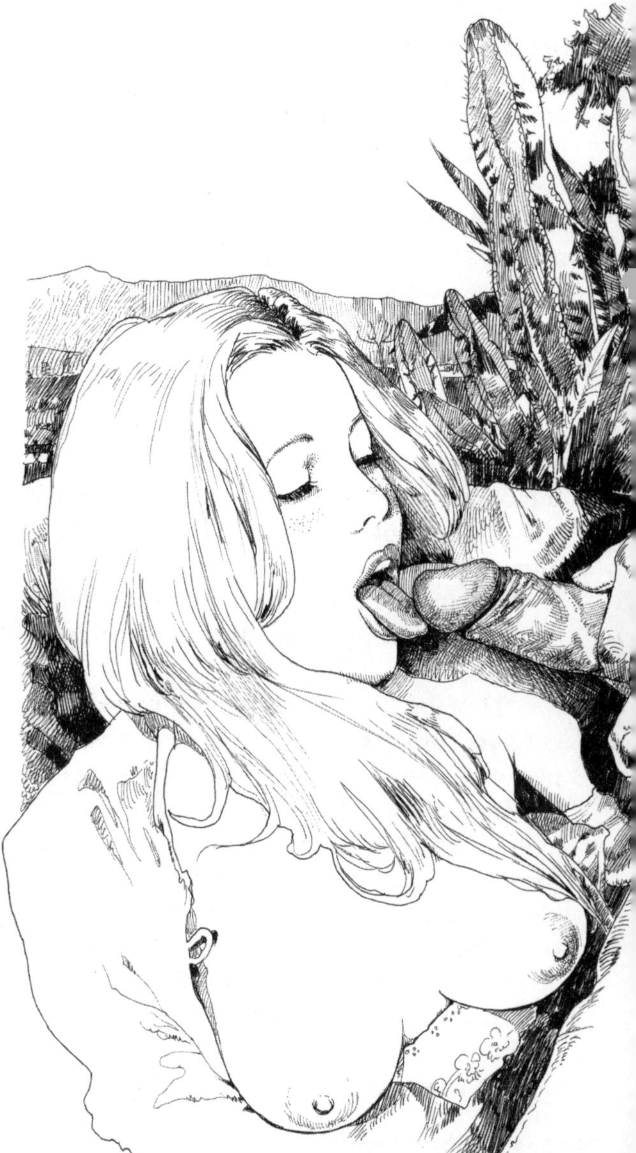

thrilled by what he was doing, Seth caught his upthrust pecker between her satiny mounds. He pushed her breasts together, enfolding his hot, throbbing shaft. Its bulging head stuck up out of her valley and, as Seth began hunching, Billy Jo watched the rosy, mushroom-shaped prominence rise and fall as its stalk stroked the inner walls of her breasts.

"Lick it as it comes up!" Seth ordered.

"No..."

"Lick it!"

Billy Jo bent her head, stuck out her tongue, and swiped at the upward thrusting cockhead. After doing this several times, she let out a little moan, bent farther, and captured the entire meaty glans in her mouth.

Seth fucked his cock up and down between her tits and into the rosy, elastic circle of her lips.

"Now – tell me what you...want!" he snarled, grasping her long blond hair and pulling her head back.

She stared at his lean, hard face, her eyes misting as her scalp hurt and her body throbbed. But she was loving this. Every word of humiliation turned her on more.

"Fuck me! Fuck me!"

Seth grinned evilly. "Where do you want my cock? Say it!"

"Inside me!" Billy Jo panted. "In my... belly! All the way in!"

"In what?"

"In me! In my..."

Seth gave her hair another jerk.

"In my cunt!" Billy Jo cried. "Oh shit, fuck my cunt!"

"With what? With what?"

"With your cock, you bastard," Billy Jo howled. "Stick your cock in me! I want your beautiful, big, sweet prick!"

"That's it, baby!" Seth exclaimed, letting go of her hair and pushing her onto her back on the grass.

He backed up, gripped the thin band at the top of her panties, and quickly peeled the garment out from under her hips. He turned her panties inside out as he hauled them up her tapering legs which Billy Jo lifted to assist him. Seth tossed her pants aside and pushed her thighs wide apart.

The lips of Billy Jo's pussy were so puffed with desire that they couldn't remain closed. Seth gazed delightedly at her coral inner folds which were running with viscous fluid. Her clit was sticking up.

Her little oval hole was throbbing, heaving.

Seth pushed down his pants and shorts, then scrambled between her thighs, tilting his cock, to her opening. He rammed his stiff dick all the way up her slippery channel, drawing a gasp from the thrilled young woman. His fat cockhead stretched her tissues wide apart.

Supporting himself on straight arms, Seth stroked his immense tool in and out of Billy Jo's quivering, throbbing quim. Her intimate membranes molded themselves to his ramming organ, seeming to suck it deeper and deeper. His forceful plunges bumped her womb. His heavy balls plopped against her super-sensitive asshole.

Wild with passion, Billy Jo gripped Seth's arms just below the shoulders, digging her fingernails in. She bowed her back upward and swung her head from side to side as she hunched against him, panting and moaning.

Suddenly he stopped fucking her and pulled his pecker out. The wet-red organ, rigidly upthrust and quivering with sexual power, swayed and bobbed as he backed off the startled girl.

"What are you doing?" she demanded. "Put it back, you prick. Fuck me, damn it!"

"Roll over," Seth snapped, pushing at her hip. "Get on your knees and shoulders."

"Why?" she asked in an anguish of frustration. But she did as he had directed.

Seth stared at her round upthrust ass, lusciously split into two perfect cheeks with a deep alluring crevice between. Her small, brown asshole winked at him. Below it, surrounded by fine blond hair, was the pink elliptical slash of her labia.

Grasping his cock, Seth moved forward and sank into her pussy from the rear. Billy Jo's eyes opened wide, the expression on her pretty features almost comical in its look of gratified lust. He began to fuck her, slamming his straight, hard belly against her buttocks.

Billy Jo gasped in rhythm with his jarring thrusts. Her hot nipples skidded in the grass. She felt deliciously humiliated positioned this way, out in the open, her ass in the air and Seth ramming into her as if she were some bitch on heat or – worse still – some heifer mounted by a bull.

Billy Jo's passion quickly surged toward release. Seth strove to achieve his climax. Neither of them heard the dull clop-clop of approaching hooves.

Hank topped the rise behind them just as Billy Jo howled, "Oooh, I'm going to come! Fuck me, you bull! Oh, you stallion! Fuck me... fuck me... fuck me!"

Seth drilled her upthrust ass like the passion-crazed animal he was. The sounds of slapping flesh were loud on the clear air. As Hank stared at the shockingly abandoned sight, his prick stiffened against the horn of his saddle. "I'll be a sonofabitch!" he muttered under his breath.

Billy Jo bawled as she climaxed. Her cuntal muscles gripped Seth's thrusting cock as if they wanted to pull it off. He jerked and growled fiercely as his balls gushed up their load of cream. Spurt after spurt of his thick, hot fluid pumped into the convulsing girl.

With a happy moan, Seth fell forward atop her forcing her fully against the grass.

Hank stopped his horse and dismounted. With his cock straining forward, threatening to burst his snug jeans, he ambled toward the passion-locked lovers on the grass.

Chapter 7

"Well, now just lookee here!" Hank laughed as he pushed his battered Stetson toward the back of his head.

Seth whirled around, pulling his slightly softened penis from Billy Jo's quaking hole releasing a gush of pearly jissum that coursed down the inside of her thighs. The sated girl stared at Hank over her shoulder with dazed eyes.

"Git out of here!" Seth snarled at his brother. He quickly stood and stuffed his wet, reddened penis into his briefs as he pulled his pants up.

Billy Jo was able to collect herself sufficiently to turn onto her bottom. She clapped a hand in front of her blond-tufted loins and extended an arm across her bobbling breasts. Hank grinned as his eager blue eyes caressed her. A hump remained at the front of his pants.

"I said git!" Seth demanded angrily as he approached Hank.

"Just cool down, brother," the huskier young man soothed. "We're gonna have us a little talk."

Billy Jo uncovered her breasts and scooted forward, titties shaking, to snatch her pink panties off the grass.

"Don't put them on!" Hank told her. "Let's all just take it easy."

"What have you got on your cruddy mind?" Seth asked.

Hank's eyes twinkled. "The same damned thing you had on yours – gettin' myself a piece of – "

"No!" she exclaimed, fumbling with her panties.

"I told you to leave those fuckin' pants alone!" Hank said, rushing over to her. He snatched the silky undergarment from her hands. He held her pants up and looked at them. "Man, they're sure wet!" He chortled as he ran a thick finger over the slippery, gleaming crotch, then lifted the panties to his nose and sniffed them. "Mmmm, smell good, too!" Hank said. He balled the panties and stuffed them into his pocket.

"Billy Jo don't have to mess around with

you," said Seth.

Hank looked at him. "Oh, don't she?"

"Shit, no!"

"Well, I'd just give another thought to that if I was you, Seth old stud. I saw you two screwing, and if I don't get my piece I'll blab the whole thing to Danny."

"Oh, please don't!" Billy Jo cried, genuinely concerned that he might and that this was all getting out of hand.

"Course, there is another way," Hank said, looking at Seth.

"What're you getting at?" his older brother asked, squinting.

Hank suddenly became subdued. "Well, I was gonna talk to you today, Seth. Looks like now's the best time for it. I, uh, changed my mind about stayin' here at the ranch. I'm for sellin' out."

Seth's eyes widened. "When did all this happen?"

"Just last night. I was with Viv, you know."

Billy Jo wondered who Viv was, but didn't ask. She was worried over having been caught with Seth, and for fear Hank would make good his threat to tell Danny.

"What's that red-headed slut got to do with it?" Seth asked.

Hank's face darkened. "Watch the way you talk about her. Viv means somethin' to me."

"Sure – a cheap piece of tail."

Hank balled a fist, then slowly relaxed. A grin crept over his broad face. "You ain't gonna rile me up – not now, not when I'm in the saddle."

"What are you talkin' about?" Seth snapped. "Make it plain."

"Okay – either you agree with me that we ought to sell the ranch, or I'll tell Danny about you and his bride."

Seth stared at his younger brother for several moments, then said, "Maybe you just better go ahead and tell him."

"Think good," Hank advised. "It'll bust the family wide open. Danny won't want to stay here after that. He'll agree to sell out, even if you won't. And it'll take only two of us to convince Pop. That's majority rule."

"Why do you want to sell all of a sudden?"

Hank shuffled his feet. "Viv and me are fixing to take off. We need some money to get us started."

"You want to give up your interest in the ranch just for a few weeks with that babe? Shit, she'll leave you as soon as the money runs out."

"She will not!" Hank declared vehemently. "She's... gonna be my wife."

"Hank, you don't even know her," Seth said with weary patience, as if talking to a child.

"I know all I need to know. Now, are you

going to agree to sell or not?"

"Can't I... please get dressed?" Billy Jo inquired plaintively. She was still sitting naked in the grass.

"Don't be in a hurry," Hank said, tossing her a grin. He returned his attention to Seth. "Well, what's it gonna be, brother?"

"Go ahead and make it with Billy Jo," Seth said. "We can think over the other."

"Seth, what are you saying?" the indignant girl exclaimed.

"What's it matter to you – another piece more or less?" Seth retorted. "I've got important things at stake."

Hank glanced at the pretty girl who was trying to conceal her voluptuous charms as she cowered in the grass. He wet his thick lips, then turned away.

"Naw, I don't think I'd better." He looked at Seth again. "If I was to screw Billy Jo, I wouldn't have no leverage on you."

He hesitated, and his face slowly brightened. "But hell, it don't make no difference, does it? If Danny finds out we both fucked his sweet bride, he'll be all the more anxious to get away from us. He'll want to sell out for sure."

Something like desperation gripped Billy Jo. The thought of having sex with her other brother-in-law, after she already had 'sinned' with Seth, was bad enough; but the prospect that Danny would find out about both transgressions and perhaps never speak to her again was unbearable.

There was only one thing for it: she struggled to her feet and began to run, this time not wanting to be caught. Hank took off after her. Seth stood and watched, realizing that his best bet was to let his brother take Billy Jo and hope her tight little cunt would get his mind off Viv. There was something funny about that redhead, anyway. She just didn't ring true.

Billy Jo dodged through the trees, her white buttocks wiggling and quivering, her lovely titties bouncing wildly. As her thighs scissored together, Seth's sperm dribbled down between them, creating a slimy slickness.

Running fast, despite the lustful swelling in his pants, Hank gained on the frantic girl. Finally he grasped her around the middle and hauled her to the ground, falling atop her.

"Please... please!" she cried.

"What the... hell are you fussing about?" Hank panted as he rolled her over. "You put out... to Seth. What's wrong with me?"

"I hate you!" Billy Jo exclaimed, grappling with him. Tears of anger welled in her eyes. It had all gone so terribly wrong. "I hate both of you!"

"Now just simmer down..."

Holding her firmly against the grass as

he straddled her, Hank smeared his wet mouth onto hers. His tongue stuffed its way between her lips. His hand, between their bodies, clutched a pliant, full-mounded breast. Powerless to resist him, Billy Jo felt her resolve melting just as it had done with Seth. She didn't want to give in, but in the end her body simply overruled her mind.

She loved the humiliating incursion of Hank's tongue, the sucking of his slobbery lips against hers. She loved his hand on her breast, squeezing and punishing the sensitive organ. Her nipple stiffened against his palm, and her pussy began to generate a fresh supply of love cream.

Hank didn't prolong the deep kiss. After only a short while, he slid backward on Billy Jo's voluptuous young body and began paying oral attention to her tits, licking and tugging at her nipples as he batted the wobbly boobs about.

She didn't fight Hank, even though her arms were free. What was the use? Her own traitorous body was as much to blame for her degradation as Hank was.

Seth came strolling up. The lanky man stood with his hands thrust into the hip pockets of his jeans, his pelvis arched insolently forward, as he watched his younger, huskier brother wallowing in the creamy billows of Billy Jo's chest. She stared up at Seth, her eyes wide and helpless. She breathed through parted lips.

"Get her to suck your dick," Seth told his brother. "She likes that."

She moaned softly.

Hank lifted his head. He stared at Seth. "She did that for you?"

"Hell, yes," Seth smirked proudly.

"Damn, I'd really enjoy a blow job. Viv won't..." Hank caught himself before saying more, but the information was out.

"Billy Jo will," Seth laughed. "Won't you, honey?" He nudged her with the pointed toe of his cowboy boot.

"No!" she exclaimed, eyes flashing sulkily. Now that the stimulation had momentarily stopped, the strength of her resolve was returning.

"Show her your pecker," Seth advised his brother. "Once she gets a look at it, you won't be able to keep her from going down."

Billy Jo shuddered. But as Hank, grinning in lewd anticipation, began opening the front of his pants, her eyes were drawn to the widening gap. When he reached inside to take out his organ, she tensed. Her blood quickened.

Seth watched with amusement. When Hank's cock swung into view, stiffening to a firm erection, though smaller than Seth's had been, Billy Jo felt a fluttery sensation.

"You don't have to sit on her," Seth said.

"Shit, she'll get up and run again," Hank replied, laughing as his naked cock stuck out.

"No, she won't. Will you, honey?" Seth gave Billy Jo another poke with the toe of his heavy boot.

Her only answer was to sigh. But she kept staring at Hank's prick.

"Get off her," Seth told his brother.

With obvious misgivings, Hank dismounted.

"Now lie on your back," Seth said.

"Aw, now wait a minute..."

Hank stretched out next to Billy Jo, watching her all the while. Her sense of enjoyable humiliation increased. Seth was trying to make her suck Hank's penis of her own accord, and she wanted to believe she wouldn't do it without a show of reluctance, but she didn't trust herself any more.

"Okay, go after him," Seth told her.

Billy Jo stared at Hank's horn-like erection which angled backward toward his head. The thing was very stiff. Its bare rosy knob enticed her.

"Get on your hands and knees and bend over him," Seth instructed patiently.

It was obvious that he was enjoying the situation. So was Hank, who eyed Billy Jo while he grinned hopefully, saying nothing. So was Billy Jo.

Suddenly she thought, oh shit, I don't care!

Lunging onto her knees, her breasts leaping then dropping to dangle over the prostrate man, Billy Jo bowed her head. Her silken blonde hair brushed over Hank's belly and thighs.

He tensed and his eyes grew hot as Billy Jo grasped his cock and held it perpendicular to his body. He watched her luscious pink lips part and her mouth open.

"Ah... man!" Hank exclaimed, blood racing, as his cockhead was suddenly engulfed by Billy Jo's warm mouth. Her tongue pressed against him. Her copiously flowing saliva bathed his glans.

She sucked ravenously on Hank's cock, thrilling to the raunchy taste and the uniquely pleasurable sensation of having the thrusting, bulbous projection in her mouth.

Billy Jo loved the sense of degradation that the act gave her, made all the more intense by the fact that Seth was watching.

I'm a pig! she thought. A hot young pig, and Seth and Hank know it. Poor Danny! Too bad he can't know it too!

She drove her encompassing mouth as far down Hank's upthrust cock as she possibly could, her wet lips sucking slickly around the bone-hard shaft. The head of his organ touched the opening of her throat, but she didn't gag. She wished she could take his prick all the way to her pussy by way of her mouth.

"Get your hand in his pants!" Seth exclaimed, his eyes twinkling fiendishly as he watched the lustful display. "Play with his balls."

Oh, yes! Billy Jo thought. His balls! His beautiful big hairy balls!

She dug for Hank's testicles but was disappointed to find they had contracted into knobs that clung tightly to the base of his shaft. She caressed them avidly, however, enjoying the abrasive coarseness of his scrotum against her hand.

Hank derived an even greater thrill in reverse. He groaned and writhed, wondering how long he could hold out. Billy Jo's lips were working near the base of his cock, gliding and rhythmically contracting against the film of her saliva which trickled down his stalk. His ballooning cockhead bobbled on the base of her tongue and into the tightness of her throat as she lapped against his shaft.

Billy Jo suddenly disgorged the slippery organ. She let it stick straight up in front of her face as she licked anxiously up and down its sides. Hank's masculine aroma flooded her nostrils – a not unpleasant mix of fresh sweat and leather on clean skin.

Seth's passion was reborn as he watched the suddenly sex-crazed girl eat his brother's cock with abject abandon. She engulfed the glans again, pumped her head up and down several times, then let the stalk escape once more and resumed licking the rosy, gleaming glans as it waggled back and forth across her face.

Seth walked around behind her and eyed her twisting, shivering ass. He dropped to his knees, opened the top of his jeans and pushed them down, together with his briefs. His cock snapped forward to point menacingly at the kneeling girl.

The lush roundness of her white, quivering buttocks made Seth recall the thought he'd entertained when he'd watched her wriggling over the top rail of the corral the other day. He grinned fiendishly, then spat on his hand and rubbed the slimy fluid over the end of his prick.

Billy Jo had resumed sucking Hank's cock, bobbing her head in long, looping strokes as she skidded his glans along the full length of her tongue, her stretched lips hungrily gobbling at his rigid shaft. Her ass waggled to and fro in front of Seth.

The lanky cowboy grasped her buttocks with both hands, spreading them wide apart to expose her small, puckered asshole. He poked the tip of his prick against the enticing indentation.

Billy Jo felt the strange contact, but

she was too immersed in the excitement of mouthing Hank's cock to think of anything else. She didn't even tense her anal muscles.

With a deft twisting thrust, Seth broke through the narrow aperture, opening her asshole wide as he drove his bulging glans into her rectum.

"Aaaaaagh!" Billy Jo exclaimed around Hank's prick as she felt the painful penetration of her rear.

But the intense hurt eased immediately after it had begun, and she felt only a shocking fullness as Seth's huge, stiff pecker sank into her squishy guts. Her asshole remained widely stretched around his shaft, but she had passed turds that big. Seth's immense glans was inside her where the constriction was not so intense.

Eyes watering, her entire body throbbing wildly, Billy Jo went on sucking Hank's upthrust cock, pumping her mouth even more avidly on the thick stick. The husky cowboy was clenching his fists, desperately trying to hang on. His nuts churned feverishly as Billy Jo caressed them.

Seth grunted with delight as he fucked his big dick in and out of his sister-in-law's twisting, hotly grabbing rectum. Her anal ring gripped him so tightly around his shaft that he knew he wouldn't be able to last long.

Billy Jo writhed between the two horny

pricks – one in her mouth and the other up her asshole. The mingled sensations of almost unbearable fullness in her rectum, degradation and wildly uninhibited passion were overwhelming in their combined force. She began to climax. Bucking and heaving, she took Hank's hot cock into her throat and fucked backward against Seth's brutally skewering rod. Her asshole spasmed around him.

Seth shot. As his semen burst searingly into her bowels, she the cum-laden balls that lay so tight at the base of Hank's prick. He jerked and sprayed her throat with a thick gush of cum. Billy Jo gurgled and gulped, desperately trying to keep pace with the ensuing spurts of his jism. But she couldn't swallow it all and some of the milky slime flooded out of her mouth and down Hank's twitching shaft. Seth was still quivering in Billy Jo's rear, spilling the last dregs of his sperm.

Her orgasm – the strangest, yet one of the most satisfying of her varied sex life – sent undulations rolling through her from throat to tail. When the vibrations finally ceased, she felt emotionally drained, yet full of warm semen in two places where nature had never intended it to go.

Billy Jo collapsed to the grass, letting Hank's softening penis flop free of her lips as

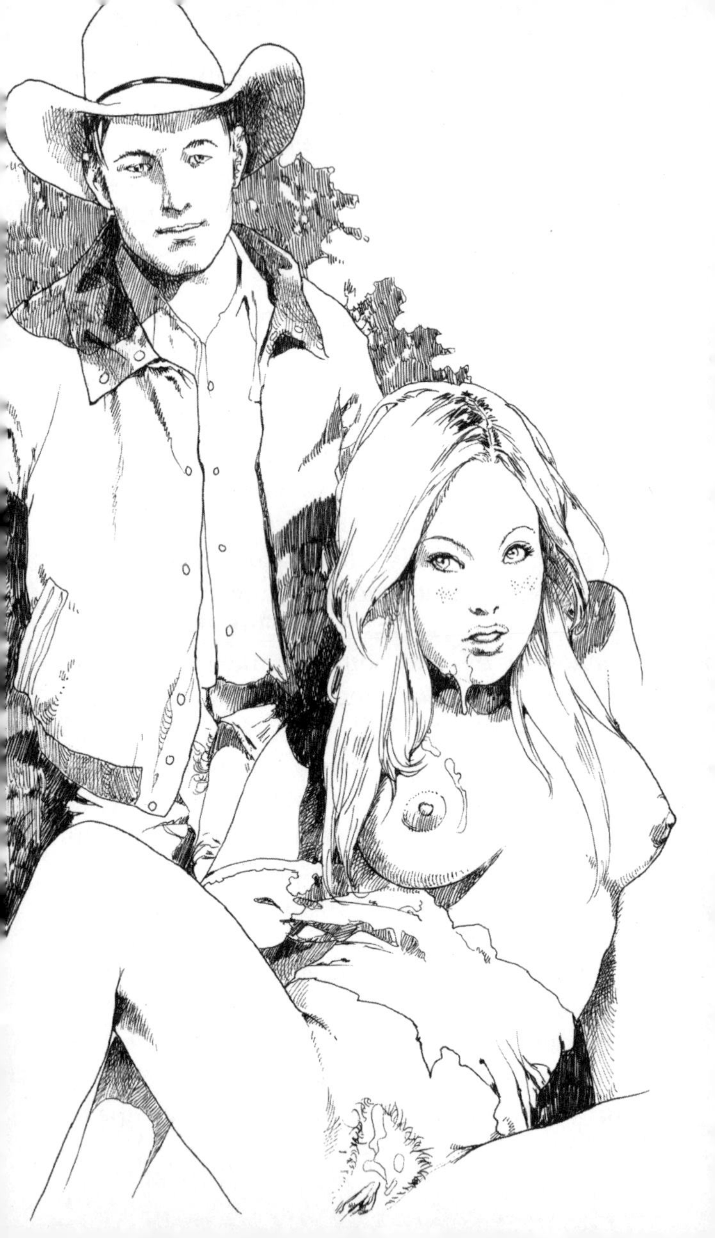

Seth withdrew his stained tool from between her buttocks with an obscene little sound.

Chapter 8

The driver of the black Cadillac Eldorado parked with accomplished ease and got out of the big convertible in one fluid, graceful movement. She stood for a moment, elegant and poised in a simple but flawlessly cut navy suit and pillbox hat, and adjusted her dark glasses against the glare of the evening sun, then set off down the street, her hips gently swaying.

When Alice McCluskie thought about it later, the whole episode seemed like some sort of erotic daydream; satisfying, liberating in some parts, sordid and tawdry in others - definitely a hit and miss affair. In truth, she felt a little dirty. She had gone to see Reed for a routine meeting; there were papers to sign, her allowance to discuss and he needed to go through some management accounts with her as a matter of course. Alice had heard rumours that Reed had been giving her estranged husband a hard time by playing some dirty tricks: hardly the way to treat a neighbouring fellow-rancher, especially one with such close ties to her. It had to stop.

It was late when she got to the ranch office on Mulberry's Main Street and Reed was the only one there to greet her; both secretaries had gone home.

Reed stood up behind his desk, and smiling, took her hand and shook it warmly. Although she found him less than handsome, she had to admit that he had a certain magnetic aura; despite being slim and wiry, the dark-haired ranch manager exuded a powerful masculinity that she found almost... attractive. He was always well turned out, with his neat little moustache and carefully groomed hair; his Western-style jacket and shirt, the string tie and immaculately pressed chinos and polished boots had obviously come from an expensive style shop in San Antonio or Austin.

"Come in, Mrs. McCluskie," Reed said in a mellow voice that suggested refinement. "Close the door, if you will please. Sit down." Reed gestured toward a comfortable-looking leather chair in front of his desk.

Rex Reed looked at the handsome raven-haired woman who sat before him. She must be forty by my calculations but doesn't look a day over thirty, he thought. And those big, beautiful melons! No hiding them even if she does get her clothes made in Austin! But it was Alice McCluskie's strong, near-perfect facial features that had always captivated the ranch manager. A generous dash of Hispanic blood gave her the dark, sultry looks of a Latin temptress: her high fringe and well-defined eyebrows completed the look of a woman full of intriguing spirit. Alice had felt his eyes taking inventory of her body as she walked to the chair and sat. Her moderately short skirt slid well above her knees, which were sheathed in sheer panty hose, and her brown eyes coolly returned his avid gaze.

"Why, Rex," exclaimed Alice, "you're being formal as heck. Since when have you started callin' me 'Mizz McCluskie'?"

Reed leaned back in his chair and steepled his fingers under his chin, his brown eyes twinkling. "Well something tells me this is a formal visit, Alice…"

Alice took a deep breath. She didn't smile. "Oh. You mean about what I've been hearing about you and Gus. Yes. It's true I wanted to know why you've been giving my husband and his family so much trouble."

"Oh?" Reed chuckled a bit uneasily. "Well, I'm not an ogre. I bear no ill will toward your husband's family, I assure you. On the contrary, I've made them a very generous offer for their ranch."

"But they don't want to sell."

"Did they appoint you as their agent to come and tell me that? Hell, always knew that old Gus McCluskie was all hat an' no cattle!" Reed's eyes continued to twinkle.

"No," Alice said, bridling at the insolence of the man. "This was my own idea. Besides, we have other business. It's hardly the sole purpose of my visit."

The slender ranch manager leaned forward. "Your husband doesn't know about it?"

Alice shook her head impatiently and spoke with authority. "I hardly see what that's got to do with it. Look, Rex. If I wanted to I could *order* you to stop whatever it is you're doing to Gus and my stepsons. Hell, Rex, I could *fire* you! But I don't want to interfere in your otherwise exemplary running of the *Lazy Q*. So, please: just stop all this shenanigans over at *Los Altos*."

Reed's gaze slid down to her breasts, caressed them through her close-fitting blouse, then dropped to the warm roundness of her hips and tapering thighs. Alice tingled under his frank examination.

"You're a very beautiful woman," Reed said. "How old are you, if I may ask?"

Alice flushed. "Forty-one."

"Why, Alice, you know something? You don't look a day over thirty."

Alice felt flustered and even a little irritated. She knew this form of flattery was intended to win her over. And with unerring accuracy, Reed had gone for her most vulnerable point – her feelings of inadequacy and loneliness that been so prevalent of late. Hell, she thought, who are you fooling, Alice McCluskie. You need a man, and Rex knows it. From the way he had looked at her, she could tell that he wanted her body and she knew he was man enough to just take it. The thought made her shiver with suppressed excitement.

"Look, Rex..." she began.

"Alice, I'm not sure how to put this but, for a long time now, I've been very attracted to you, and I've always hoped that..." Rex let his voice tail off suggestively.

"Yes?" Alice felt her cheeks glow pink. Suddenly she felt like a teenager on her first date. Her nerves were very alive and she shuddered. The critical moment had arrived, and Alice still wasn't sure where she stood with the man. He might only be mocking her. But she doubted it. She had to make up her mind, it was up to her... she could just put him in his place with a word or...

She stood.

Reed tensed visibly. His voice was slightly husky as he said, "Come closer."

Alice moved up beside his chair. He swivelled to face her. Electric impulses raced along her taut nerves.

Looking her in the eyes, Reed curled his hands around the backs of her knees and began slowly gliding them up her sleekly stockinged thighs. Alice's inner trembling increased. She felt slightly weak as well as an incredible current of sexual exhilaration course through her body at his sensitive touch.

Rex could tell by the way her eyes were half-closed that he was getting to her. She was no longer the tough, articulate female boss she had seemed a few moments ago.

His hands reached the tops of her full, firm thighs. Her skirt was bunched on his arms, exposing most of her lovely legs to his avid inspection.

Rex's penis stirred in his pants.

As he raised his hands a little farther underneath Alice's skirt and wrapped them around the firmly bulging cheeks of her fine, generous bottom, his cock stiffening and straightening out in his chinos. He squeezed and rolled her full, womanly buttocks, which were sheathed in pantyhose over light briefs.

Alice was becoming as aroused as he was. She no longer cared about any ranch business – or even about the *Los Altos* business. Everything had to be for her pleasure – whatever she wanted. She quickly removed her dark blue suit jacket and tossed it so that it fell over the big leather settee.

As Reed fondled her pliant ass, the sexy, mature rancher's wife unfastened her blouse and took it off. Reed's eyes were on her tits, which overfilled her snug bra, the creamy flesh bulging above the rims of the cups. Alice reached behind her and unhooked her bra clasp. The cups surged forward. She took the limp harness away, letting her titties swing free full, their stiff pink nipples acting like magnets to his eyes.

"My God!" Reed exclaimed. He pulled her against him, his fingertips pressing her silken briefs into the crack of her ass as his warm palms compressed the resilient mounds.

Alice bent slightly, shoving a breast against Reed's mouth.

He sucked at her luscious nipple, his tongue stroking the firm rubbery projection as his lips skidded moistly against the rim of her areola. Alice's pussy began to dribble. Her head grew light.

Reed switched to her other fleshy boob, letting the sucked one bob quiveringly away. Alice shoved her dry nipple between his lips, and he quickly moistened it, making it tingle in rigid arousal. Reed's moustache tickled her breast as he sucked her nipple deep. The hot bud throbbed against his lapping tongue.

Giving a twist, Alice jerked her tit from his mouth. She dropped to her knees on the carpeted floor. Thrilled, Reed swung his thighs wide apart so that the uninhibited woman could move closer.

Alice did so, her brain turning giddy with excitement. It wasn't only sex that was stimulating her; it was the fact that she was becoming desired once more; after months, no, *years* of neglect, finally someone was appreciating her. Reed was obviously eager for her to continue.

Her hands lit in his lap, feeling the hardness of his sex through his clothes. She quickly unzipped his fly. Reed breathed hard as he watched her delicate, feminine hand glide through the fly of his trousers to enter his shorts to grasp the bent shaft pressing against the knit fabric.

Alice grasped his cock and swung the horny thing into view. Reed had a foreskin which covered the head of his dong, except for the moist pink crest which peeped out through the hood's ruffled lip.

Alice had never seen a prick that looked just like that. As she hesitated, Reed clutched the upthrust shaft and retracted its velvety cover. The pale-pink head of his penis bulged in manly splendour. Its heated scent rose to Alice's nostrils.

Reed waited.

The woman gazed at his prick, which now looked like the others she had known, except that its pink skin appeared more tender. She bowed, parting her moist lips, and captured the meaty glans in her mouth.

"Ah!" Reed exclaimed, digging his fingers into her luxuriant black hair, clenching great bunches of her lustrous black tresses.

His hands massaged Alice's scalp as she began to suck his cock, her head rhythmically plunging and rising as the encircling band of her lips skidded up and down across the firm, sensitive ridge of his corona. She drew in his male flavour and breathed his aroused scent. Her pussy salivated more, wetting the crotch of her briefs and plastering the lacy material against her humid cuntlips.

Alice writhed, her mouth screwing fervently up and down his shaft as she warmed to her work. Panting with excitement, Reed tousled her lovely hair.

Finally Alice held just his glans within her mouth. She bathed the bulging knob in her slippery saliva as her lips rhythmically contracted behind its rim. He felt the firm edges of her teeth. Her abrasive tongue swabbed the super-sensitive tip of his peter.

She lifted her head. She was breathing as hard as he, and her eyes wore a passionate glaze.

"Well?" she asked, her voice tense and husky.

"Yes!"

"Do you want me to go on?"

"Oh, God! *Please!*"

Inwardly, Reed was exulting. It was true that he had always lusted after Alice, his old boss's daughter. But he had never expected her to be this hot. For chrissakes, she made Viv Lanier look like a girl scout. His mind raced ahead. This might be the way to do it, he thought. Get the bitch so hot for him that sooner or later she'd just sign over her rights to the ranch. He'd keep her on an allowance, of course and if she became trouble, why, he'd just cut her off. Hell, this was a lot simpler than dealing with her father and brother had been...

"Go on!" he rasped at Alice.

She hesitated. This was pure, rash, bestial sex. With an employee, what's more. But his large cock, standing strong and straight, enticed her.

Alice bowed and waggled her little pink tongue back and forth across the head of Reed's prick.

"Good – " he said as a blissful tremor passed through him. His cock twitched.

Alice began kissing just the tip of it, encircling the moist crest with her soft, sucking lips. Her tongue beat a tattoo against the tip of his organ as she drew in his stimulating flavour.

She lunged, taking the entire glans and part of the shaft into her mouth. Her tongue stirred against the bone-hard, quivering column as she sucked. She suddenly let the pecker escape. The thing swayed and twitched in quivering stiffness.

"Oh shit!" exclaimed Reed. "You're driving me crazy!"

She feverishly licked up and down Reed's fat, rosy shaft, causing the upthrust column to rub back and forth across her nose and cheeks. When her mouth reached the very bottom of his shaft, Alice was frustrated by the presence of his clothes. She dug into Reed's pants and shorts, grasped his nuts, and wrenched them into the open.

The impassioned woman rolled the contracted, coarse-textured scrotum in her hand as she alternately sucked and licked Reed's glans. Finally she capped her mouth over the head of it once more and sucked wildly on the bulging meaty knob as her wet lips worked slurpingly behind the ridge of the glans.

Reed groaned, arching upward in his chair, and his cockhead skidded to the back of Alice's tongue. She felt a strong tremor shake him, and suddenly her mouth was filled with his spurting cream. The slimy fluid slid down her throat as she gulped, and some washed forward along her hotly lapping tongue to ooze out around her lips and dribble down her chin. With her head spinning madly, Alice continued to suck the ejaculating male until his balls were depleted and his dong began to wilt.

Alice let the organ flop away and wiped

her chin with two fingers. She stuck the fingers into her mouth and sucked them clean.

"My God!" Reed groaned, breathing deeply. "It's never been... so good!"

"Take your clothes off," Alice panted. "Lie down on the floor with me."

"I don't know... if I can go again."

"Yes, you can," Alice insisted, tugging at him.

Reed slid out of his chair and lay on the floor. Bending over him, titties shaking, Alice helped him off with his shoes, trousers and shorts, then his jacket, tie, and shirt. She left his socks on.

She quickly skinned out of her skirt, pantyhose, and briefs.

They rolled together on the carpet, Alice finally straddling him and feeding him her dangling tits. Reed sucked and licked at the elongated pink points of her bobbling boobs. She backed up and kissed her way from his neck to his nipples, then to his belly button, which she licked and sucked.

Alice rubbed her satiny, firm-soft breasts back and forth across his flopping penis. She caught his flaccid but sizable organ between the mounds and caressed it by rubbing her titties up and down along its sides.

Reed was breathing hard and turning his head to and fro.

Alice burned with the need to screw him.

Her need to filled, to be fucked, was very great. Her only purpose was to get the man ready to fuck.

She backed further down and fervently licked his meaty cock. She held it up and attacked his scrotum, which was now velvety soft and elongated. She licked the hairy sac all over, then seized a bulging nut in her mouth and sucked it.

"*Ohhhh!*" Reed exclaimed, bucking upward against her face.

Alice sucked his other ball, then nuzzled beneath them. She pushed his legs wide apart and licked deeper into his crotch. Her moist, passionate tongue swabbed the crinkled dimple of his anus that nestled in the hairy valley between his lean, muscular asscheeks, giving her a new burst of flavour. Alice pursed her soft lips around the man's asshole and sucked, battering at his rectal gate with her tongue-tip.

His cock strengthened, waving to and fro, half-hard. When Alice's wet tongue twisted through the ring of his anus and slithered up his ass, Reed's prick assumed bolt stiffness.

"God *damn!*" he cried. "Fuck me, you wild bitch! *Fuck* me!"

Alice leaped astride his loins, immediately sheathing his pecker in her hot, clasping quim. She bobbed up and down, titties flopping in luscious fullness as Reed's thick shaft stretched her silken, slippery channel with deeply penetrating strokes. She squirmed, grinding her hot, hairy cunt around his upthrust cock.

"I love – it!" she cried. "Screw me... *screw* me – "

Reed heaved and bucked, trying to drive his cock all the way up to her throat. Its tip managed to enter the tight little gate of her womb as Alice ground down hard, massaging his balls with the soft undersides of her buttocks.

Reaching up like a drowning man, he grasped her bobbing tits and squeezed hard.

"Oh, shit!" Alice exclaimed. "That's... so incredible... I'm coming! I'm... "

Reed knifed upward, throbbing in the middle of her belly. His semen splashed into her convulsing womb and streamed down his quivering shaft, mixed with her own hotly gushing product as her cunt muscles rippled, spasming to a rhythm of its own.

The man groaned blissfully, his churning balls spewing up their last drops of jism. When he went limp, Alice fell forward atop him. He grasped the rubbery pillows of her ass.

"Damn... never had it... so good!" he rasped at her ear.

The copulation had been very satisfying for Alice, as well. But she wanted more. She wondered if Reed had it in him.

He rolled her off him and sat up.

"That was great, baby," he said with a satisfied smile. "You made me happy as a gopher in soft dirt."

Alice blinked. "Do you mean it?"

"If I tell you a hen dips snuff, you can look under her wing. There's one thing, though."

"What's that?"

"You didn't give me a chance to kiss your sweet twat. It's been a long time since I've had a chance to go down on a real woman's one."

Laughing happily, Alice fell onto her back and spread her thighs, drawing her knees up. Reed knelt and noisily attacked her moist and marvelously fragrant crotch.

His moustache tickled thrillingly as his tongue scoured up and down her velvety cuntlips, licking up every drop of girl juice and semen which had spilled from her still-throbbing vessel. Then he spread her hairy outer labia wide apart, exposing their pink, smooth inner sides. He licked that slippery meat and proceeded to the wiggly folds of her vestibule, sucking up the thick juice that dribbled between them. Finally he lodged his tongue on Alice's palpitating clitoris, fluttering in and out until she had another come, accompanied by a little gush of juice that he eagerly licked up and swallowed. She flopped wantonly about, her big tits lurching and quivering.

Reed moved forward atop her, his cock unbelievably stiff again. He sank his rod into her narrow, slick crevice and fucked her for fifteen minutes, non-stop, until they both exploded in a final gut-wrenching orgasm which left them exhausted.

Alice had been the first to move. Leaning up on one elbow she gave him a shy grin while she traced a pattern on his smooth, muscular chest. Eventually she rose to her feet and started to put her clothes on. Rex followed suite. They both seemed a little lost for words.

Finally Alice said, "Wow. That was incredible Rex. You've made me feel like a real woman again. I'm grateful." Although she meant them, the words came out as somehow self-conscious and insincere.

"You always know where you can find me, *Mrs*. McCluskie," said Rex with a sort of mock gallantry, making a sweeping bow.

As Rex locked up the office and they said their goodbyes and left for their cars, Alice felt strangely empty inside. Sure, the sex had been good, in fact it had been thrilling. But somehow it left her with a bad taste in her mouth. Perhaps it came from screwing the hired help, she thought, a little grimly. What's more, her shrewd female instincts told her that Rex was somehow not to be

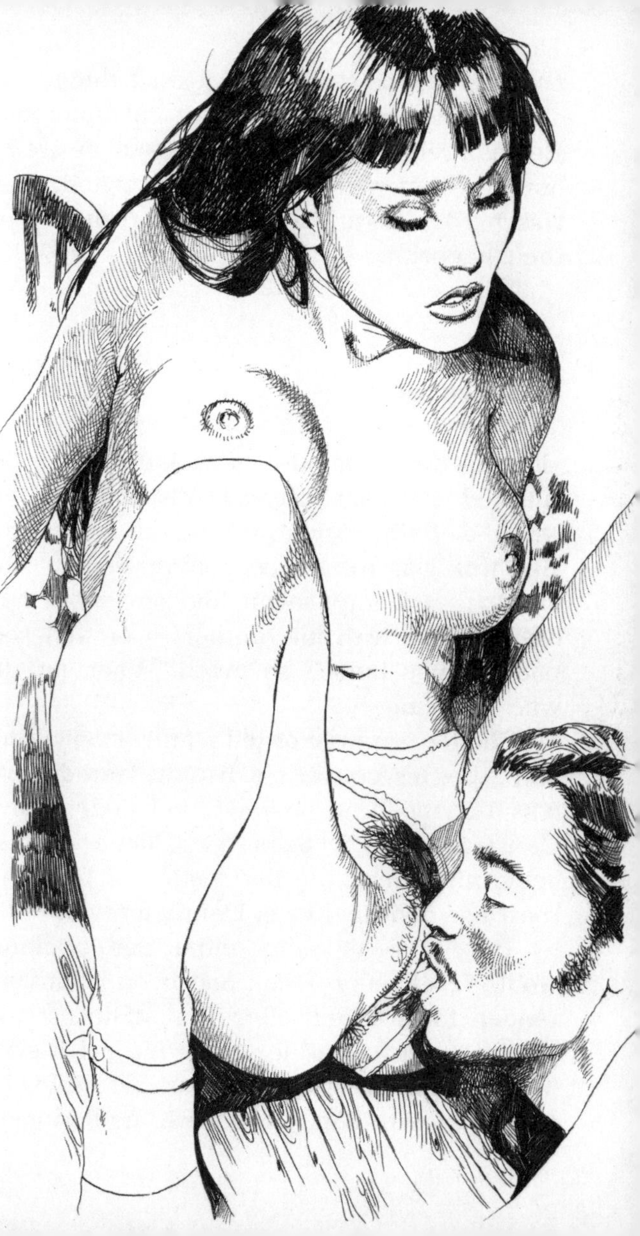

trusted. Maybe she should just sit things out a while and see happened. But she knew that Rex had rekindled the fires of sexual desire in her, and that was a blaze, once started, that was hard to extinguish, like a brush fire in the Chaparral.

Chapter 9

During the remainder of that day, Billy Jo suffered a certain physical discomfort as a result of Seth's unnatural assault upon her. But this was insignificant compared to the worry that Danny might find out about her orgiastic sex with his brothers – or that she had enjoyed herself so much. What sort of wife was she?

She had an urge to tell Danny everything and to beg his forgiveness. But she feared there was a chance that he would not understand. Confession might ease her shame, but it could also mean the destruction of her new marriage and the loss of Danny forever.

Billy Jo didn't believe either Seth or Hank would tell Danny. Hank had been positively tender toward her after the affair on the prairie, as if he had forgotten his girl friend, Viv, and his previously announced desire to run away with her. As for Seth, he had good reason not to tell Danny what had happened, because he didn't want Danny and Hank to line up against him in favor of a sale.

As evening came on, Billy Jo's driving urge was to make up to her young husband for the adulterous sins she had committed against him. That seemed the best way of relieving her guilty conscience.

They spent the evening together, watching TV on a portable set which Danny's father had provided. When the network fare ended at eleven o'clock, Danny asked his young wife to turn off the set.

After doing so, she lay down beside him on the bed, snuggling close. Even with his leg and hip in a cast, Danny's nearness warmed Billy Jo in a deeper and more meaningful way than Seth or Hank had been able to do. They had aroused and thrilled her, but she didn't have the slightest feeling of love toward either of them. Paradoxically, her love for Danny had increased as a result of the experiences she'd had with his brothers.

If only I didn't feel so horny all the time! Billy Jo thought.

The young bride's need to overcome this painful lust inspired her to be especially attentive toward Danny. She kissed and caressed him as they snuggled together. She thrilled as he toyed with her titties. She had removed her bra before coming to see him to make matters as easy for him as possible. After he had rolled her lusciously resilient mounds through her blouse, Billy Jo unbuttoned the front of the garment and let her breasts spill out.

"Wow, this is what I want!" Danny huskily exclaimed as he palmed the wobbly, rounded flesh.

Billy Jo's nipples bristled passionately against her husband's caressing hand. He plucked at the thrusting rosy tips, rolling them between his thumb and finger, then using them as little handles to shake her lovely boobs.

Billy Jo was growing hot. She wished with all her heart that Danny was free to fuck her. If only they could have lived normally as man and wife, she might never have let another man touch her.

Danny's hand slid down her front, and Billy Jo worked herself toward the head of the bed. This gave him easier access to her loins and permitted her to shove a bobbling, stiff-tipped titty into his month. As he licked and gently tugged on her firm, tingling nipple, his eager hand moved up underneath her dress. He petted her warm, soft pussy through the narrow band of sleek fabric that passed between her legs.

"Get inside my panties," Billy Jo murmured. "Let me have your finger."

Danny hesitated, saying with an embarrassed laugh, "I don't know if I'd better get so excited. Remember, you told me you didn't much care for jacking me off."

A daring idea occurred to Billy Jo. "Maybe there's... something else we can do tonight."

"Baby, if you're talking about fucking," he said, his lips brushing her tit, "there's just no way. You can't get on top of me with my leg hiked up in the air, and I sure as hell can't get on top of you."

"There's another way for us to have fun," Billy Jo replied, her excitement increasing. "But get into my pants first. Finger me."

"Hey, you've gotten more broad-minded during the last couple of days," Danny said with a happy chuckle.

Billy Jo writhed inwardly. "It's just that I miss you so, honey. I miss making love to you the way we did every night before you were hurt."

"Don't you think I miss it?" Danny replied, a husky edge to his voice, as he lifted the crotchband of her panties and touched his young wife's dewy, hair-lined slit. "This especially! Oh Christ, how I'd love to stick my dick into it!"

"I *want* your big dick!" Billy Jo exclaimed in a tone that let him know she really meant it. To reinforce the point, she snaked a hand into his pyjamas and grasped his stiff,

Ranchers' Dirty Wives ★ 155

warm rod.

"Oh, wow..." Danny said gratefully.

His middle finger wormed its way into her slippery snatch, and he went back to sucking her pointed breast. Billy Jo stroked his hard cock and tickled the bulging head with the tips of her fingers.

After a while Danny took his mouth from her tit and panted, "Oh God, I need to get my rocks off!"

Billy Jo took a deep breath. Her brain was swirling giddily. Now that the moment to carry out her daring idea had arrived, she was concerned about Danny's response.

"Promise you won't be sore?" Billy Jo asked. "I don't want you to think I'm some kind of slut."

"Baby, I'll love anything you want to do," he assured her. "Just do it!"

Billy Jo sat up, taut tits quivering, and looked at his luscious prick as she drew the stiff rosy thing out of the folds of his pyjamas.

"This is so nice!" she exclaimed, her voice husking up. "If I can't have it inside my body, I can at least..."

She bowed her head, breasts swooping, and to Danny's immense surprise engulfed his throbbing cockhead in her mouth.

"Aaaah!" he exclaimed, and a happy jolt went through him. "Oh, baby, I never thought you would... ooooh!"

She was licking and sucking at his smooth, slippery glans with such obvious desire and relish that Danny had to steel himself against the wonderful thrills that resulted. He was about to shoot off.

Billy Jo tingled with delight as she pumped her encircling lips across the ridge of his cockhead and ran her gliding, fluttering tongue all over the knob. Danny's prick was somehow so much better than either Seth's or Hank's! It was the only cock she really wanted, and she enjoyed it nearly as much this way as she would have if Danny had shoved it up her cunt.

The sensitive nerve ends on Billy Jo's lips and tongue reveled in the marvelous excitement of encompassing and stroking her handsome husband's hard penis. She took more and more of the wondrous shaft into her mouth, letting his cockhead glide far back on her tongue as she lapped against his coronal ridge and sucked avidly at his thick, slippery stalk.

"Uuuh... uuuh!" Danny panted. "Oh, God damn! Oh, baby, you'd... better stop! I can't... take any more! I'm going to..."

Billy Jo didn't stop. She sucked and licked his stiff dick even more passionately, mouth-fucking it with long, rapid strokes as her restless tongue tried to taste and caress every inch of the thrusting organ, even letting it slip half-way down her throat which constricted to massage its sensitive tip.

That did it.

"Aaaah!" Danny exclaimed. His whole body went tense, and his eyes rolled back. "No! Oh, SHIT! It's... wonderful... aaarrrgh!"

His throbbing prick erupted in Billy Jo's mouth, splashing his thick, warm semen over her tongue and into her throat. The thrilled girl gulped and sucked him even harder. She kept swallowing happily as his cum streamed down to her stomach. In the midst of his vigorous ejaculation, Billy Jo came, her whole body blossoming with luscious warmth.

She continued to suck and lick Danny's cock until she was sure she had gotten all the tasty cream he could possibly give her. When his organ began growing soft in her mouth, Billy Jo released it and raised her head. She ran her tongue over her lips, swallowed a final time, and smiled at her blissfully happy husband.

"I love you!" Danny exclaimed with deep feeling. His eyes warmly mirrored the emotion that filled him as he caressed Billy Jo's silky golden hair.

"And I love you!" Billy Jo replied with equal fervor. "Only, you! Forever!"

Danny drew her down beside him, and they kissed. The faint foreign taste on Billy Jo's tongue gave him a strange added satisfaction.

What she had done had proved her love for him more strongly than anything else possibly could have, Danny felt – and by kissing her immediately afterward he was demonstrating his appreciation and understanding.

The married lovers clung together, their lips moving warmly, their tongues in moist embrace. The rest of the world seemed so far away that it might as well not have existed.

Chapter 10

After saying good night to her husband, Billy Jo went to her own room and immediately to bed. With her guilt eased and her body pleasantly relaxed after her soft but satisfying climax with Danny, the young bride had no trouble falling asleep.

It seemed only minutes later, though actually it was about two hours, when she was jarred awake. Arms were around her, and a hard column was thrusting against her belly.

"Hank!" she exclaimed, staring directly into his face in the dimness. "Get out of here! You can't just... "

His thick lips sealed her mouth, preventing further protests. Billy Jo's brain reeled as his aggressive tongue stirred her mouth while his hand palmed the shivery mounds of her bottom.

It's starting all over again! she thought with alarm. No, I can't let it!

But the old problem remained: If she were to resist, there would be a fuss and Danny would surely find out. Also there was the more subtle but equally troubling problem of her own sensual responses. Hank's kiss and touch were already stirring her up.

What's wrong with me? Billy Jo wondered desperately. A man only has to touch me, and I'm ready to fuck or suck! That isn't normal. I must be some sort of sex-fiend!

But her self-recrimination didn't change the way she felt. The feeling grew stronger as Hank's lascivious kiss and impudent petting continued. Soon Billy Jo's loins were on fire, and she had to have the only treatment that could extinguish the flames – a cock, properly applied, between her legs. After two consecutive orgasms without having her pussy pierced, the passionate young woman desperately needed to be fucked.

"Come on and stick it in me!" she panted as she broke away from Hank's kiss and grasped his horny prick.

"Suck it a little first... just a little," he begged, his laboured breathing revealing an excitement at least as strong as hers.

"I want you to fuck me this time," Billy Jo said, dropping all pretense of reluctance.

"I'll fuck you, don't worry! That's why I came here. But put your sweet lips around it, baby. Just for a second."

Billy Jo slid toward the foot of the bed and tilted Hank's pecker. She bowed, her golden hair brushing softly, seductively across his belly, then seized his meaty prickhead in her mouth. She nibbled on the rubbery glans, sucking and swallowing. She played with Hank's nuts.

"Baby... yeah!" He tousled her silken hair. "God, you do that good! Oh shit, I love it!"

Billy Jo loved it, too. But she wanted to do more than suck him. She had to have his rod inside her.

After several slurping, gliding plunges of her encircling lips on his firm prick, she raised her head. She threw a leg across him and mounted up, aiming his sturdy lance into the aching wet hole amid her blonde pubes. She dropped until she was sitting on Hank's balls and his hard cock was sticking all the way up inside her.

"Jesus, you're tight!" he exclaimed. "What a pussy!"

"Shut up and fuck!" Billy Jo demanded, realizing that she sounded like the worst kind of tramp, but not caring any more.

She began to twist her hips and bob up and down on Hank's upthrust prong. He joined the salacious rhythm, bumping into her snug, slippery sheath each time she lowered her crotch.

Billy Jo and Danny had screwed this way a couple of times during their honeymoon, just for variety, but he had preferred to be on top. Billy Jo rather liked to top-ride, because it let her control the pace of the copulation.

Hank gazed at her big tits bobbing in the moonlight, then grasped them and kneaded the full, firm mounds like baker's dough as Billy Jo posted on the saddle of his loins. His thick cock voluptuously stretched the tissue of her pussy as it rammed up and down, in and out. When she rotated her channel around him, the stretching was even more luscious.

As the excitement mounted, Billy Jo fell forward onto her arms, thereby bringing her hot clit into firmer contact with Hank's stroking shaft. She gasped and writhed, shaking her head and wobbling her large tits in his grasping, milking hands.

Neither of them noticed the opening of the door and the arrival of a third person in the room. Seth stared at the moonlit spectacle on the bed, and a fit of jealousy overwhelmed him. Where did Hank get off, taking over his territory this way? He had let Hank have her on the prairie because it had been necessary, but that didn't mean he was going to give his younger brother free rein.

"What the hell's going on?" he barked, not

realizing how stupid the question sounded.

Billy Jo stopped screwing and stared at Seth, her mouth falling open.

"Aw shit, what're you horning in for?" Hank growled.

"You're the one who's horning in," Seth said angrily, "and I don't like it."

"Why don't you ask Billy Jo how she feels about it?" Hank suggested, breathing hard. "I know how she feels. Her cunt is grabbing onto me like crazy!"

"Shut up, both of you!" Billy Jo whispered urgently. "Do you want Danny to hear?"

As it happened, however, Danny wasn't the one they had to worry about. He was soundly asleep. The boys' father, plagued by insomnia because of his problems with the ranch, had heard footsteps in the hall for the second time within the span of a few minutes. The footsteps had moved in the same direction each time and therefore could not have been made by the same person leaving his room and returning. Gus concluded that both his elder sons were up and about.

He immediately thought about Billy Jo. From the time she had arrived at the ranch, Gus had noticed both Seth and Hank eyeing her. And during the last couple of days she had seemed nervous, as if reluctant to look either him or his sons in the eye. When he had asked her if everything was all right, she had assured him it was, but he had been unconvinced. With Danny flat on his back, his beautiful young bride offered a powerful temptation to a couple of horny bucks like Seth and Hank. Gus understood, because his own loins had responded to Billy Jo's plump, writhing ass and erect, quivering tits.

The old rancher got out of bed and put on his robe. Moving quietly, he left his room and walked down the hall to the room Billy Jo was occupying. Standing close to the door, he listened.

"... don't you ask Billy Jo how she feels about it?" Hank was saying. "I know how she feels. Her cunt is grabbing onto me like crazy!"

Gus stiffened, his leathery face turning red with rage. Hank obviously had gotten to Billy Jo, and it sounded as if Seth was trying to horn in. Gus could hear Billy Jo's voice, but it was pitched softly and he couldn't make out what she said.

Considering only that he should put a stop to the outrageous adultery, for Danny's sake, Gus opened the door and entered Billy Jo's bedroom.

The eighteen-year-old blonde had resumed actively screwing Hank, even though Seth was standing next to the bed and staring at them. All three were oblivious to Gus's entry into the room.

The furious intensity of Billy Jo's grinding atop Hank, her white back undulating in the moonlight and her buttocks bobbing up and down, struck Gus motionless. It was clear that Danny's bride wasn't being forced; she was the aggressor in the powerfully erotic scene. Gus felt heat surge into his loins. His old pecker, which rarely saw sexual action any more, began to stiffen and tent his bulky robe.

Seth also was hard with excitement as the young fuckers on the bed strove to a heaving, quivering finale. Billy Jo's passionate wail mingled with Hank's lusty groan as he spurted his warm cream deep into her belly. They sighed in unison, and Billy Jo fell motionless atop him.

When Gus finally found his voice, he barked in a furious, rasping whisper, "Hank! Seth! Get outa here!"

Billy Jo gasped. She rolled off Hank and desperately tried to cover herself with the bedclothes. But by that time Gus had seen all of her, including the hair-fringed, gaping pink hole where Hank's cock had been.

As Hank scrambled off the bed, sweeping his robe from a nearby chair, Seth faced his father defiantly.

"What's the idea of breaking in here?" the elder son demanded.

"Keep your voice down!" Gus snapped.

"What's the idea of you being here in the first place?"

"That's Billy Jo's business, not yours."

"Come on, Seth!" Hank urged, struggling into his robe. "For cripe's sake!"

Gus whirled on his younger son. "You're the worst! You bedded your brother's wife."

"Seth screwed her before I did," Hank hissed.

"Is that true?" Gus asked Billy Jo. His eyes condemned her.

The thoroughly shamed young woman wished that she could die. "Yes... yes, it's true!" She buried her face in her hands.

Seth reluctantly – turned toward the door, following his embarrassed brother.

"Wait!" Gus whispered urgently. His sons faced him. "Not one word of this to Danny, understand? And both of you leave Billy Jo alone from now on."

"Yeah, Pop," Hank said, eyes downcast.

Seth was silent. He left the room behind his brother.

Gus turned toward Billy Jo who lay crumpled on the bed, sobbing gently. The bedclothes covered her bottom, but her white, graceful back gleamed enticingly in the moonlight.

Gus's erection had lapsed. However, he remained uncomfortably aroused. "Why'd you do it?" he asked tensely.

Billy Jo raised her head and looked at him. "Oh, Gus, I'm so sorry! They were after me and... Oh, I miss Danny so!" Again she pressed her face against the bed and sobbed.

The middle-aged man felt compassion toward her. Danny had told him she was a virgin on their wedding night, which meant she had been a good girl until Seth and Hank had led her astray. It was a cruel twist of fate that had caused Danny to be injured right after instilling her with such an urgent need for sex.

Recalling how passionately she was screwing Hank, the old rancher wondered how he would be able to keep her away from his able-bodied sons until Danny recovered. If he didn't figure out a way, Gus felt, the family would be torn apart.

The solution suddenly occurred to him. At first he was unwilling to accept it, but common sense as well as the heat in his loins argued in its favor. Danny wouldn't be capable of understanding, Gus realized. But Danny wasn't going to find out, if he could help it.

Gus approached the bed and placed his hand gently against Billy Jo's back. She stopped crying and looked up at him.

"Don't blame yourself," he said, his tone surprisingly tender. "I reckon you couldn't help givin' in to Seth and Hank."

"Do you really mean that? Oh, Gus!" Grateful for his understanding, Billy Jo wanted to throw herself into his arms. But she restrained the impulse just in time, realizing she was nude beneath the sheet which she held around her.

The silver-haired man smiled at Billy Jo in the dim light. There was warmth in his crinkly blue eyes. "I'm gonna help you stay away from Seth and Hank. You want to do that, don't you?"

"Yes!" Billy Jo eagerly replied. "Danny's the only one I love."

Trembling with a carnal urge too long suppressed, the fifty-seven-year-old man took off his robe. Billy Jo's eyes widened as she stared at his long, meaty penis that was jerking into full stiffness and the big dangling balls that hung low beneath it.

"Gus! No! Oh, my God!" She scooted backward against the wall, clutching the bedsheet in front of her.

"Shhh!" Gus said. "Don't let Danny or the other boys hear. They wouldn't understand. But this is the only way."

Billy Jo's brain swirled wildly, unable to come to grips with the shocking reality Gus was presenting. He was Danny's father. He couldn't be asking her to have sex with him.

He sat on the edge of the bed and reached for her. Billy Jo cringed. Gus took hold of the sheet which was her only concealment and began drawing it away. Billy Jo continued to clutch the thin cover. But as she looked into her father-in-law's eyes and realized he was the only security she had, her fingers relaxed their hold. The sheet left her.

Gus gazed at her luscious young beauty – big tits, high and pointed, belly firm and gently rounded, hips full, blond hair bristling wispily where her thighs and belly joined – and he was filled with a desire such as he hadn't known in years. His old cock stiffened and stood up from his lap, the bald knob suffused with rosy warmth, the brown stalk hard as in the days of his youth.

Billy Jo stared at the evidence of her father-in-law's arousal, and she began to react as she had to every stiff prick she had seen at *Los Altos* Ranch. She couldn't help herself.

Gradually she was making her adjustment to the inevitable. There didn't seem to be anything that could be done about it. If Gus, who was old and wise, could understand and accept her for the passionate creature that she was, why shouldn't she accept herself?

She threw her arms around the middle-aged man, her naked breasts squashing against his firm, hairy chest. He snuggled closer to her as they sat on the bed, and she felt his hard cock standing against her belly. His mouth captured hers, his firm lips sucking at her sweetness. His tongue thrust between her teeth to caress the silken sides of her mouth.

Billy Jo was launched on another passionate ride. She clutched Gus's cock as if it were a lever to direct her giddy flight. The feel of her cool, delicate fingers encircling his manhood gave him a marvelous new thrill. He felt the virility which he had feared was slipping away from him permeate his entire body, giving him a warm, lusty glow.

He stopped kissing Billy Jo and pressed her onto her back against the bed. He began to caress and kiss her lush body.

Gus had almost forgotten how delightfully firm and resilient big teen-aged titties felt. But now the memories of his youth came flooding back to him as he wrapped his gnarled hands around as much of each boob as he could hold and squeezed tenderly. Billy Jo's urgent pink nipples thrust even higher than before, and he brushed his lips across them, marvelling at their fresh firmness. He drew Billy Jo's nipples into his mouth and took long, voluptuous sucks at each of them as her hand stroked his horny shaft.

She was doing some marvelling of her own. Somehow she hadn't believed that a man Gus's age could produce a hard-on that would rival that of her twenty-year-old bridegroom or his slightly older brothers. But the proof was in her hand, and she was enjoying it.

Gus moved down along her body, forcing her to relinquish her hold on his staff. He licked and sucked at the satiny skin around her navel, then dug his tongue into the dainty cup. Billy Jo squirmed with delight, causing her tummy to quiver against his face.

He had a definite destination in mind. Though at least one of his sons had fucked Billy Jo within the last few minutes and presumably he deposited his sperm in her sexual crevice, Gus felt he must taste and orally caress her pink-petalled flower of desire.

First his chin, then his lips invaded the tuft on her mound. Billy Jo held her breath. Gus clutched her firm, smooth thighs from underneath and lifted them into the air, spreading them wide apart. Her glorious scent touched his nostrils as he bowed his grizzled head. Then his lips and lapping tongue invaded her dripping wet, slippery softness, and he was in heaven.

Billy Jo was very close to paradise herself as she thrilled to the gliding, fluttering, twisting explorations of her father-in-law's eager tongue between the passion-puffed labia of her cunt. He circled and lapped at the thrusting tip of her clitoris, causing her to moan with delight. Gus caught the already inflamed pea-like protrusion between his lips and sucked at it, making Billy Jo's passion build.

She wanted to bob her hips but somehow was able to restrain the urge, fearing Gus would lose his luscious hold upon her if she moved. She panted and made little whimpering cries. Finally Gus skidded his tongue down her velvety, slick trough and into the flaring elliptical hole of her vagina.

Billy Jo had to move now. Letting out a voluptuous groan, she pressed her wet, meaty cunt hard against Gus's loving face and rotated her hips, her buttocks wiggling above the mattress. His tongue plunged in and out of her palpitating, grabby hole, and the motions of her hips returned his passionate oral fucking.

"Oh, that's... wonderful!" she panted. "Wow! Oh, Daddy... daddy... that's so... good!"

Though Billy Jo's silken thighs were brushing warmly across his ears as he slurped at her tasty twat, Gus heard what she called him. He was thrilled all the more. Clutching the cheeks of her wriggling ass in both hands, the impassioned man fluttered his fucking tongue at rapid speed in her syrupy, sweet box, and she came.

A ball of fire seemed to burst in her belly, sending down a shower of fresh viscous fluid into Gus's wildly lapping tongue. The heat radiated through Billy Jo's entire body. She moaned with bliss.

Old Gus guzzled down his daughter-in-law's creamy goodness, then sent his tongue scouring along the plush, hair-covered portals of her pussy, gleaning every drop which had splattered out. He licked her clit a final time, twisting his tongue around the sensitive little knob and pushing its fleshy sheath as far back as it would go.

Gus straightened on his knees. Billy Jo lay in an utterly abandoned pose, panting.

"Fuck me... fuck me..." she breathed heatedly. "Stick it into me! I neeeed it!"

He was ready. His phallus stood so high and hard, so choked with blood, that it felt as if it might crack right off. But there was something else he wanted to do before he sank his shaft into the luscious girl.

Holding one of her lovely legs high in the air, he licked and sucked along its wonderfully smooth, soft inner surface. Then he gave Billy Jo a twist, and she flopped onto her stomach.

The passion-gripped girl feared that he intended to invade her tight rear hole as Seth had done. Hot as she was at that moment, she would have accepted the hurt of being sodomized in order to enjoy the thrill of penetration. But it very quickly became apparent that Gus had no such brutal purpose. The sudden pressure of his whisker-bristling face against her soft, quivering buttocks told Billy Jo that he only wanted to kiss her ass.

Pleased, she bowed her back and thrust her plump, firm buttocks against her father-in-law's face, wriggling the wealth of springy softness against his leathery, stubbled cheeks. His wet tongue swabbed her twitching asshole. Then his lips suctioned around the little puckered orifice and he kissed it lingeringly, drawing up a faint flavour that in other circumstances would have been offensive but which only fed his mad passion at that delirious moment.

Finally Gus raised his head, smacking his lips over this latest treat. Billy Jo rolled onto her back and reached for his lean, strong body.

"Fuck me!" she cried softly. "Oh, Daddy, you've got to fuck me now!"

Gus groaned as he settled himself between her uplifted, widely spread thighs. He grasped his cock and pointed its blunt, bloated head into the flaring mouth of her soft, wet pussy.

As the mature man's thrilling hardness invaded Billy Jo's narrow, slippery quim, stretching the tunnel wide, she hooked her legs around his hairy thighs and wrapped her arms around his torso. Lying against her, his cock sunk into her belly to his balls, Gus felt a wave of bliss that was reminiscent of much younger days.

If he had thought about the matter, he

couldn't have convinced himself at that moment that he was acting on Danny's behalf – to service Billy Jo's needs so that Seth and Hank wouldn't get to her. But fortunately he was too excited to reflect on anything. The pleasure of the moment had him in its horny grip, and he wanted only to ride the wondrous surge of passion to its natural culmination within the sweet young girl on whom he lay.

He began to fuck her, moving his deeply sunk, rigid prick just an inch or so in each direction at first. But he bore perfectly against Billy Jo's clit. This and the pumping agitation of his thick cockhead in the center of her belly gave her a combination of luscious sensations that proved wildly exciting.

Billy Jo dug her fingernails into Gus's flesh and ground her sucking cunt around his hard shaft.

"Oh, Daddy... Daddy!" she cried. "I love it! Screw me! Fuck me all night long!"

Gus's answer was a groan against her ear. His wet tongue licked the delicate whorls, and he sucked her dainty, sweet-scented lobe.

Gradually the slow, stirring strokes of his deeply penetrating prick became longer and more avid. This enlarged the area of Billy Jo's sensuous response, and she derived the added thrill of feeling her father-in-law's big balls bouncing against her asshole as their bellies slapped.

She hunched with him, in perfect tempo. Soon their hips were pumping wildly together as they both worked for the reward of passion.

Billy Jo reached it first, her buttocks writhing and bumping above the bed as her cunt grasped spastically around Gus's bobbing cock. Her wet tissues sucked at his penetrating manhood as her muscles rippled up and down the length of his rod.

"Oh!" she exclaimed. Then, as the orgasm grew in force and warmth, she babbled, "Oh my God... wow! Daddy! Lover! Fucker! Oooooooh!"

"Aaaagggh!" Gus rasped, and slammed her buttocks hard against the mattress as he nailed her deep. His thick, bone-hard pecker spewed forth a rich flood of long-stored semen.

When the storm had finally ebbed and Gus dismounted from the thoroughly gratified young woman, he said, "Remember now, you can come to me whenever you need someone. I'll always take care of you, and Danny will never know. That's better than foolin' around with Seth and Hank. Young bucks like them are dangerous."

"Yes... yes, I understand," Billy Jo replied, wanting only to drop off to sleep.

After Gus had put on his robe and left the room, it took her less than a minute to slip into peaceful slumber. She didn't dream.

Chapter 11

Billy Jo awoke to the feel of a hard cock pumping in her vagina.

She blinked up at Hank's fleshy, smiling face. He was propped on straight arms, his light hair falling over his forehead as he rammed his sturdy dick in her palpitating pussy.

"You shouldn't... be here!" Billy Jo panted. "You shit – Wow! Oh, baby, that feels so – "

She was off again, writhing and bumping as her hot cunt milked at Hank's penetrating pecker. They came together, her wet pussy gobbling at the base of his shaft. Billy Jo shook all over, and Hank ground his moist mouth onto one of her vibrating tits, licking and tugging at her nipple as he squirted the last drops from his balls.

"Baby, I'm crazy about you!" he breathed heatedly against her ear after their combined orgasm had finally tapered off.

"I thought... you were in love with Viv," Billy Jo said, not really caring, but wondering at his sudden about-face.

"She's nothin' compared to you!" Hank said. "You're terrific, baby! I never was in such a hot, grabby cunt!"

Billy Jo began pushing him away. "Don't say things like that! I'm married to Danny, and he's the man I love."

"But I can at least share you until he's up and around, can't I?" Hank asked earnestly as he looked down at her pretty face.

"No! You heard what your father said last night."

"Damn it, he don't need to know! I was real quiet coming in here."

"Hank!" Billy Jo exclaimed, wanting to tell him his desire for her was hopeless, but not having the strength to do so after he had given her such a glorious release. Gus's solution hadn't worked out as he had thought it would.

Hank felt he had solved all his problems, at least for the next month or so. He got ready to drive into town, determined to tell Viv good-bye. He hadn't really wanted to give up his interest in the ranch, anyway, and now he didn't have to.

He even dared to hope that after Danny had recovered, he and his younger brother could somehow share Billy Jo's favours. He had read a book about such things, and he didn't see why an arrangement like that wouldn't be possible for Danny, Billy Jo and him.

He called on Viv at the small hotel in Mulberry where she was staying. The pretty redhead was surprised and apparently not too pleased when she opened the door of her room and saw Hank standing there.

"Honey, our date wasn't until tonight," she said with a frown.

Hank didn't smile. "Yeah. Well, that's what I came to talk about."

Viv backed up and let him into the room. She closed the door.

"I've been thinking things over," Hank began. "I'm afraid things ain't gonna work out for us."

Viv stood quietly, watching him and saying nothing.

"I like you a lot," Hank added. "But... well, I want to stay on at the ranch."

Viv moved forward and slid gracefully against him. He felt her firmly thrusting tits and the teasing curve of her belly.

"I know how it is to break away," she said gently. "But you're going to have to do it some time. And what we've got isn't going to happen again, for either one of us."

"Yeah, honey, but..."

Viv's moist, enticing lips brushed his, then caught hold, and her tongue slithered into his mouth. Though he had been with Billy Jo just a few hours before, Hank responded.

He tried to push Viv away, but she was determined, wriggling her lithe, slender body against his bulky form. Her questing kiss warmed him to the tips of his toes.

"There now," Viv finally said as she backed up, smiling proudly. "You can't tell me good-bye after that, I'll bet."

Hank was surprised by her attitude. He had expected her to be all broken up by his announcement that they were through. She hadn't been. Still, she was working to hold onto him. The whole thing seemed cool and calculating, somehow.

"I...I still can't go away with you," Hank insisted.

Viv's blue-green eyes narrowed. The young cowboy thought for a moment that she was going to lash out at him angrily. He almost hoped she would. That would make it easier for him to turn around and leave.

But Viv did something that shocked and thrilled him. Dropping to her knees on the carpet, she immediately unzipped his fly.

"Hey, what're you – "

That was all Hank could say before the aggressive young woman drew his growing but still-supple penis out of his pants. She looked at the rosy head as she held the organ around its base, the knob hanging in mid-air. Then she bent and planted a moist, tingling kiss on the tip of his peter.

A thrill went through Hank, and his cock started to stiffen out. Viv smiled up at him.

"It likes that," she said. "How do you

suppose it would like it if I..."

She capped her mouth over the ballooning head of the organ which now stood stiffly out from the front of Hank's jeans.

"Wow!" he exclaimed, and his hands lit in Viv's hair.

She sucked his cock with long, looping lunges, the glans skidding along her tongue and into the opening of her throat as her lips gobbled along the spit-slick shaft. Thrills rocketed upward in Hank's body, making his head light.

Suddenly Viv stopped sucking him and let his horny pecker snap upright. She rose to her feet, smiling foxily.

"Now why don't we get into bed and fuck?" the glamorous young woman suggested.

Hank had to struggle to adhere to his purpose. But his mind had been firmly made up, and he had the Hinshaw toughness.

"Naw," he said, shaking his head and backing up. "I've got to go." His cock wilted.

At this point he fully expected Viv to curse him. But her eyes merely glinted with new determination. She dropped to her knees in front of him again.

Scooping one hand into his clothes and bringing out his soft, hairy balls, she used the other to stuff nearly his entire penis into her mouth. Her wild tongue lashed the flaccid but meaty organ as she sucked urgently at its base, her nose rubbing against the coarse fabric of his jeans.

Hank released a voluptuous groan, and his cock became pipe-like once more, forcing Viv to back up. She tugged at his tensing nuts and rolled them as she licked and sucked at the knob of his penis.

Though he clung to his decision to tell Viv good-bye, he knew he wouldn't be able to leave her until she had brought him off. He began to rock on the balls of his feet, fucking his stiff dick in and out of the girl's pink, moist lips.

Viv tried to withdraw as before, thinking that now she could get him to agree to go to bed with her. But Hank clutched her head and held her firmly in place. He kept stroking his iron-hard penis forward and back, in and out of her mouth.

Viv was dismayed. The last thing in the world that she wanted was to suck this dirty cowboy to a climax. But she seemed to have no choice. His big dick was sticking into her face, pumping like crazy, and he had such a firm grip on her head that she couldn't get away.

Her efforts to resist had stimulated Hank all the more, and he was only a few strokes away from a climax. Fucking Viv's mouth even faster, he strove for the beckoning prize. His tightening balls still swung, slapping the girl's chin as he rhythmically rammed his pecker into her throat.

Viv gagged and gurgled, desperately trying to keep from vomiting. Her eyes watered. Suddenly Hank gave a lusty groan, and the cream bubbled up from his balls to stream hotly down the tube of his cock. The thick slime splashed into Viv's throat.

Horrified, she tried to keep from swallowing the nasty stuff, but couldn't. One gulp went down. Hank, however, let go of her head in his excitement, and she was able to back up. She took his next spurt on her tongue. Closing her throat, Viv held the bland-tasting, salty-sweet semen in her mouth. Hank spurted again, filling her mouth even fuller of the stuff.

Finally she was able to back up sufficiently to dislodge Hank's prick. It swayed away, dripping the last of his charge. Semen drooled over Viv's pink lip and down her chin.

She struggled to her feet and rushed into the bathroom. Hank stood with a strangely bemused expression and listened to her spitting furiously into the john.

By the time she returned to the bedroom, his penis was restored to his pants and his fly was closed.

"That, uh, wasn't very nice," Viv scolded mildly. Then she forced a smile. "But I'll forgive you, darling... this time."

"Sorry, if you didn't like it," Hank said,

turning toward the door. "I was trying to leave before, but you wouldn't let me."

"You mean, you're still going to walk out? After that?"

"I've got to," Hank said, opening the door. "Sorry to hurt your feelings, but..."

"Why you miserable creep!" Viv exclaimed.

At last Hank had drawn from her the explosive response which made him feel better about telling her good-bye. He grinned and stepped into the hall.

"Prick!" she screamed after him.

An elderly maiden lady, just entering the hotel's small, unattended lobby, stopped in horror. Hank tipped his hat as he edged around her and left the building. Viv slammed the door of her room.

"Well, I never!" the old maid exclaimed. She marched to, the hotel desk and began beating on the bell to summon the manager.

* * *

It was mid-afternoon at the ranch when Seth looked up from the work he was doing near the barn and caught a glint of sunlight off an approaching car. He recognized the sporty machine as that of Hank's girl friend.

Since his younger brother was out on the range rounding up some strays, Seth put down the harness he had been mending and ambled over to the open area next to the house where he waited to greet the visitor.

Viv brought her car to a stop and smiled at him. "You're just the man I want to see!" she cheerfully announced, swinging the car's door open.

Seth ogled her lovely legs as she brought them around. Again she was wearing a miniskirt that was so short it revealed a flash of panty crotch-pink today. Seth's penis stirred.

"How come you want to see me?" the lanky young man inquired. "I thought you and Hank was..."

"Hank's very immature, I'm afraid," Viv said. "I've always liked... older men, anyway." Her hands lit on the buttons of Seth's work shirt. She toyed with them while smiling up at him.

Considering that Hank had taken Viv away from him at the beginning, then had muscled in on Billy Jo, the elder brother would have been happy to beat Hank's time, if it were a question of that. However, Viv's pitch was just a little too blatant.

He had been suspicious of her from the start, but he hadn't been able to figure out her game.

"Ain't you got enough facts yet for that story you're writin'?" Seth inquired coolly.

Viv took her hands away from him. "Well,

not quite." She looked around uneasily. "Where's Hank, anyway?"

"Out on the range. He won't be back till supper time."

Viv smiled. "Oh, that's good!" She took Seth's arm and turned him around. "Let's you and I walk over to that big old haystack next to the stable."

Seth went with her, though his mind churned with suspicious resentment. Where did she get off anyway, he wondered, wiggling her butt around there, first making a play for Hank and then for him? What did she think he was – some simple booby who would be so grateful for the chance to screw her that he wouldn't ask any questions?

When they reached the large pile of straw where Seth had watched her surrender to Hank the other day, she drew him down beside her.

"Now, isn't this nice?" she purred, practically flashing a neon sign that read Kiss me!

"You sure you're a writer?" Seth stuck a straw into his mouth.

Viv blinked. "Why, yes. I told you that the first day I was here."

"What kind of a story are you writin'? Maybe I'll want to read it some time."

"Do you read much?" Viv asked, chuckling. Her eyes seemed to mock him.

"Quite a bit," Seth replied evenly. "The nights around a ranch are pretty dull."

"Your nights don't have to be dull from now I on," the red-haired girl said boldly, placing her hand on the warm, tightly packed crotch of Seth's jeans.

He sprang at her, pushing her onto her back in the straw. "What the hell's your problem, baby? Are your pants so damned hot you've got to throw yourself at every man you see?"

"Seth!" she exclaimed, breathing hard as she stared up at him in surprise. "What an awful thing to say!"

"That's how it looks to me. First you go after Hank and let him screw you fifteen minutes after you meet, and now you're onto me. Why us, baby? Ain't there any hot cocks in San Antonio – or wherever the hell you come from?"

Viv was speechless. She decided she had underestimated Seth, and perhaps Hank, also.

The lanky man slowly released her and leaned back. "You're a damned good-looking babe and – don't get me wrong – I wouldn't mind playing with you. But the whole thing seems kind of funny."

"All right." Viv sat up. "Hank and I had a fight. I wanted to hurt him, and I thought the best way to do that would be to have an affair with you." She suddenly smiled. "But I like you, anyway. I did from the first. It was only after Hank mentioned that you had a girl friend that I even looked at him."

"What girl?"

"Billy Jo, I think Hank said her name was. You remember him telling me."

"Billy Jo's my kid brother's wife."

"Oh." Viv's pink lips pursed.

"That still don't answer the question of why a gal like you is so easy to make. Baby, you're no dog. If you was, maybe I could understand."

"Okay, forget it." Viv stood and brushed the straw off her. "You've made me feel cheap, and I don't care for that."

"Another thing," Seth said thoughtfully as he remained seated, sucking on the piece of straw. "Why was you so hot to take Hank away from here?"

"I'm not going to stand around here any longer answering a lot of stupid questions."

Viv turned and started to leave. Seth leaped off the straw pile, caught her by an arm, and spun her around. She gasped and stared at him.

"Who sent you to see us?" Seth asked, getting a sudden brainstorm. "Was it Rex Reed?"

"What if it was?" Viv snapped angrily. "It didn't work, so that's that. Now let go of me!"

Seth's studied calm ignited into anger.

The cheap cunt had nearly torn his family apart, making Hank threaten to tell Danny about Billy Jo and him, and forcing him to throw Billy Jo into Hank's arms. He wasn't about to let her off easy.

"What's the connection between you and Reed?" Seth demanded. "Are you just some whore he hired?"

Viv's eyes blazed, and she swung her free arm, slapping him across the face.

Seth's anger turned to rage. He swept Viv off her feet, whirled around, and tossed her into the straw. She landed on her fanny, her lovely legs in the air. Her short skirt skidded to her lap, exposing strips of bare thigh between the tops of her hose and the elasticized edges of her pink nylon briefs.

Sputtering with indignation, Viv rolled over in an effort to get up. Her skirt wound around her middle, baring her bottom. The shapely cheeks quivered, the crack between them enticingly visible through the sheer nylon.

Before Viv could rise to her hands and knees, Seth landed beside her. His hand at the middle of her back held her down as he gazed at the inviting target of her lightly-covered ass.

The lean, hard-faced cowboy raised his hand and brought it down stingingly against Viv's bottom.

"Oh!" she exclaimed.

Fired by the springy quiver of her asscheeks and by the sound which his hand had made when he had smacked them, Seth raised his hand and brought it down again – harder this time.

"Ow!" Viv bawled. "You dirty bastard!"

"How much did Reed pay you to break us down?" Seth snarled. "Was it worth this?"

He spanked her sleek, quivering panty seat again.

"He didn't pay me, God damn you! I'm a..."

Again his hand struck her bouncy bottom.

"*Aieee!* ...real estate broker."

"Just working for commission, huh?" Seth said. "Well, this is it!"

He spanked her a fifth time.

"Let me up! I'm sorry... I'm sorry!" Viv began to sob.

By this time Seth was so involved in the excitement of the spanking that he couldn't stop. He wanted to hurt Viv even more.

He grasped the elastic band at the top of her panties and stretched it back, causing the flimsy garment to skid out from under her tummy. The slender redhead's white ass was bare. The satiny skin bore pink splotches where his hand had struck. Seth let the elastic snap against Viv's thighs just below the tops of her stockings, and he raised his hand above her once more.

As she writhed impotently in the soft straw, he spanked both bare buttocks, then just the left, then the right. The pink splotches turned an angry red.

The humiliated and painfully chastised young woman kicked and sobbed.

"What the shoot's goin' on?" Hank asked excitedly as he loped up.

Seth glared at him and continued to hold Viv down. "I didn't think you was comin' back till night."

"The strays was easy to find. Man, what're you doin' to Viv?"

"Oh, Hank, make him stop!" she pleaded tearfully. "He's killing me!"

Seth grinned lustfully as he looked at her rosy-streaked ass. "Ain't that a picture?"

Hank squatted in the straw. "What're you swattin' her for?"

"Because she came out here slingin' her stuff at me after you and her broke up. And guess what I found out – She's working for Reed!"

"No bull?"

"She admitted it. She's a fuckin' real estate broker. If she could have got us to sell, she would've made a fat fee. Now she's just getting' her ass burned, and she don't like it."

"Oh, please... please!" Viv moaned. Her

buttocks quivered as she squirmed.

Hank grinned. "So she went after you, huh? Maybe she'd like to take on both of us... at once."

"You fiends!" Viv shrilled. "I'll have both of you arrested!"

"And have the whole story of what you and Reed was trying to do come out?" Seth asked. "Not likely."

"Come on, man," Hank said eagerly. "Let's jazz her!"

"No!" she cried.

"How do you want to do it?" Seth asked.

Hank pulled her bruised buttocks apart, exposing her pink little asshole and the red wisps surrounding the bottom of her cuntal slash. "Well, she's got two holes. That's just enough for two peckers, wouldn't you say?"

Viv was too shocked and terrified to make a sound.

"Your arithmetic's pretty good," said Seth. "Which hole do you want?"

"I'll take her pussy."

"That's fine with me," Seth replied. "I always kind of liked them old dirt roads."

Viv found her voice: "No! Oh God, no! Listen... I'll take on both of you, but one at a time. Okay?"

"Listen to how eager she is," Seth said, still pressing the small of her back.

"You think we ought to have pity on her?"

Hank asked.

"She didn't have no pity on us."

"I'll take you both at once," Viv said quickly, sniffling back her tears. "I'll suck one of you while the other screws me."

"Hey, that sounds pretty good," said Hank.

Seth seemed to consider the proposition. Finally he said, "Okay, but I figger she ought to suck both of us."

"Yes... yes, I will!" Viv exclaimed. "Just let me up."

"First you've gotta take off all them clothes," Seth insisted.

"All right!" Viv said. "Anything."

"Be ready to grab her if she starts to run," Seth told his brother, releasing the pressure on her back.

Viv quickly rolled over and sat up. Her fancy hairdo had gotten mussed, and there was straw in it. Her tears had caused her mascara to run.

"Help her off with her blouse," Seth said.

As the girl sat helplessly in the straw, Seth took hold of her pullover at one side while Hank grasped it at the other. They whisked the garment up over her head.

Viv's titties were cuddled in a low cut pale pink brassiere. Hank reached around her and fumbled the fasteners open, then whipped the flimsy garment away. Her long, pale tits jiggled, their very pink nipples sticking out.

"Let's take them pants off," Seth said, wrapping his hand around the soft crotch of the panties that were halfway down her thighs.

As he pulled the pants away, Hank bent and licked at a titty while squeezing the other in his big, rough hand.

Viv whimpered in degradation, but she didn't dare complain for fear the coarse cowboys would give her the shocking treatment they had first threatened.

"What have we got here?" Seth said, roughly pulling her stocking-clad legs apart. He dug a hand down between the bare tops of her thighs and rubbed her velvety, hair-covered cunt.

Viv squirmed in a vain effort to avoid the humiliating pawing.

"Well, are we gonna get us a blow job or not?" Hank asked as he raised his head from her breasts.

"I'm ready," Seth said.

Crouching at either side of Viv, the two men unlimbered their pricks. Wide-eyed, she glanced from one thrusting pecker to the other, both of which were aimed threateningly at her. It was easy to see that Seth held at least a two-inch advantage over his brother. Seth's rod was the longest Viv had ever seen.

He crawled closer, his stiff prick nodding. Hank followed suit, and the dismayed girl had both dongs poking at her face, so close that she could smell their aroused fragrance.

"Okay, baby," Seth said. "Start licking."

There was nothing Viv could do but obey. She stuck out her rosy little tongue and swiped it across the tip of Seth's dick. He clutched his rod at its base to hold it steady.

"Mine now," Hank said, holding his organ and leaning closer.

Viv closed her eyes as she licked his cock. But there was no way she could close her nostrils to the raunchy fumes that emanated from the spit-moistened, passion-hot peter.

"Back to me," Seth ordered.

The humiliated girl had to open her eyes to see where to lick. As her tongue glided over the crown of Seth's cock, he pushed forward. His fat glans shoved Viv's tongue back into her mouth and followed, plugging her face quite thoroughly.

Quivering at the brink of nausea, Viv sucked the meaty, juice-exuding glans. Suddenly Seth withdrew and pushed her face toward Hank, who immediately shoved his prick into her mouth. She was forced to turn back and forth, from one thrusting dick to the other, licking and sucking.

She didn't catch the signal which Seth gave his younger brother. When Hank flopped onto his back, his upthrust cock swaying like a flagpole in a hurricane, Viv took advantage of the opportunity to mount him and encase his penis in her silken, slippery box. That was one, at least, that she wouldn't have to suck any more.

Hank pulled the impaled young woman forward atop him, her titties compressing against his chest. He spread his legs well apart, to allow room for Seth to kneel between them.

The lanky cowboy dropped to position, his monstrously long, virile organ nodding. Its head still gleamed with the viscid glaze of Viv's saliva.

Seth eyed her lovely buttocks, split as she lay atop Hank, his shaft stretching the rosy orifice in her titian curls. Her cute little asshole winked from between the white mounds which still bore the pink splotches caused by Seth's spanking.

Taking a firm grip on his lengthily protruding prick, Seth wiggled forward and placed the tip of the tool against Viv's defenseless anus. As soon as she felt the contact, the frightened girl tried to squirm forward, but Hank's encircling arms held her securely. There was no way she could avoid Seth's twisting thrust.

Viv bawled as the fat, slippery head of his pecker painfully bulled its way through the sphincter of her ass and sank into her hot rear chamber.

"You're killing me!" she wailed.

Paying no attention to her anguished cries, Seth began fucking her virginal asshole, thrilling to the tightness of the elastic portal and to the compressed condition of her rectum, caused by the presence of Hank's thick shaft up her cunt.

As Seth screwed her rear, the other man stroked up and down in her pussy, jostling Viv and increasing the pain of Seth's unnatural penetration. The hapless young woman moaned and sobbed as the two pricks pumped inside her at the same time, rubbing each other through the thin membranes separating the chambers that they occupied.

Seth forged deeper and deeper into Viv's ass, grunting as her spasming tightness gave him an extremely voluptuous sensation. Hank similarly was enjoying his thrusts into her tighter-than-usual vagina.

"Oh, I can't stand it!" Viv cried as she writhed in a futile effort to escape from the dual impalement, especially Seth's searing incursion up her butt that seemed to have set her guts on fire.

But the brothers kept fucking her, bouncing her, jostling her – pounding their hard meat into her with ruthless abandon.

Viv's moans tapered off, and she began panting.

Seth could hardly believe it when he felt

her ass push backward against his horny penetrations. She worked avidly forward and back, first pressing against him, then against Hank.

"Fuck me... fuck me!" she breathed, the words barely intelligible. Her cries quickly grew to a crescendo until she was screaming, "Fuck me... screw me... rip me! God damn you motherfucking bastards... Bull me! Ram me! Tear... me... apart!"

Hank and Seth all but granted her insane wish as they fucked her cunt and asshole furiously, each ramming as the other withdrew for yet another plunge. Viv hunched forward and back between them, bawling and squealing. Her long, pear-shaped breasts flopped wildly about. Her pussy rippled around Hank's slippery, hard incursions as her anal muscles gripped Seth's penetrating red-hot poker.

Finally she let out an air-splitting shriek and climaxed, spasming in both holes at once as she shook all over. Seth groaned and spurted his hot sperm into her guts as Hank let go in her vagina. The three lust-locked lovers rolled together in the straw, oblivious to everything but the mind-boggling thrills that coursed through them.

Later Viv pulled her clothes together and scurried back to her car, her hair wildly disheveled and her makeup streaked on

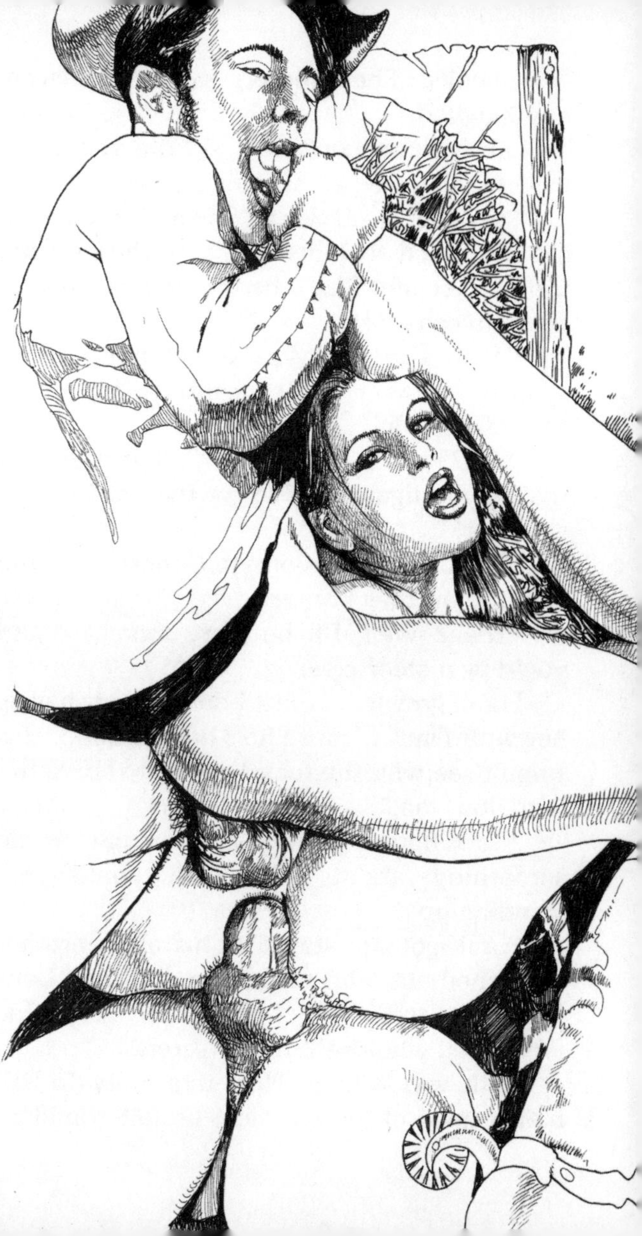

her cheeks. The brothers sat in the straw and laughed.

"Do you reckon she'll sic the sheriff on us?" Hank asked as his laughter subsided.

"Shit, no!" said Seth. "She and Reed have got too much to hide. Anyway, she had the time of her life. She'll be thinking on this for years to come."

"Well, I'm glad I'm rid of her," Hank replied. "Now I can concentrate on taking care of Billy Jo."

"You?" Seth snapped. "What the hell makes you figure you've got the inside track with her?"

"I was in her room this morning," the younger brother bragged.

"Yeah? Well, I'll be there tonight – and you'd best steer clear."

Hank growled, "Shit! I don't mind sharing her with Danny, cause he's her husband. But I don't see why the fuck I've got to share her with you, too."

"You figure you're big enough to do something about it?" Seth challenged, standing up.

Hank got up, stared at his older brother for a moment, and then turned away. "Let's leave it up to Billy Jo. I reckon she can decide for herself who she'd rather screw."

Seth was willing. Now that Billy Jo had had a taste of his big dick, he felt confident that she wouldn't settle for less.

There would be trouble after Danny got up and about. But Seth would ford that stream when he came to it. If the final outcome were to split up the family and leave him with both the ranch and the girl, he could live with that. His main problem, Seth believed, would be to convince his old man not to sell out to Reed.

Maybe Billy Jo could help, Seth conjectured. He had never heard of a father and son sharing the same woman, but he didn't see any reason why it couldn't be done. And his father wouldn't offer too much competition.

With this thought to stir his imagination, Seth went back to work.

Chapter 12

Billy Jo was a busy girl during the next few days, entertaining both of Danny's brothers and also his father. She concentrated her efforts on seeing that old Gus didn't find out she was still bedding Seth and Hank, while keeping it from the boys that she was taking care of their father and each other. Her ingenuity was taxed to the utmost.

But the rewards made it all worthwhile. Billy Jo revelled in an almost constant sexual

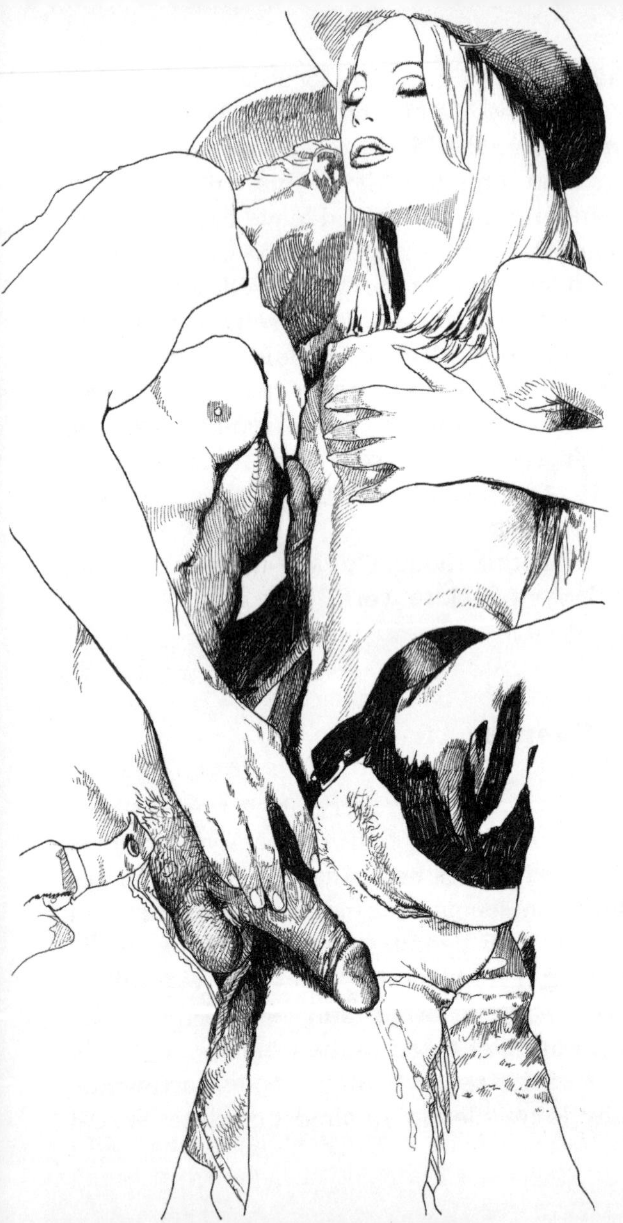

high – getting screwed on the range, in the haymow, and on the straw pile by day, and ending up in Gus's bed at night. She made it a rule that no one was to visit her room and enforced the ban by keeping a chair propped under her doorknob. This helped her keep each McCluskie from finding out she was entertaining the others. Moreover, as confidante to the three brothers and their father, now she was never more informed about the ranch politics, about Reed and Vivienne Lanier's involvement, about the failed marriage of Gus and Alice. Sometimes Billy Jo felt that she knew more about the McCluskies than each of them knew about themselves – collectively, at least.

Billy Jo also took care of Danny by hand and mouth, and in a spiritual way she found this the most enjoyable activity of all. Her love for her handsome young husband remained untouched by her other sensual experiences, and his appreciation of her new lack of sexual inhibitions gave her added pleasure. They were as happy together as his physical condition would permit.

However, this contentment was soon blasted by the arrival in the mail of a menacing notice from the local water district. In precise legal language, the McCluskies were informed that the district's board of directors had voted to divert Coyote Creek, which flowed across the rear of the Los Altos Ranch.

"Hellfire, they can't do that!" Hank exclaimed when his father brought the matter up for discussion that evening. "We need that water for the back range. It'd cost us a fortune to pipe well-water back there for the stock."

"I reckon they can do it right enough," Gus said with a sigh. "They tell us here in the notice that they'll put in a ditch from the new creek for our use, but we've got to pay a big assessment for the construction cost."

Seth said, "It's that sonofabitch Reed again! With him running most of the land in the county, he runs the water district, too."

Hank glanced from his brother to his father. "Ain't there nothing we can do about it?"

"I'll see a lawyer," Gus said without enthusiasm. "But the district's probably within their rights, long as they're willing to put in a ditch for us."

"This is going to bust us for sure," Hank declared. "That bastard Reed! He's going to get his fuckin' way after all."

"Watch your language, boy," Gus scolded. "Billy Jo's here."

The young woman had been sitting quietly at the side of the room, listening to the conversation among Gus and his sons. Now that everyone was looking her way, she spoke up.

"This Reed doesn't sound human. He must be interested only in land and money. Can't you talk to Alice? Surely she wouldn't want to force you into selling *Los Altos*?"

A look of thunder crossed Gus's weather-beaten features. The boys looked embarrassed.

"Hell, I'd rather die than go running to Alice. She probably wouldn't understand anyhow. Say it was outa her hands. There's talk that my... wife and that little rat are..." his words died on his lips, as if talking of his estranged wife in this way was somehow too painful to continue.

"I'm sorry Gus. I really shouldn't have brought this up." Billy Jo responded, shocked at how deep the older man's pride ran. But an idea was germinating in her mind.

"I reckon the time has come when we're gonna have to sell out," Gus said disconsolately. "Do you boys agree?"

"It sure looks that way," Hank said, figuring Billy Jo would go with him.

Seth nodded and looked at Billy Jo. He believed she would choose to leave with him.

"Gus, have you talked with Danny about it?" the young woman asked.

"Not yet. I was fixin' to do that later."

"Let me talk with him," she said. "I know he's had his heart set on staying here."

Billy Jo left the living room and went

upstairs to see her bedridden husband. His eyes lit up when she entered the room.

She sat next to his bed and held his hand. As she told him about the notice from the water district and related the tentative decision reached by his father and brothers, Danny's expression clouded.

"God damn it, I don't want to sell out!" he exclaimed angrily. "We hadn't ought to let Reed do that to us."

"You're right," Billy Jo agreed. "But the question is, how can we stop him?"

"There ought to be a way."

"Maybe there is," Billy Jo said thoughtfully. "I hope you don't mind, honey, but I'm going to take a break for just a few days – I'm going to check into *Mon Plaisir*. Your father told me that Alice and Matt would be staying there while the *Lazy Q* house staff are on their annual vacation, and, whatever it takes, I'm going to make sure she knows just what's going on. Call it a diplomatic mission if you like, but I haven't met your stepmother or your youngest brother yet, and I'd like to; anyway, by the time I get back you'll be good as new. Almost. But don't tell Gus, OK?"

"That's fine with me, baby." Danny was looking distractedly off into space. "You go on do that. You need a rest. Maybe you can get Alice back on our side."

* * *

Later she got Hank to drop her at the hotel.

Billy Jo realized that what she had in mind was a long shot gamble. But she felt it was worth trying, for Danny's sake. Though Gus and his other sons were prepared to sell the ranch, Danny wanted to hold on – and what he wanted, she wanted too.

PART II

Chapter 13

Alice watched her stepson watching the girl floating in the pool.

She didn't blame Matt. The girl was very pretty, with long blonde hair and a lovely body. And these days Matt was old enough to be interested in girls in 'that' way, she thought, a little sadly. No. Looking at his expression now, she was sure. He *was* interested in girls in 'that' way.

The girl with honey-coloured hair that fell over eyes lay on the airbed and dangled an arm in the water. She was the prettiest by far that Alice had seen in Mulberry's 'luxury' hotel, *Mon Plaisir*, where she and her stepson had come to stay. Her skin was a wonderful golden colour, her body enviously slim but with some very beautiful hollows and hills and curves. Her bikini was almost nonexistent. The bottom was a simple, tiny patch of bright red and the top hardly a band a cloth that just barely covered her large, flawless breasts. They're big for a slender young girl like that, she thought. But not as big as mine...

Alice liked looking at the girl, too. She had never denied the beauty of the female form and she always enjoyed looking at cute girls.

The only thing she knew about the girl was her name, Sam. It was a slightly masculine name for such a pretty girl, but somehow it suited. She guessed it was short for Samantha: Sam looked to be perhaps eighteen, twenty at the most. It seemed she was staying at *Mon Plaisir* all by herself.

Alice's suite was on the second floor, with a pleasant balcony overlooking the big pool and patio area. She sat out there on the balcony now, looking down at Sam and her stepson. Matt was in a lounge chair, pretending to doze, but his interest in the girl was obvious. It was the middle of the day, and the few guests staying were out except for Alice, her stepson, and Sam.

It wasn't long before Alice noticed the front of her stepson's bathing trunks bulging. She frowned momentarily as she realized Matt had a hard-on. But her frown changed to amusement when she noticed that Sam was, evidently, teasing and tantalizing the boy with her lovely body.

Alice didn't mind a little flirting. In fact she enjoyed flirting herself. The girl on the raft seemed to know just what to do with Matt, working on his young hormonal turmoil to arouse him to the point of that hard-on. Sam was on her back as she floated lazily in the sparkling water, legs apart.

It was exciting to watch Sam tease her

stepson. Watching them, Alice found that she, too, was being turned on. She wasn't sure it was because of her stepson's cock or the sweetness of Sam's body, and didn't really care. A ripple of heat flowed through Alice's body and she found herself becoming wet between her thighs, her nipples straining, hard.

The ringing of the telephone irritated Alice, especially when it turned out to be a wrong number. Sighing, she stepped back onto the patio and looked down.

Sam's tits were naked!

The girl had taken her bikini top off, and it now floated on the surface of the water. Her firm tits rose up into twin points, with fantastic pink nipples. Alice noticed Matt was no longer trying to sneak peeks at Sam, but was gazing at her openly, his mouth slack with adolescent lust. Alice had evidently missed something when the phone rang.

Sam was not in the least bashful about letting Matt see her lovely breasts. Alice saw the girl was watching Matt, a smile playing about her moist lips. Either Matt was so awed by what he was looking at, or his mind had suddenly become numb – he just sat there with his cock straining at his trunks, making no effort to conceal it. Alice's reaction to this was a deep tickling sensation between her thighs, and she was acutely aware that her labia and clit were becoming wet and swollen inside her panties.

Sam was delicately moving her fingertips over her tits, drawing them up over the swelling curves and around her rigid nipples. Alice gasped, knowing Sam was going out of her way to tease Matt, being bold and blatant and wanton. She felt a moment of concern for her stepson. The girl shouldn't tease a boy Matt's age, even if there was only two years' age between them! A man would be different, felt Alice, but for a boy of Matt's age, something like this could be potentially disturbing.

Was it really only a tease, or something else? Sam didn't look like a sly prick-teaser. Surely Sam would not tantalize a boy that way unless she was willing to fuck them. Alice wondered if her stepson would be eager to fuck the girl, or if he would be too shy. From the expression on his good-looking face, Alice didn't think shyness was a problem. She grinned to herself: Matt would be like a raging bull if he could get his hands on Sam's lovely tits. His cock seemed ready to burst the seams of his trunks and Alice gazed at the outline of her stepson's prick. Even from this distance, she could see it was big.

Why do I want to see his cock? Wasn't Rex Reed's enough for me the other day? she asked herself, unable to make her eyes move from it.

A hand movement from Sam brought Alice's eyes to the pretty girl. Sam was looking at Matt, too, her eyes steamy even from this distance. Alice watched Sam drawn a pattern along her flat stomach, just above the top of her bikini bottom, then down along the crotch and briefly caress the inside of one thigh.

Alice found she was being turned on as much as her stepson by this girl's wanton display of open sensuality. She could not resist touching one of her own large, soft breasts, moulding her palm around it and squeezing gently. The pressure on her tit sent waves of steamy desire down her body, causing her cunt to twitch. The crotch of her panties was wet, almost soaked, with the seeping fluids of her excited cunt.

Alice's eyes began to blaze with passion, watching Sam now more than her stepson. Sam was tracing her finger about the crotch of her bikini, openly stroking her pussy as Matt gawked with desire. Sam pulled her finger along the bulge of her cunt, right where the slit would be, and Alice heard her stepson grunt. Matt was almost sitting up, braced on one elbow. Everything about his posture indicated an obviously horny fascination. He was stroking his hard-on through his swimming trunks.

Sam slowly shoved her fingers under the

top of her bikini bottom and Alice watched. Plainly, Sam was touching her pubic hair.

On an impulse, Alice looked around. There was no one else in the hotel, she knew, and the maids had already cleaned the rooms, still she darted her eyes from balcony to balcony, then back to the pool. Matt was too absorbed in watching Sam, and the girl was much too busy to look up at Alice. Lifting her skirt to her waist, Alice ran her palm between her legs and rubbed at her cunt, feeling her sopping, slippery cuntflesh through the thick, deliciously wicked and exposed. If either or both of them at the pool looked up, they might have seen Alice's long, slender thighs and the crotch of her panties, seen her rubbing her cunt. But they didn't.

Again Alice heard her stepson grunt. It came out more as a moan of torment than anything else. Immediately after the grunt, the sound of Sam's tinkling laugh drifted up to Alice. It took a moment or so for Alice to realize what had happened.

Matt had come in his trunks!

She saw the dark spot spreading from where the tip of his cock was outlined underneath the light blue material: the horny sixteen-year-old had come off watching Sam tease him.

"Was it a good one, Matt?" Alice heard Sam ask. "Did you come nice and hard?"

Alice saw her stepson nod his head.

"I told you I'd show my titties to you, didn't I?" Sam said to Matt. "Now do you believe me?"

Matt nodded his head vigorously as Sam retrieved her floating top and put it back on.

"I came too, you know," Sam said as she tied the halter over her shapely young breasts. "As it happens, I come quite often…" Her voice tailed off dreamily.

This had been going on a while, Alice realized, frowning. She had paid no attention, and here this pretty young girl was playing around with her stepson, making him ejaculate inside his trunks. But it was so open! Right there at the pool with the sun burning down on them. Of course there was no one around to see – except Alice. Still, someone might.

Alice felt admiration for Sam, admiring her boldness and wanton behaviour. Sam was doing things that, recently, Alice had only fantasized about. Somehow Alice felt an empathy with Sam. She hardly knew the girl, but felt as if they could be very close, kindred spirits.

Alice had forgotten her dress was at her waist and her hand was between her thighs. Quickly, she shoved her skirt back down and smoothed it over her hips. She watched Sam paddle to the edge of the pool and climb out. The back of her tiny bikini had snuck into

Ranchers' Dirty Wives ★ 217

the crack of her ass, and the white, creamy ass flesh was an erotic contrast to the golden colour of her thighs. Sam wiggled her ass at Matt before she pulled the bikini out of the crack of her ass and blew him a kiss.

"We'll do it again later, honey," she said, picking up her towel and stepped into her own apartment on the bottom floor.

Alice watched her stepson stand up, his cock looking as if it were still very hard. She watched him gaze in the direction where Sam disappeared, rubbing the front of his trunks. Then he started for the stairs to come up for a late lunch.

As Matt ate a sandwich and drank a glass of milk, Alice found herself looking at her stepson in a different way. She had assumed that her youngest stepson was still immature in some ways, but apparently this was no longer the case. He was not so young as to ignore a pretty girl like Sam. Nor was he too young to get a hard-on and come in his pants. Alice still felt excitement rumbling through her body as she looked at him, visualizing his cock gushing creamy come juice. The scene in her mind created a beautiful storm between her thighs, and she was surprised to find that she had almost come, too.

After his late lunch, Matt mumbled something about changing out of his trunks. She watched him go down the short hall to his room, her eyes on the tightness of his young ass and strong thighs.

When he didn't return to the living room after about ten minutes, Alice followed him. He wasn't in his room, but his trunks were on the floor. She picked them up, turning them inside out and looking at his still wet come juice. Taking them to the bathroom to place them in the hamper, she shoved the door open and stepped in – stopping in her tracks.

Matt was sitting on the toilet, his legs spread and his cock hard. To Alice, it looked impressively large. He was, or had been, jerking off frantically. The boy gave a yelp of surprise when his stepmother entered and saw what he was doing. He tried to cram his stiff cock down between his legs, but it jerked upright again, as if it had a mind of its own. He tried once more, and the same thing happened.

Alice laughed, a low, throaty sound. "I guess you can't hide it, can you?" she said.

"Aw, Alice," Matt blushed.

"A hard-on isn't anything to be ashamed of, Matt," Alice said, surprising herself with her choice of words. "Nor should you be ashamed of playing with it."

Red-faced, Matt lowered his eyes, but his cock kept standing up straight and hard. He closed his thighs, but it didn't help at all. His balls squeezed up from them.

Alice stared at her stepson's cock and balls, an itch tormenting the palms of her hands. "I know how good it can feel," she went on, her voice dropping to a husky murmur. "I understand the feeling very well, honey. I know you can't leave it alone when you get hard like this. I know you have to touch it... play with it..."

I should go now, she thought to herself. Leave, right *now!* But as she whispered, her eyes burning on his magnificent cock, she just moved farther into the bathroom, getting closer and closer to her stepson. His trunks had dropped from her hand, forgotten. She was a foot away from him now, her knees shaking as she stared down at his cock. The head was rosy and swollen, and it was dripping from the little hole at the tip, the shaft throbbing dangerously.

She hardly realized it when she began to sink to the floor, bending her knees, squatting at her stepson's side, her hand resting on one of his hot knees. She licked her lips as she stared at his cock and balls; they seemed disproportionately large for one so young. She looked at the thick bush of wiry hair at the base of an otherwise hairless stomach. Maybe not so young, she thought.

"I know the feelings a boy gets sometimes," she murmured with a thick voice, her hand moving slowly up his trembling thigh. "It's difficult to ignore, honey. Girls get that way, too. And it's nothing at all to be ashamed of."

The tip of her fingers barely touched his balls and she heard Matt gasp and lifted her eyes to his. Matt was looking at her now, his eyes unfocused but very, very hot. She felt his balls writhe against her fingertips, and she lightly brushed at them. Christ, the forty-one year-old thought, first I'm getting lesbian crushes and now I'm seducing my own stepson. What's *wrong* with me? I should stop this – *now!*

But her fingers didn't stop trailing past his balls and they moved tentatively, slowly up the underside of his throbbing cock. She was breathing hard as she watched her hand, her gasps matching the pants of her stepson. She felt the heat of his cock against the tips of her fingers and, reaching the swollen head, she swirled a thumb around the smooth head and finally over the wetness of the precum that was oozing from his cock's tip. Matt was shaking, making strangling sounds in his throat as he watched, disbelievingly, as his stepmother caressed and stroked his hard cock.

Alice squatted at his side, her knees showing as her skirt slipped back. A few inches of her thighs could be seen, and Matt snuck peeks at them. Alice very lightly enclosed her stepson's cock with her fist, moving it up and down slowly, feeling the hardness, the heat, the powerful throbbing of it. Her cunt was on fire again, and she could feel the wetness in the crotch of her panties. She could smell her own musky arousal.

Tightening her fist, she started jerking her hand up and down, twisting it. She squeezed her stepson's cock, feeling it swell and burn against her hand. Alice began to whimper softly as she stroked Matt's cock, little mewls of raw desire coming from somewhere within her. Gripping Matt's cock tightly now, she pumped in short, jerky thrusts, watching his cock drip more and more. She ran a tongue over her luscious lips as excitement built up throughout her body. The pulsations of his cock seemed to be increasing significantly as she jerked up and down, but she was so fascinated to be holding his cock she paid no attention to it.

Suddenly, unexpectedly, Matt came.

"Ohhh!" Alice cried out, jerking back, but not in time to miss the first gush as it splattered over her face, dripping sluggishly down her cheek and the side of her nose. Fascinated, she watched the rest of his come juice boil from his quivering penis, spurt after spurt. She jacked him off furiously now, moaning as prodigious amounts of his semen began to land on his lower stomach and upper thighs and her hand. "Oh, my *God!* Look at it, Matt! God, you're coming so much, honey!"

Alice pressed her thighs together convulsively. She could feel the beginnings of a cum as her entire vulval area was squeezed by her muscular contractions. She ran her fist up and down his spewing cock fast and hard, and gave a low moan as her cunt went into fiery convulsions of a sharply enjoyable orgasm.

She jerked on his prick until he finished cumming. Then, without another word, she stood up and moistened a cloth. She wiped her face, his stomach and thighs, then his cock, and last her own hand. Tossing the cloth into the bathroom sink, she quickly left the small tiled room, throwing an amused glance back at her stepson sitting on the toilet, looking happier than a rooster in a hen house.

Chapter 14

To her surprise, Alice felt no guilt about jacking her stepson's cock off. On the contrary, it not only excited her to the point of orgasm, but it made her seriously consider fucking him.

While the domestic staff was taking a summer break at the *Lazy Q*, they had booked into *Mon Plaisir* for a couple of weeks; it was by far the best hotel for miles around.

It was fairly small – only fifteen or twenty suites, built on two stories in a square around a nice large pool and gardens. Matt and Sam were the only young ones there, the few other guests were adults, mainly retired couples. Most, as far as Alice could see, seemed to go on excursions during the day.

Being without boys and girls his own age did not bother Matt. He had always been a loner. He never seemed to have much interest in life on either ranch – hers or her ex-husband's. He was a good student, but thought sports were stupid. He preferred his books to chasing balls or trying to hit one with a piece of wood. His intelligence was far above average, as was his maturity and self-possession for a boy of that age. He had a powerful telescope set up in his room that he studied the heavens with and she knew that he had dreams of becoming an astronomer some day.

Alice had been separated from Gus McCluskie for over a year now. After her father and her brother were so tragically killed, she had moved into the big ranch house on the *Lazy Q*. Matt had been the youngest and there was an amicable arrangement between his father and his stepmother about dividing his time between the two neighbouring ranches. Staying here in Mulberry he could walk to the shopping mall near-by, or could go to movies when he wanted; his generous allowance was spent on astronomical equipment and books about the stars and planets.

Matt was at the movies this night, and Alice was alone in the suite. She was pleased that her stepson acted no differently toward her since she had jacked him off earlier in the day. In fact, once he got over his surprise, it was as if it were something she did for him on a daily basis. She was delighted that he showed no feelings of shame, or treated her as if she was something to be ashamed of.

She went into his room, suddenly eager to use his telescope to look at the stars. He actually had two of them set up. The larger, more powerful one, and a small one next to it. Both, she noticed, were not aimed into the sky now but downward. Curiously, she peeked into the larger telescope.

It had been adjusted to peer into a window directly across from their suite. All she saw was a closed curtain with shadows moving behind it. But it had been set in place for some reason, Alice knew. Turning to the smaller one, she peered into it and found herself looking directly into Sam's bedroom!

A shiver went through Alice as she saw Sam sitting on the couch, apparently reading. The girl was in her robe, with her long legs propped up. One lovely tit was exposed, as were her thighs. Matt had shown his stepmother how to adjust the focus and pull in a bright, detailed image so as she peered into the eye piece, Alice turned the focus knob and found she could see Sam's tit perfectly. With her pulse racing and her own tits swelling, Alice moved the telescope slightly, focusing it upon Sam's thighs. The image seemed close enough for her to reach out and touch.

The young girl moved a hand along her thigh, sliding her robe away from her body as Alice watched. Alice noticed she could almost count the pores on that creamy, exciting flesh. As the robe parted, Alice began to moan softly. She was looking directly at the honey-coloured curls of Sam's cunt. Each strand seemed to leap out at her. She began to breathe heavily when Sam drew her hand up her thigh and toyed with the lips of her cunt. There was something intensely erotic about watching Sam without the girl realizing she was being seen.

As her own cunt started twitching, Alice watched as Sam parted the pink lips of her cunt and exposed her small, but obviously swollen clitoris. Sam stroked it slowly, spreading her legs widely, her book forgotten now. Alice's eyes were straining with eager pleasure as Sam slowly dipped a finger into her cunt and moved it back and forth, her rounded hips writhing in self-induced pleasure. The image of Sam was so sharp and seemed so close, Alice was sure she could hear the soft moans of ecstasy Sam must surely be making. She could see that wet finger glistening as it went in and out of her pink, hair-rimmed cunt, and could almost hear the moist sounds of it.

As often as Alice had used her own fingers on her pussy, she had not once thought it would be exciting to watch another girl finger-fuck herself. But as she watched, her own cunt was convulsing between her thighs, boiling with wet heat. This was the girl who had only this afternoon wantonly teased her stepson into discharging inside his bathing trunks, and now she was finger-fucking herself with the drapes open. Remembering the things she had heard at the pool, Alice wondered if Sam was aware that Matt had his telescope trained on her window, and that she finger-fucked herself as another means of teasing him at night.

She watched Sam with pleasure, seeing the rounded hips arch up as the girl apparently came. Sam pulled her finger from her cunt and Alice watched in delight as the girl licked it, running her tongue about the wetness and finally plunging the finger in and out of her mouth rapidly as if she were simulating fellatio.

When Sam finally turned out her lights and went to bed, Alice turned her attention back to the larger telescope. This time she saw that she had missed the opening in the curtains across the way. Through a small but revealing slit she could see the bed in that room, and she gasped loudly. On it was a woman she had exchanged smiles with a couple of times in the hotel lobby, spread out with her hairy cunt revealed. Then she saw a man move between the woman's thighs, his cock hard and his hairy balls swinging. Alice's pussy throbbed as she saw the woman grasp the man's cock and stuff it into her cunt. The man's cock slipped all the way in and the woman's legs wrapped around his waist. Alice watched his balls bounce and his clenched asscheeks rise and fall as the couple started fucking vigorously.

Alice shoved her hand under her skirt and inside her panties, finding her cunt wet and hot to the touch. She rubbed at the puffy lips of her cunt as she watched the man and woman fuck. She imagined the man's cock thrusting into her own cunt as she rammed two fingers into herself.

With her hand flying under her skirt, Alice panted with steaming excitement, watching the man and woman fucking so eagerly, wishing she was there on her back with his cock plunging so powerfully into her pussy, probing and stretching and filling her. His balls bounced about, banging against the woman's lifted ass, and then a hand came down and around and started twisting and squeezing his scrotal pouch. Alice was so excited she could almost feel the heavy-looking balls in her own hand. The woman's face could just be seen past the man's shoulder, and Alice was certain the woman was screaming out her ecstasy. At least her mouth was open and her eyes were wide and glazed.

Alice spread her feet on the floor and half bent her knees as she fucked herself frantically. She had merely pulled her panties aside, so excited she didn't want to waste time removing them. If she did she might miss the finish of the man and woman across the way.

She was disappointed when she saw the man's naked ass slam hard between the woman's legs and his body go stiff. He was coming, and it was over much too fast for Alice. She kept watching them as they relaxed, and then the man lifted from between the woman's legs. The woman stayed on the bed, her legs wide, and Alice watched her hairy cunt expel a little gush of silvery come juice, her hand moving about the thick curls of her pussy.

Still excited, Alice turned from the telescope, her hand still inside her panties. She pulled the drapes and turned on the light, looking about her stepson's bedroom. She seldom had reason to enter it. Matt always made his own bed and kept his room neat and clean. Now she looked around. Near the telescopes she saw where her stepson sat as he jacked off while he watched either Sam or the couple. The fact that her stepson was peeking into windows at night did not disturb Alice. She, too, had found how exciting it could be. She wasn't sure she wanted anyone to peek in at her, but it was fun to watch others in secret.

Turning off the light, she went back to the living room, and just in time because Matt came in as soon as she sat down.

"Enjoy the movie, honey?" she asked him.

"It was okay," he said, flopping down on the couch and slumping forward, his legs apart. Alice found her eyes moving to the front of his pants, wishing his cock was hard. "It wasn't as good as I thought it would be. Hey, it's a good night to study the stars."

He jumped up instantly and went to his room. Alice knew he would be disappointed. Sam and the couple across the way were all through for the night.

"Alice, have you been in my room?"

She looked up. Matt was standing there, his expression hard to read. "Yes," she said slowly, "I was there, honey," she said. "I thought it might need some straightening up. Do you always leave your curtains open?"

She looked directly into his eyes, letting him know she had discovered he was looking at more than stars. Matt gazed back at his stepmother unflinchingly.

"Some stars you see," she said in a low voice.

"You saw?" he asked.

Alice nodded her head. "I saw Sam and I saw the couple across the way," she admitted. "How long have you been peeking on them, Matt?"

"Long enough," he said boldly.

Alice gave her stepson a conspiratorial grin. "Kind of exciting, isn't it?"

A similar grin spread over his face. "Did it excite you, Alice? I mean, watchin' them do those things?"

"Very much," she replied, her eyes moving down his body to the front of his pants, noticing he was swelling up there. "I sort of, you know, enjoyed it. I enjoyed it plenty."

"Want to see someone else?" Matt asked.

"You mean there's more?" Alice asked, getting to her feet. "In this complex?"

"No, over at that tall building," he said. "It's an office building."

"At night?"

"Come on and I'll show you," he said excitedly. Before he turned, Alice saw that his cock was bulging out hard now.

She walked into his room, seeing he had

left the lights off but had pulled his curtains open again. She watched him work with the powerful telescope, getting it adjusted on the tall office building a block or so away.

"There. Take a look, Alice."

Peering into it, Alice saw a man, apparently a janitor, his cock out of his pants, one hand jerking on it as he dusted about desks. Soon, the man stood behind the desk with his cock over it, and she saw him come off, spurting come juice onto the polished desk top.

She laughed. "That's one way of getting back at the boss, I guess."

"He does that every night about this time," Matt said, standing close to his stepmother.

She could almost feel the heat coming from her stepson's body and it made her shiver. She stepped aside as he made another adjustment with the telescope, and then she saw he had aimed it farther away from the office building. It was a very powerful telescope, and she found herself peering into some bedroom window. A young boy and girl were there, both naked and feeling about each other. She watched until the girl was spread across the bed, her legs wide. When the boy started to shove his cock into her cunt, Alice let her stepson look.

Matt was breathing hard and hotly as he looked at the boy and girl fucking. Alice, at his side, was shaking. She moved her hand to the front of his pants, brushing it over his throbbing hard cock. She felt her stepson's body jerk, but he made no move to turn away or push her hand from him. She placed her palm against his hard-on, moving it slowly in circles as he watched the young couple fuck a few blocks away.

Feeling intensely aroused, Alice stepped behind her stepson, pressing her body against his back, her hands wrapped about him, one at his chest and the other cupping his cock. "If I did it once for you, I could do it again, baby. If you like..." she whispered into his ear.

"Uhh, yeah," Matt replied, moving his hips into his stepmother's caressing hand.

Alice ran her tongue about her stepson's ear as she began to open his pants. She slipped her hand inside and felt his cock hot and hard. Bringing it out of his underwear with difficulty, she closed her fist around it and began to stroke back and forth, pressing her pussy against his ass cheeks.

"Do you like this, Matt?" she murmured huskily at his ear. "Do you like my hand on you this way?"

"Yeah, Alice!" he grunted.

She cupped her hand about the swollen head of his cock, feeling the wetness smear her palm. She twisted her hand, feeling the hot, smooth, slickness of him. Her cunt was bubbling with a heat that threatened to scald the hair-lined lips. She worked on his belt, opening it, then shoved his pants downward, his shorts with them. Cupping his balls in one hand, she jacked his prick with the other, but even this wasn't enough for her. She lifted her dress and pressed her pantied cunt upon his naked ass, feeling her thighs on his. Matt's young body shook with pleasure as her hand moved back and forth.

"They're finished," he said in a choking voice.

"I'm not," she whispered at his ear, darting her tongue into it. "I'm not finished yet, darlin'."

She turned him, moving her stepson toward his bed. He sat down and she dropped to her knees before him. Spreading his legs, she grasped his cock once more, and as Matt lay back, Alice leaned down and kissed one thigh. She jerked and pumped on his cock, sucking at his flesh, her tongue swirling about the sensitive inner surface of her stepson's leg. Old Gus McCluskie had enjoyed this very much, and she had no doubts his youngest son would, too.

Squeezing his cock as she pumped it, Alice breathed hotly as her tongue moved upward, licking and tasting his young, firm thigh flesh. She wasn't sure just how far she would go but at the moment she was prepared to go all the way with her tongue.

"What... what are you gonna do, Alice?" Matt asked in a voice that sounded strangled.

"Hush," she whispered. "Just enjoy it, honey."

She jerked on his prick as her tongue moved from thigh to thigh, now halfway up them. Her cunt was fiery and wet as she licked and sucked at the flesh of his legs, her hand moving up and down his beautifully hard cock. Although it was dark in the room, with only enough light to make out indistinct details, Alice could see her stepson's balls a few inches from her face. She gave a whimpering sound and stroked her tongue about his balls, causing her stepson to jerk with unexpected pleasure. The sounds of his panting breath excited her, letting her know she was providing a great deal of ecstasy for him.

Swirling her tongue expertly, she flicked the tip against his balls, running it around them as she jerked her fist on his prick. She was pleased to find her stepson's balls tasted so good! She started licking them, her tongue going up and down, moving them about her lips. Matt was opening and closing his legs about her, arching his cock up and then dropping his ass. Alice shoved her hand under him and cupped a young, firm ass cheek, squeezing it as she tongued the boy's delicious young testicles through his scrotal sack. She knew, by the hard throbbing of his cock and the way his balls jumped and writhed against her tongue, she would have him coming off quicker than she wanted.

Yet she wasn't sure how far she should go. It might be better to go slow, or it might be better to go fast. The desire to gulp his young cock into her mouth and suck him frantically was strong, and she fought against the urge.

To have his sweet, hard cock throbbing between her lips would be so good, she thought. His cock, so young and hard, would feel heavenly inside her mouth, and she was sure his come juice would taste delicious as it flowed across her tongue and down her burning throat.

With a soft groan of delight, Alice swirled her tongue about his balls eagerly, finally taking them both into her mouth, sucking hotly as her fist jerked faster on his cock. The way his balls felt in her mouth sent a fiery ecstasy down to her cunt, and Alice began cumming. The waves of steaming orgasm shot through her one after the other, a series of orgasms like she had seldom experienced. She whimpered as she mouthed his balls, her fist flying up and down his prick.

Matt was lifting his ass up from the bed, grunting. Alice dug her fingers into his naked little ass hard, sucking his balls hungrily. She jerked frantically, mentally urging her stepson to come, to gush his creamy come juice before she gave in to the burning desire to close her lips about his cockhead and let him come off into her mouth.

She felt his cock spurt, and the creamy heat of his ejaculate coated her jerking fist. She pulled his tightened balls, making him shoot with her fist, soft sounds of delight coming from deep in her throat.

"Come, baby!" she moaned. "Oh, God... come! Come hard... come all over the place!"

"I am, Alice!" Matt groaned, his ass jerking wildly.

She pumped on his cock until it began going soft and small in her fist. Then she pulled her hand away and half turned so that Matt would not notice her licking it and relishing the taste. She found tissues on his night table and, while she savoured the delicious flavours of her stepson's semen, she carefully cleaned his cock, balls, thighs, and stomach, wishing now she had been able to take all of his jizz into her mouth.

She stood for a moment looking down at him in the darkness, barely seeing him. The crotch of her panties was very wet, and giving in to a sudden impulse, she lifted her skirt and stripped her panties off. Holding them in her hand, she moved to the door. She flicked the

Ranchers' Dirty Wives ★ 237

light switch, turning the room into brightness. She saw her stepson grinning at her, his cock and balls sweetly exposed to her.

"That's better than just watchin', Alice," he said.

"I know," Alice grinned back at him. Then she tossed her cunt-wet panties at him. They landed on his face, and Matt gave a soft laugh as he drew them down to his neck. "Now, here's something you can dream on, darlin'." She turned her back to him, and gave her skirt a saucy flip, showing her naked ass to her stepson briefly. "Nice, huh?" she teased.

"I didn't see much, Alice," he said.

"Well, take a good look, baby," she replied in a throaty voice, lifting her skirt again and holding it up this time. She patted her naked ass as she arched it saucily at him. "Isn't that a nice ass?"

"Yes, Alice. It most certainly is."

Chapter 15

Three days had gone by, and twice a day Alice had jerked her stepson off, usually with his balls in her mouth. Matt, of course, was having the time of his life.

He still sat near the pool when Sam was there, and Alice had not told him what she had seen. She enjoyed watching her stepson and the pretty girl without them knowing it. At night, she and her stepson would peek into Sam's room and watch the pretty girl caress herself, finger-fuck to orgasm, then lick her fingers. The couple across the way apparently didn't fuck every night, but Alice and Matt saw the janitor jacking off on the polished desk.

After watching with the telescopes, Alice would always leave her stepson with her cunt-wet panties on his face, flip her skirt upwards and wiggle her naked ass saucily, sometimes pat it in a teasing way.

As yet she had showed him nothing but her ass, but the desire to allow him to look at her body was becoming stronger. She wondered if he would be pleased with her, if he would find her titties as pretty as Sam's, her cunt as exciting. Not that she was jealous, no, just that she wanted to excite her stepson as much as the lovely little creature did.

During the passing few days, Alice found herself drawn to Sam almost as strongly as her stepson seemed to be. The girl was certainly a beautiful one, and her legs were very exciting to look at. When Sam climbed from the air float, the bottom of her bikini was always pulled into the crack of her ass, the creamy whiteness flashing. Alice understood Sam considered her ass to be quite lovely, and in truth it was. It was a strokeable ass, tight, and very shapely. Alice wondered what it would be like to feel Sam's ass, to play with her tits and maybe, just maybe, fondle and slide a finger into her hot, sugary cunt.

Such thoughts excited Alice tremendously, and she knew her stepson was desperate to caress the older girl, too. It was in his eyes every time he looked at her, in the way his cock became so hard as he watched her, especially through the telescope at night.

The next day, shortly after noon, Alice met Sam in the hotel lobby. She had just come home from the nearby shopping mall as Sam strolled up from the opposite direction. Sam was dressed in a short tennis skirt with a matching blouse. Her golden thighs flashed prettily in the sun, drawing Alice's eyes.

"Hello," Alice said, giving a friendly smile. "You're Sam Smith, aren't you? Staying across the pool from us? I'm Alice McCluskie. We've howdyd but we ain't shook yet, as they say 'round these parts," she grinned, extending her hand.

"Why, hello there, Mrs McCluskie!" Sam said, taking her hand and pumping it sincerely as if she had not seen the woman in years. "Here, let me help you with those bags."

"Why thank you, and please – call me Alice – otherwise I'll surely have to call you Miss Smith," laughed the older woman.

Alice gave one of her bags up and followed the girl up the stairs toward her apartment. The gentle sway of Sam's tight, shapely ass cheeks drew her eyes, along with those creamy thighs. Halfway up the stairs, Alice could see Sam's panties under the tennis skirt. Already those panties had crept into the crack of Sam's ass, and the half moons of her white ass cheeks beckoned erotically to Alice's eyes. Feeling childish, Alice stooped lower to peer under the short skirt, feeling her tits swell and a hot throb start between her legs as she looked at that sweet, sweet ass.

Inside the apartment, Alice tried to keep Sam there for a while. "Have you been playing tennis?" she asked.

"Oh, no," Sam replied. "I don't play tennis. I just think the skirts are pretty, so I wear them every chance I get."

"Coffee?" Alice asked, hoping.

"That would be lovely," Sam smiled at the older woman.

Sam leaned against the sink in the kitchen, crossing her feet. There was something appealing about this casual position that caused Alice to shiver with desire as she turned the automatic coffee maker on.

"Matt isn't home?" Sam asked.

"I hardly ever know where he is," Alice said. "He's getting to be such a big boy, he thinks he doesn't have to tell his stepmother where he's going."

"I think Matt is sweet," Sam murmured. "He's such a handsome boy, too."

"Yes, he is," Alice answered, looking at the thrust of Sam's pretty tits, her eyes becoming hot.

Sam continued to lean on the sink, her eyes seeming to study Alice's face, reading her expression and understanding what was going on inside the older woman's mind. She slowly uncrossed her feet and stood upright, her shoulders thrown back to make her tits strain forward.

"Don't you wear a bra?" Alice said, mentally kicking herself for making such a personal observation. She could see the twin nipples pressing against the blouse, and her eyes burned upon them.

"I don't like them," Sam said, and Alice realized the girl's voice had dropped and become throaty.

When Alice lifted her eyes, she found Sam gazing at her intently. Alice trembled as her cunt twitched. Sam lifted her arms to Alice, a small smile on her moist, full mouth. For just a second Alice resisted, then she moved closer to Sam and her arms went about the girl. They hugged each other tightly for a long, thrilling moment, feeling their tits mashing together. Then, without Alice knowing when it happened, her lips were on those of Sam, kissing hotly. She felt Sam's lips open underneath hers, and the tip of the girl's moist tongue began playing with her tongue.

They kissed hotly, lips writhing, arms wrapped tightly around each other. Alice felt Sam's tits moving against hers, felt those nipples hard and firm. The younger girl seemed to always take the initiative; she sucked on Alice's tongue, pulling it deeply into her hot, wet mouth with a soft moan. Alice responded with an erotic gurgle of pleasure, her hands moving down Sam's back. She cupped the sweet firmness of Sam's tight ass and whimpered with pleasure when Sam pressed her lower stomach hard against her. Sam had worked her thigh between Alice's legs, and now Alice could the heat of her crotch. Sam grabbed Alice's generous ass in her hands, and while they squeezed each other's ass cheeks, they moaned and sobbed as ecstasy swelled within their bodies.

Sam lifted Alice's skirt and the contact of the girl's hot, smooth thighs straddling her naked leg sent a hot flash of increased desire through Alice. She felt the moist heat coming through Sam's panties and searing her thigh. Alice pressed her leg hard into Sam's cunt as the girl rubbed it there. Alice squeezed the resilient flesh of the girl's squirming ass, feeling Sam dig her fingers deep into her own. The women looked at each other, gazing into hot eyes as Sam rubbed a pantied cunt against Alice's thigh. The young girl's eyes glazed over and a soft sigh came from her mouth. Alice felt the hot throbbing on her leg and knew the girl had come.

Their lips met softly, briefly, in a short kiss. Sam took the older woman's hand and led her to the bedroom. With a teasing smile, Sam opened her blouse and shrugged it from her shoulders. Alice gasped as she gazed upon the shapely beauty of Sam's flawless breasts. The nipples stood up, pink and swollen, and the white band of her tits contrasted with the golden colour of her flesh. Sam cupped them and, lowering her eyes in pretended shyness, offered them to Alice.

"So lovely," Alice whispered, taking both titties in her palms and caressing them gently, her fingers squeezing just hard enough to bring coos of delight from Sam.

"Kiss them, Alice," Sam pleaded with a husky voice. "Please – kiss my tits, suck on my nipples."

The women were about the same height, and Alice lowered her face, wrapping her eager lips about one nipple, drawing it deeply into her hungry mouth, sucking hard, her tongue swirling and licking. She felt Sam's hands cupping her tits through her light-weight summer sweater, caressing and fondling them. She sucked in a wet, greedy way on the succulent nipples, her hand on the other, scooting her right hand around to knead and fondle Sam's lovely ass. She shoved her hand under the short skirt and felt the heat of her flesh. She ran her finger about the cotton panties, then pressed her fingers under it to feel the naked smoothness of Sam's ass. She sucked hungrily, moaning softly, going from tit to tit. Eventually Sam lifted up Alice's sweater to reveal her creamy, bra-encased breasts.

"Let me," Sam whispered throatily. "Alice, let me suck your nipples!"

Reluctantly, Alice lifted her face, and allowed Sam to quickly remove her sweater and bra. Sam gasped with delight as she gazed upon the lovely brunette's large tits; as they tumbled out she thumbed the big, sensitive nipples into even larger hardness.

"God, you have such beautiful tits, Alice," Sam murmured, licking her lips. "I love those big, long nipples."

As Sam dipped her head and swirled her tongue about one nipple, finally sucking it very deeply into her mouth, Alice's cunt rippled into a little orgasm. Moaning with pleasure, her fingers clutched at Sam's shoulders.

"Ooooh, I don't believe it! I think I just came!" she mumbled in astonishment.

Sam giggled happily, and Alice gasped as one of Sam's hands pressed her skirt between her thighs hard, rubbing upon her cunt.

"Oh, God!" Alice whimpered. "Ohhh, God!"

"Mmmm, nice, isn't it?" Sam murmured with her lips brushing a swollen nipple. "My, you feel so hot, Alice!"

Again their lips came together, grinding in passion, both women whimpering as they clutched at each other's ass again, rubbing their lower bodies hotly together. Nimble fingers worked briefly at the zipper of Alice's skirt and it slithered to the floor. Standing in her bikini panties, Alice stepped back and watched Sam remove her short skirt, then slide her panties down those tantalizing thighs. Her cunt hair was so blond that Alice could see the pink slit of her pussy through it.

"Take your panties off too, Alice," Sam gasped, fondling her own tits, her eyes blazing in passion. "Take your panties off so I can see your pussy!"

Alice almost ripped her flimsy panties from her body and stood proudly, her feet parted and her hips arching forward, presenting her lovely, mature cunt, thickly covered by jet black pubic hair, and the fleshy, swollen lips of her swollen sex. Sam moaned and shoved her hand between Alice's smooth thighs, feeling the wet right away, cupping her cunt and rubbing a finger back and forth between the slick, slippery lips. Alice's hand darted to

Sam's pussy, worming a finger into the tight grip of the girl's cunt.

Now both totally nude, they moved to the bed, sitting on the edge as they began to kiss hotly and wetly, their hands moving about each other's body in steaming desire. Alice thought: she's done this before; she'll know what to do. I'll just follow her lead.

Sam slipped off the bed, going to her knees. Alice watched with burning eyes as the girl parted her knees, stroking the creamy inner surfaces of her thighs. Sam traced a finger about the curls of Alice's cunt hair, parting it and looking at the tip of Alice's large, protruding clitoris.

"Ohhh! Oh, Yes!" Alice murmured when Sam pressed her wet, hot lips upon her thigh, kissing it, sucking the flesh between them, her tongue swirling. "Oh, yes, *yes!*"

Sam began eagerly licking and kissing at the inner sweetness of Alice's legs, inhaling the musky scent of her aroused sex, licking her way up between them. She was gripping Alice's trembling hips with strong fingers, and her hot breath seemed to sear the flesh of Alice's legs.

Murmuring softly, Sam nuzzled her face into the thick, steamy bush of the woman's hairy cunt, kissing, licking, following the little trail of dark hairs that led all the way up to the indentation of Alice's belly button with

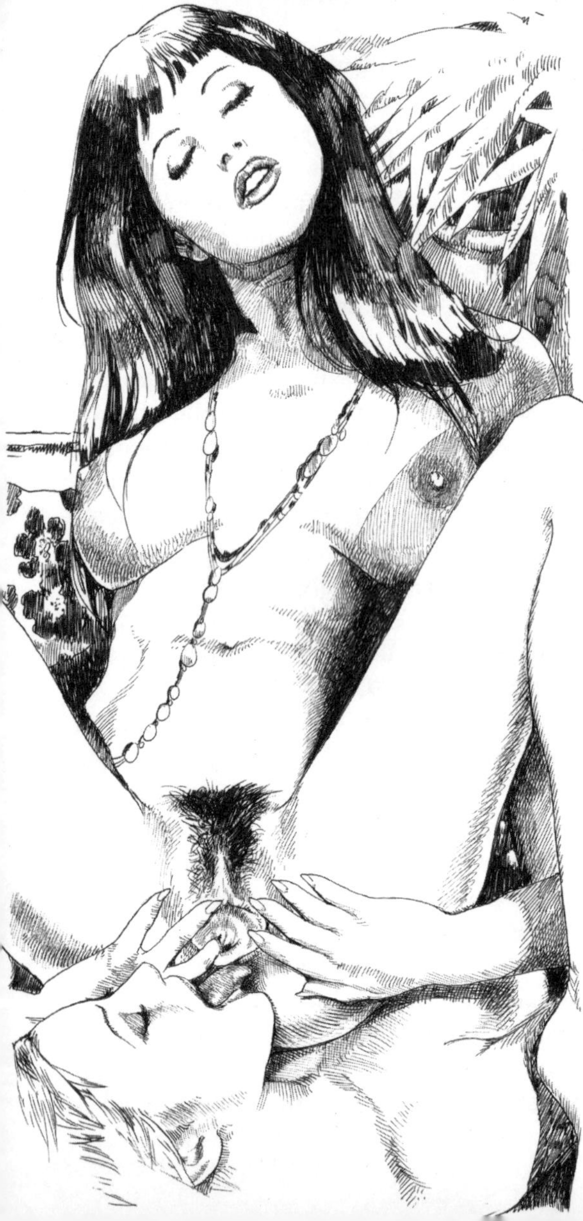

her tongue.

Alice leaned back on her elbows, her eyes closed as boiling desire bubbled through her body. Sam ran her tongue about each hairy pussy lip, teasingly. The wetness of her tongue sent chills of anticipation through Alice and she lifted her hips, writhing her crotch in search of the girl's mouth. Sam flicked the tip of her tongue over Alice's throbbing clitoris, which swelled and stiffened with pleasure; she thrust her cunt into Sam's face, grinding almost mindlessly. She choked when Sam ran her tongue along the slit of her cunt, and then shoved it into the slippery wetness.

When Sam fucked her tongue in and out of Alice's cunt, Alice moaned again, louder this time, and banged her overheated cunt into the girl's face. She felt Sam's tongue swirling and licking the sensitive labia, then close her lips about her clitoris, sucking on it hard.

Sitting upright, Alice grasped Sam's tits, urging her to climb onto the bed with her. Sam came eagerly, and they stretched out, pressing together. Alice kissed Sam's lips, wet and shining with cuntjuice; she could taste her own secretions and she loved the wicked thrills it gave her. Alice pulled Sam on top of her naked body, wrapping her slim thighs around Sam's hips and locking her ankles behind the girl's knees. Squirming together, they kept kissing wetly, pressing their bodies against each other, pubis to pubis and breast to breast.

"You feel real good, Sam," Alice whispered passionately as she squeezed the girl's firm, grinding ass cheeks. "You feel so damned good against me!"

"You too, Alice," Sam replied in a low voice.

Then Sam started licking and kissing her way down Alice's naked body again, swirling her tongue and licking at the sweet flesh, sucking a nipple, then going farther down.

"I want to kiss you, too," Alice whispered. "Let me kiss you, too, Sam. I've never..." she tailed off, feeling a little foolish and inexperienced. "I've never done this with another woman."

"That makes me want you more," breathed Sam. "Now, don't think about it... just *do* it!"

Sam turned around on her hands and knees, her lips and tongue continuously moving, tasting, kissing, licking. Alice spread her legs wide as Sam's tongue licked once more through the thick hair of her cunt, sliding her hand between Sam's golden thighs, feeling the curly blond pussy hair with eager fingers. As Sam licked up and down the slit of her cunt, Alice lifted her hips and pulled at Sam's body until she had manoeuvred them into a 'sixty-nine' position.

Closing her lissom thighs around Sam's

head, Alice watched as Sam's wide-split ass cheeks descended slowly towards her face, gazing up at the pink sweetness of the drenched young cunt, seeing it swell and glisten with arousal. The neat brown asshole above seemed to wink an invitation to Alice, and she ran her fingertip lightly over its puckered surface, watching it contract involuntarily. Sam was cupping Alice's ass, lifting her crotch up to her face and licking hungrily, sucking on Alice's throbbing clitoris. The wet slurping sounds sent an appeal to Alice's ears, as if to say "Eat me!"

Then she heard the girl actually say:

"Eat my cunt, Alice!"

"Oh, yes! I *will!*" Alice grunted eagerly, pulling Sam's rounded ass further down, thrilling to feel the warmth of the girl's dripping slit against her face.

Mouth open, she sucked Sam's cunt lips into her mouth and swirled her tongue about the sugary lips, then plunged her tongue into it. Sam's cunt was very tight, very hot, and very wet. With her hands clutching the shapely tight ass, Alice began eating and sucking and licking. She swallowed continually as the juices flowed unceasingly into her thirsty mouth. The exotic, musky odour and the slightly salty taste of Sam's cunt sent Alice's senses into a reeling ecstasy as she tried to thrust her tongue even more deeply. The blond-haired lips seemed to suck and grip her tongue as Alice plunged into it, moaning in this sweet, erotic pleasure.

With her face in Sam's cunt, Alice lifted her hips and twisted them, offering her cunt up to the eager girl's mouth, pumping her hips to fuck on that darting tongue. She clung to Sam's naked, succulent ass tightly and pressed her open mouth hard upon the sugary wetness of Sam's cunt. Sam's cunt dripped constantly, filling Alice's mouth with salty-sweet juices. Alice swallowed them hungrily, lapping her tongue inside the steaming slit for more. The satiny walls of Sam's cunt lifted Alice to new heights of sensual pleasure that she had never known existed and she sobbed softly as she sucked and licked, whipping her own cunt roughly up and down, making Sam gurgle happily. The way Sam held her naked ass, fondling the smooth cheeks as she tongue-fucked her and licked at her wild, unruly gash, soon had Alice erupting into orgasm after orgasm. She squeezed her thighs about Sam's head, sucking as hard as she could, wanting to make Sam's cunt convulse just as her own was doing. Time and again they came, bringing each other to amazing orgasms with their lips and tongues.

As they rolled apart, gasping for air, their naked bodies shaking, both had come so much that it was almost painful. Alice's face, especially around her mouth, was glistening with the wetness of her female lover's juices. She ran her tongue over her lips, finding them slightly bruised. She smiled at Sam, seeing that pretty face was also wet and shiny for the same reason. Sam was smiling with total satisfaction, her blue eyes glowing.

"My God," Alice whispered, caressing the sweetness of Sam's tanned thigh near her cunt. "You taste so good, Sam. I had no idea a cunt would taste that sweet. Wow," she said, stretching her arms above her head and giving a tired little yawn, "I feel like I've been rode hard and put up wet!"

Sam sat up, looking down at Alice, her eyes wide with surprise. "You mean... this is your first time with a girl, Alice?"

The forty-one-year-old nodded, grinning with pleasure.

"Then why?" Sam asked. "I mean, what made you want to do it?"

Alice told of watching her at the pool, of seeing her bikini bottoms pull into the crack of her ass, of the strange and growing desire to feel the saucy ass of this enigmatic young girl. She did not see fit to mention the way Sam tantalized her stepson, or how she had watched her fingerfuck herself through Matt's telescope or how she had jerked her stepson off while sucking on his balls.

Sam stroked Alice's tits. "I'm glad, then,"

Ranchers' Dirty Wives ★ 253

Sam said. "I've seen you around and you want to know something? I've wanted to suck your cunt ever since I first saw you. I just didn't know if you'd let me."

"Now we both know, don't we?" Alice laughed, rubbing between Sam's thighs. "But this doesn't mean I'm turned off by guys. I love them – especially those hard cocks they have. I love to feel a hard cock in my cunt, but now I love to feel my tongue up a pussy, too."

"We're the same," Sam laughed. "I enjoy eating pussy as much as fucking a sweet cock, too."

"Like Matt's?" Alice asked, then wondered why she had said it.

Sam's eyes grew warm as a smile spread over her face. "He's so good-looking. I wouldn't mind fucking him at all.

"Why don't you do it, then?" Alice heard herself ask.

"I thought… he's so young, Alice," Sam replied. "Would he know what to do with a girl? Has he had a piece of ass, do you know?"

"I'm not sure," Alice said. "But I think he's getting horny enough for it lately. Besides, there's always a first time, isn't there?"

Sam giggled, pinching Alice's nipple.

"What's so funny?"

"I think it's hilarious, eating your cunt the

way I just did and now thinking about fucking your stepson," Sam laughed. "Tongue-fuck the stepmother, then go fuck the stepson!"

"Anything wrong with it?" Alice asked, a little anxious.

Sam's eyes grew serious.

"Well, I don't think so, Alice, but *you* might – when you hear what I've got to tell you. We need to talk. We need to talk a lot. You see, my real name is the same as yours – McCluskie. Billy Jo McCluskie."

* * *

Later, much later, Alice said, "So Sam isn't your real name? What should I call you? Billy Jo? It's pretty. I like it."

She held her head in her hands, letting her dark hair tumble down over her face.

"Oh God, what a mess, Billy Jo. Every time I stand up my mind sits down."

Billy Jo/Sam came over to where Alice sat on the edge of the bed, sat down too, and put her arm around the shaken older woman.

"I've been an utter fool. Why didn't I see through Rex Reed? It's so obvious what he's trying to do, but I couldn't bring myself to face the awful truth that he might have had something to do with Dad and my brother's deaths. What shall I do?"

"For the time being, don't do anything,

Alice. The time to kill a snake is when he raises his head. And I something tells me that Reed is about to do just that..."

Chapter 16

That evening Alice found herself wishing her stepson would go down to visit Billy Jo.

She knew Billy Jo would fuck Matt, she had said she would, in so many words. If he would go down to visit with her, maybe he would fuck her in the living room, and she could watch them on the telescope! Somehow, the idea of seeing her stepson fuck the sweet young wife – his sister in law – sent shivers of perverse pleasure between her thighs. The idea of seeing her stepson's precious cock thrusting into the blonde-haired cunt she had sucked off that afternoon almost made Alice come as she sat looking at Matt. Soon she would have to tell him what she knew, that 'Sam' was the other 'Mrs. McCluskie'. Billy Jo McCluskie, to be exact. But not yet: it might spoil things if he knew too much too soon.

"Matt," she said softly, "have you ever thought about doing something with any of those women you've been spying on?"

"Doing what, Alice?"

"I know you've been jacking off, watching them," she said. "You jack off when you see Sam in her living room, don't you? And remember how good it makes you feel when I suck your balls and jerk you off after we look at her? Doesn't that make you wish you could fuck her?"

Matt's eyes became round as he looked at his stepmother. Alice saw the effect her words had on him by the way his cock started swelling inside his jeans. She grinned.

"Well, don't you think it would be good to stick your cock in her blond cunt, darling?"

"Yeah, that would be great, Alice!" he said enthusiastically. "But I don't think Sam would let me. I think she thinks I'm just a kid and she's not gonna want to fuck a kid like me."

"I wouldn't be too sure about that," Alice said. "I have a hunch she might let you."

"Really?" Matt asked, eagerness in his voice.

"I'm sure Sam would let you fuck her," Alice said, her voice firm. "Listen, why don't you go visit her now? You can find out if she will."

"Aw, I wouldn't know what to do, Alice," he said.

"Leave that up to Sam, baby," Alice replied. "You don't have to do anything but get a hard-on. I think she'll do the rest."

"You mean it?" he asked again, his eyes glowing, his cock straining at his pants. "You think she'll fuck me, Alice, really?"

"Why don't you take that hard-on you're getting down there and find out?" she smiled at him. "Once she sees your hard cock, I bet she won't be able to keep her hands off it."

"Like you, Alice?" Matt laughed.

"Mmm, like me."

Matt got to his feet, pacing up and down the living room, excited, his cock bulging in his pants. "I'll do it," he said. "I'll go see her. Maybe she'll let me fuck her. I hope she'll let me put it in her! Gosh, I bet she's good at it, Alice! She looks and acts like she'll love getting fucked!"

"Go find out," Alice urged, watching his excitement and his cock swell. "Go on before you come off in your fucking pants, baby!"

"Aw, you wouldn't let me come in my pants, Alice," he said, arching his hips toward her.

"Don't be so sure," she teased. "You make my panties wet all the time, don't you? It would only be fair if you cum off in your pants." She ran her hand over his hard-on. "Mmmm, you've got a nice, big, hard cock, baby. If you don't go on and see if Sam will fuck you, I'm going to take your cock out and play with it myself."

"I'm going!" he said.

Alice watched her stepson run out the door. Then she hurried to his bedroom quickly, entering the darkness. The small telescope was still trained on the living room of Billy Jo's suite. She peered through the lens, seeing its occupant sitting on the couch in her robe as usual. Then she saw the girl look up and knew her stepson had knocked on her door.

She watched the cute young blonde invite Matt into her suite, taking his hand and bringing him to the couch. Alice noticed that Matt still had his hard-on.

Billy Jo sat down beside Matt and turned to face him, one leg up on the couch, the robe parted to expose her golden, creamy thighs almost to the 'vee' of her pubic curls. Alice sensed that her stepson was more nervous than a long-tailed cat in a roomful of rockers: he kept glancing at the girl's legs. She saw her laugh reassuringly, then lean over and kiss Matt's cheek.

Already Alice's cunt was wet, dribbling and throbbing with sexual heat. It wasn't everyday a stepmother could watch her stepson's first fuck, she thought, pleased. Billy Jo took Matt's hand as they sat talking, placing his palm on her knee. Matt was quickly losing his nervousness, Alice saw. Billy Jo pulled Matt's hand up her thigh a ways as she leaned over and kissed him, on his mouth this time. As she leaned forward, her robe came apart, revealing her beautiful tits with their rigid, rubbery nipples.

She wished she could hear them talking, but since she couldn't, looking at them and playing with herself was the next best thing. She slipped a hand into her panties and slid a finger into the warm wet groove of her cunt. She saw Billy Jo lift her stepson's hand and curl his fingers about one of her tits, and then she dropped her hand right on top of Matt's raging hard cock. Alice was proud of her stepson, watching him boldly stroke and fondle Billy Jo's luscious titties. When she saw her opening Matt's pants, taking his young cock out, Alice almost came, her cunt boiling with that sweet, deliciously wet sensation.

The younger Mrs. McCluskie closed her fingers around her youngest brother-in-law's cock, jerking up and down on it. Alice knew what she was feeling. As she jacked on his hard cock, Billy Jo ran her tongue over Matt's lips. Finally she drew back, opening her robe and letting it fall away. Alice watched her stepson look at Sam's naked beauty, his eyes glowing with eager excitement. He looked upon her blonde-haired cunt intently, then moved his hand up her thigh and stroked it, finding the entrance to her vagina and pumping one of his fingers in and out. Billy Jo leaned back on the couch, spreading her slender legs wide and arching her cunt up to Matt's thrusting finger, gripping his erection tightly.

Alice was hardly breathing as she saw Billy Jo stand her stepson up, open his belt, and shove his pants down. Matt's manhood stood out, straight and lovely, his balls appearing very full. Alice squeezed at her own tits as she murmured, "Fuck him, Billy Jo! Take his cock in your sweet cunt and fuck my stepson! I want to watch this beautiful shaft fuck your tight slit!"

Whether it was because she had said those words or because she was watching Billy Jo play with Matt's cock and balls, Alice felt an small orgasm shudder through her cunt. She moaned softly, watching Billy Jo spread her legs and push Matt to his knees between them.

Using two fingers, Billy Jo spread her pink, wet inner labia, and holding Matt's prick at the base, rubbed his swollen, dripping piss hole about the fiery slit of her pussy, mashing it against her swollen clitoris. She was looking into Matt's face as she did this, her lips parted and her tongue moving about them. Matt was staring down at what she was doing with his cock and her cunt, his hands holding her hips as though she would jerk from him.

The image was sharp, and Alice sucked in a hiss of air as she saw her stepson's cock sliding into Billy Jo's cunt. She could almost

Ranchers' Dirty Wives ★ 261

hear Matt gasp with ecstasy. Billy Jo closed her eyes as Matt's cock entered her, and it was obvious to Alice that the girl was sighing with pleasure. For a long moment, Billy Jo held him inside her cunt, then she placed her hands on his narrow hips, moving him back and forth, lifting her cunt to his prick. Alice watched her stepson catch the rhythm, and then he was fucking Billy Jo, his cock sliding deeply and wetly. She churned her hips up and down, fucking back at Matt vigorously. Alice could almost hear the wet sounds of her stepson's cock penetrating that sweet tight cunt, and she yet again shoved her hand under her dress to rub at her own dripping pussy.

Observing her stepson's small ass bunch and tighten, his cock moving in and out sent ripples of desire up and down Alice's spine. She watched as Billy Jo moved hips up and down, grinding into Matt's plunging cock, his balls slapping against her delectable, pert ass. Now she could see his cock glisten with the wetness of Billy Jo's cunt, could almost see the way that tight pussy sucked at his prick. She no longer held Matt's hips now, but clutched at her own large, firm tits, twisting and pulling at her pink nipples, her head turning from side to side, her long honey-blonde hair flopping over her face. Billy Jo was thrashing her naked ass about wildly, and Alice knew instinctively that the girl was either coming or very close to it.

Then the girl thrust her cunt hard onto Matt's cock, clutching his tight, muscular buns. Alice saw her stepson ram his prick deeply, his young body shaking, and then turning rigid.

"He's coming in her," she whispered excitedly to herself, her eye glued to the telescope. "Matt is shooting his precious come juice in her tight, wet cunt!"

A powerful orgasm shot through Alice as she watched Billy Jo and her stepson coming together. Matt's cock stayed inside her cunt for a long time, with him slumping over the girl's lovely body. Alice was glad to see Billy Jo caressing his back and ass while he rested, her thighs moving gently against his hips.

After watching her stepson pull his pants up and seeing Billy Jo lead him to the door, hugging him tightly against her naked body to kiss him good-night, Alice left the telescope and her stepson's room.

She was in the living room when Matt came in, his face glowing happily.

"She let me, Alice!" he said exuberantly. "Sam let me fuck her! Ohh, it was sure good, too! I liked it so much."

Catching his excitement, Alice grabbed him and hugged him tightly. She ran her hand along the front of his pants, feeling his cock and balls. She kissed him wetly on his mouth, darting her tongue into it for a moment.

"Was it that good, baby?" she laughed. "Did her cunt feel real hot and wet to you? Was it a tight pussy?"

"Yeah, man!" Matt said. "Sam fucks good, Alice! I thought she was gonna fuck my cock right off... almost pulled my balls in it!"

"I supposed you're tired now, huh?" she teased him. "I suppose all you want to do is go to sleep, right?"

"Not me," he said. "I want to stay awake and let the feeling stay as long as it will."

She squeezed his cock and balls through his pants, then turned him loose. She pretended to pout. "Now I won't have any fun with you, I guess. You're probably not interested in my hand-jobs anymore."

"I am, Alice," he said. "You can always jack me off and suck on my balls. I like that, too."

She gave a sigh of pretended negligence. "Well, I suppose I could jack off the paper boy, or find me another fellow who will let me have some fun, too."

Matt hugged his stepmother tightly. "Aw, Alice. You know you can jack me off. Here..." He opened his pants and pulled his cock out. "You can do it for me now."

Alice looked at his cock. It was still wet from Billy Jo's cunt.

"You're not even hard for me," she pouted.

"You've always had a nice hard-on for me to play with, honey. I guess Sam has fucked you out, after all."

Matt stroked his cock, standing in front of his stepmother.

"Oh, let me do that," Alice growled good naturedly, her cunt steaming again. "Take your fucking pants down and let me do that for you."

Matt shoved his pants down and Alice sat him on the couch, dropping to her knees between his legs. She licked at his flesh, watching his cock grow, swelling and pointing toward his stomach. She cupped his balls gently and caressed them, stroking her other hand along his pussy-wet cock. She could smell the arousing scent of her young neighbour's cunt on him.

Shoving her face between his legs, she lapped about his balls, tasting Billy Jo's juices there. That added to her erotic pleasure. Taking his balls into her mouth, she began to pump at his once more hard cock. The piss-hole flared and dripped a single drop of pearly white semen, lubricating her hand and making her fist slide smoothly on his prick. She guessed it was all that was left of his earlier cum.

"Mmmm, you taste so good!" she moaned, drawing both his balls into her mouth, her nose brushing the base of his cock, once again inhaling the scents and flavours of the young girl's cunt mixed with his own thick sperm.

Letting his balls drop from her mouth, she kissed the base of his cock. "Knowing you were down there fucking her made me so hot, baby," she murmured. "I wanted to play with myself, the way we've watched Sam do."

"Why didn't you, Alice?"

"Because... well, because, that's all."

"Just thinking about it, huh?"

"No," she confessed. "I watched you in the telescope. I watched it all – the way she fucked you, your cock going into her cunt, you both coming."

"You did?" His eyes glowed.

"You don't believe me?"

"Sure, I believe you, Alice," he said. "I'd have been watching if I was you."

Alice stood up, lifting her skirt slightly and shoving her hands under it. Without letting her stepson see her cunt, she pulled her panties off. As she lifted first one knee, then the other to remove her panties, Matt caught a brief flash of her hairy cunt.

"See, I'll show you how hot I got," Alice laughed, rubbing the crotch of her panties against his face. "Tell me if I was hot or not? Those panties are almost soaked!"

Matt held them off his face, looking at the lacy crotch. They were drenched with the juices of his stepmother's cunt. Giggling a little crazily, Alice shoved the wet crotch against his lips, rubbing it back and forth.

"Have a taste of cunt, darling. *My* cunt!"

Matt laughed, his hand on the back of his stepmother's as she rubbed her panties at his mouth. Playfully, Alice shoved the cunt-wet crotch of her panties between his lips. "Taste that cunt... it's second-hand pussy, but it's better than none!"

Her finger had shoved the wet crotch of her panties into his mouth, and she felt Matt sucking at it. "Mmmm, you like the taste, don't you, Matt? I'm surprised you didn't get down and lick Sam's cunt."

"I sure thought about it, Alice," Matt laughed and pulled her panties out of his mouth.

She watched Matt rubbing the wet crotch of her lacy panties about his mouth, then turned to see his cock throbbing up strong and hard. With a soft mewl, she went to her knees and shoved her face into his crotch, licking and kissing his sweet balls as she began jacking him once more. His cock throbbed so sweetly in her fist, and he was dripping an awful lot. He was still rubbing her panties about his lips, and she watched him suck at the cunt-wet crotch as his eyes gleamed down at her.

"Tastes good, Alice," he moaned, arching his hips up into her hand, twisting his crotch at her mount. "I like it, your pussy taste."

"Mmmm," she moaned around his balls.

The taste of Billy Jo's cunt lingering on him gave her a much more intense sensation than ever before. It added to her oral pleasure, doubling it now that she had sucked her cunt herself. She wondered, briefly, what her stepson would say if he knew she had licked that blonde cunt earlier that day. She was sure it would excite him. Maybe she would let him know about it later.

His balls were tightening inside her mouth as she sucked them, and the throbbing of his cock was increasing. She ran her fist up and down faster as Matt twisted his crotch against her face. His balls seemed to fill her mouth and a hot, burning desire to take his cock inside her mouth and suck his come juice down her throat came over her.

Before she could make up her mind, Matt gave a grunt and come juice spurted from his cock. Alice moaned around his balls as she saw her stepson stuff the cunt-wet crotch of her panties into his mouth, sucking at them, his cock spurting thick, creamy come juice into the air. She watched it drop down to splash onto his stomach, her hand, and even some on one of her cheeks. She clutched his cock tightly as he came.

Releasing his balls, she gazed up at him, her panties dangling from his mouth. "Nice, isn't it?" she murmured. "You can suck my wet panties anytime you want. But I get to do this, too."

Her tongue flicked from her mouth and into the come juice smeared on his stomach. She lapped it up, swirling her tongue about, then lightly lapped it across the wet slit of his cockhead. As she swallowed the come juice and her tongue touched at his piss hole, Alice squealed when a powerful orgasm sent her ass cheeks wiggling as her pussy clutched in burning ecstasy.

"Oh, God... I came!" she whispered. "I came, baby!"

Tiredly, she rested her cheek on his cock and balls, feeling wonderful. She felt Matt's hand on her head, running his fingers through her thick dark hair. She turned to look up at him, her chin touching his balls, her lips at the base of his cock.

"You're so sweet, Matt," she whispered, kissing the base of his cock with her moist lips. "God, I can't believe how sweet you are."

Matt smiled at her, rubbing his cock about her lips.

"That's enough," Alice said softly, getting to her feet. "If we don't stop now, I might fuck you myself."

"I will if you will, Alice," he laughed.

She grinned at him. "You'd fuck your own stepmother, honey?"

"If you'll let me," he said.

Alice studied his young, good-looking face. "I believe you would."

"Try me," he laughed, arching his cock up. "Just try me and see!"

"Well, at least you can suck on my cunt-wet panties," she laughed. "That's better than nothing, isn't it?"

He nodded, running his tongue along the lacy crotch, then rubbing them about his face.

"I think you really do like to suck on my fucking panties," she said.

"Only if they're nice and wet like these, Alice."

"I'll make sure they are from now on," she said, leaning down. She pulled her panties away from his lips and kissed him. "I'm tired and ready for bed. I know you're going to have some very sweet dreams tonight, after fucking Sam and getting me to suck your balls and jack you off again."

Alice walked to the short hallway, starting toward her bedroom.

"Alice?"

She stopped and turned.

"You didn't show me your ass," he said. "You've always shown me your ass before going to bed."

It was true. Each night after they watched the others through his telescopes, and after she had sucked on his balls and jacked him off, she had flipped her skirt up over the pale moons of her ass and let him have a peek, whether she was wearing panties or not.

Grinning at him, she flipped her skirt up, wiggling her naked ass for him, then started once more toward her bedroom.

"Alice?"

"What?"

"I wanna see your pussy."

Alice faced her stepson, a burning excitement flowing through her body, the hairy lips of her pussy starting to throb again.

"Please," Matt asked in a soft voice. "Let me see your cunt. Just once, Alice."

Chapter 17

Alice stared at her stepson.

He was still sitting on the couch, his pants at his ankles, stroking his cheek with her panties now.

"Please," Matt said again. "Let me see your cunt, Alice. You see my cock! It's only fair."

Matt was right. She knew she should let him look at her pussy if he wanted. There was no doubt that he was very interested in seeing her. The idea of her stepson looking at her, between her thighs, at her big, hairy cunt, was exciting, exciting enough to create a fire there. She felt her clitoris throbbing and the cheeks of her ass clenching. Her eyes moved to his naked cock, and she was surprised to see it stir, starting to swell again.

"Why, honey?" she asked.

"I wanna see it, that's all," Matt said.

"If I let you see my cunt," she replied in a slow, very low voice, "what will you want to do next?"

"I just wanna look at your pussy, Alice, that's all."

Alice knew what he would want to do next. The thought of her stepson sliding his cock into her cunt and fucking her sent chills of hot anticipation through her. She was facing him now, and her fingers started inching her dress up. Matt's eyes grew hot as he saw her thighs, then almost bugged out when she pulled her dress up to her waist. A shiver went through Alice as her stepson looked at her pussy. She parted her feet, standing in a wide-legged stance, shoving her hips forward. The thick triangle of her cunt hair was not like Sam's. It was thick, all but concealing her cuntlips. Holding her dress with one hand, Alice shoved the fingers of her other hand through the curls of her pussy and parted them, showing the dark pink, wrinkled inner lips of her cunt to her stepson.

His cock jerked into full-blown hardness before her eyes.

"Gosh!" Matt groaned as he gazed at his stepmother's pussy. He ran his tongue over his lips. "You're so pretty, Alice. Your cunt is so pretty and hairy! You look wet, too."

"I am wet, Matt," Alice said in a throaty, almost choking voice. "I'm very wet."

"Alice, I'd..."

She waited, but he didn't go on. She knew, though, what he was going to say. He was going to say he wanted to fuck her, and Alice knew that if he asked, she would give him anything, her cunt, her mouth – her body – in anyway Matt wanted. But he didn't finish saying it.

Holding her skirt at her waist, Alice gazed at his cock, imagining what it would feel like sliding into her cunt. The cock of her stepson... fucking her. The lips of her pussy throbbed with a painful desire to have his prick inside her. She moved her fingers about her distended clitoris, feeling his eyes on her cunt.

"Yes darlin'? You'd what?" she asked, her voice husky and filled with desire. "What would you do, honey?"

Matt gripped his cock hard, making the head swell. He ran the crotch of her panties over the head of his cock, caressing himself with the nylon, his eyes never moving from between her legs.

"Are you going to fuck my panties?" she asked, arching her eyebrow at him. "Or fuck me?"

"Gosh!" Matt groaned.

They gazed at each other. Alice wanted her stepson to make the first move, and Matt was waiting for his stepmother to do something. He kept caressing the crotch of her panties about the head of his cock, and Alice stood with her skirt still bunched up at her waist, slowly rubbing at her swollen, very inflamed clitoris. Matt watched his stepmother's hand, and she watched her panties move about his cock.

She was hardly aware that she was moving, stepping toward him. She walked with her cunt tossed forward, her eyes blazing on his prick. Matt was hardly breathing as his stepmother came toward him, unable to take his eyes off her fingers and what she was doing with her hairy pussy. His balls drew up at the base of his cock, his fist squeezing hard.

Alice stopped when her feet touched his. Matt was on the couch with his ass hanging over the edge, his cock standing up so hard. He pulled her panties away from his cock and dropped them on the floor, his hands resting on his thighs, waiting as he looked up at her.

"Oh, damn!" Alice whispered, staring at

Matt's cock as if seeing it for the first time. The heat in her cunt was unbearable. She clenched the cheeks of her ass, running her tongue over her lips. "Oh, shit, Matt!"

"Alice, please," he whispered.

She knew what he wanted without the words – he wanted his cock inside her cunt, wanted to fuck her, to fuck his stepmother!

"Baby," she murmured softly, smiling down at him. "Baby, oh baby!"

Alice spread her legs around his, then climbed onto her knees above his upstanding cock. Letting her skirt go, she reached behind her back and unbuttoned it, keeping her eyes on his. Lifting her arms from the dress, she let it fall to her waist, her titties free and naked against him. With her cunt only a few inches above his cock now, Alice cupped her tits in her hands, caressing them. She twisted her hips, doing an erotic and quite lewd bump and grind as her stepson licked his lips, his eyes burning between her slim thighs.

"Put it in, baby," she whispered softly.

Matt seemed mesmerized, unable to move.

"You can put your cock in me, Matt," Alice said in low voice. "Stick it in my cunt, Matt. You can fuck me."

His hands moved, sliding up her inner thighs until he grasped his cock. Alice sighed as she settled her cunt against the swollen prickhead. She felt her stepson's rubbery glans spreading the lips of her cunt, stretching them apart as her ass moved downward slowly, very slowly. Again she sighed as his rigid shaft moved deeper, throbbing along the sensitive lips of her fiery cunt.

"Ohhh, yes!" Alice hissed, settling down on his cock. It was deep inside her pussy now and she could feel his balls pressing the cheeks of her ass. "Ooooh, yes, baby!"

A shiver rippled through Alice's body and her tits jiggled, her nipples hard. The sensation of her stepson's cock inside her cunt was amazing, truly fantastic. It seemed to fill her cunt nicely, hotly, making it throb sweetly. The way his prick stretched the hairy lips of her cunt almost caused Alice to cum as soon as the head had slipped into her.

Alice closed her eyes as she felt her mind spin with the sweetest of all ecstasies. A faint dizzy feeling came over her as she sat astride his hips, his cock so very deep up her pussy. Her clitoris was being pressed against the base and into those wiry hairs, tingling deliciously. Matt's hands had been caught as she lowered her ass onto his cock, and they felt good, too, against her inner thighs. Another shiver shot through her, this one making her ass shake. When the hot cheeks of her naked ass brushed about his balls, Matt groaned in pleasure.

Opening her eyes, Alice fought to focus

them. She looked into her stepson's face, his expression filled with awe and ecstasy. Shrugging her shoulders to make her big melons jiggle, she cooed softly.

"Oh, yes, honey! Oh, my yes! Yes, yes, yes!"

Matt seemed to be trying to speak, but the words wouldn't come out. He opened and closed his lips like a fish out of water, his eyes taking on a dazed dullness. His cock seemed to lurch inside her cunt, fiery in hardness. He managed to pull his hands from between her hot thighs and his crotch. When he rested his palms on her thighs, his fingertips just touching the thick hair of her cunt, Alice began to sob softly.

"Please don't cry, Alice," she heard her stepson say.

"I'm not crying, darling," she replied, her voice quivering.

"I heard you," Matt insisted.

"Well, if I'm crying, it's because I'm so damn happy!"

She fell forward, hugging her stepson against her tits tightly, cupping his chin and smearing kisses about his face. His cock throbbed inside her cunt, and Alice felt her pussy respond by gripping it tightly. She looked into his eyes again, holding his cheeks. She saw the desperate heat there, his hungry desire to fuck her, his stepmother. Smashing her lips against his, Alice kissed her stepson fiercely, lips open, her tongue licking about his mouth.

She moved her ass, lifting it until she held the swollen, sweetly rounded head between the scalding lips of her intensely hot, very wet, cunt. With a screwing motion, she ran her pussy down again, sinking completely.

"Ooo, baby, baby!" she gurgled hotly, still holding his young face in her hands. "It's so good, Matt! Oh, you're so good! So hard inside me! I can feel your cock throbbing, beating like a heart in my cunt!"

Sitting on him, his balls pressed against the creamy smoothness of her ass, his cock far inside her cunt, her clitoris scraping the base, Alice wiggled her hips, a sort of sideways sliding motion with her cunt. Matt moaned with ecstasy, his fingers digging into her flesh near her hips. Alice sat upright on her stepson, her shoulders back, her tits thrusting out with impossibly hard nipples. She lifted her dress, and all Matt could see was the dark thick hair of her cunt pressing against him. He was unable to see his cock inside his stepmother's cunt, or the pink wetness of her pussy. All he could do was feel, and that was almost enough to make him come.

"Like it, honey?" she asked, smiling down at him, cupping her tits in her hands, her eyes blazing with heat. "Does it feel good to you?"

"Oh, Alice!" Matt wailed with delight. "You're awfully hot and wet! It feels like I might shoot, Alice!"

"Oh, you can't come yet, darling," she whispered. "We've just started to fuck. No, don't come off yet."

Using her thighs, Alice began to lift and lower her crotch on her stepson's cock, fucking him slowly. His hands had slipped up to her waist, shoving her skirt away. She watched his eyes as he gazed at the thick bush of cunt hair that was moving on his cock, seeing the way her fiery cunt was devouring the hard heat of his prick, leaving it glistening wet with the seeping fluids of her succulent pussy.

Matt arched his cock up as his stepmother's cunt came down on him, dropping his ass when she lifted, watching with enormous eyes. Each time Alice's pussy went down, she wiggled and rubbed before lifting again. Both stepmother and stepson began to gasp with increasing ecstasy. Friction seemed like steam as her cunt held his cock, sliding up and down it smoothly.

"Oh, God, it's good!" Alice moaned, leaning forward again and bracing herself with her hands on her stepson's shoulders. "You feel so fucking good in my cunt, Matt! Ooooo, baby, let's fuck! Let's fuck and keep fucking and never stop fucking!"

Her ass was moving faster now, lifting

and plunging in quick darting motions. Each time her cunt slammed down, Alice grunted, bringing yelps from her stepson.

"Hold my ass!" she screamed. "Hold your stepmom's ass! Oh, Matt, grab my fucking ass!"

His hands moved past her hips and palmed a twisting, plunging ass cheek in each. His fingers dug into the tight flesh, almost inside the crack of her churning ass. Alice whimpered and hissed and wailed, thrashing up and down her stepson's cock in demented ecstasy. The moist sounds roared in her ears. Her cunt was blazing hot now, the hairy lips clinging to his cock very tightly as it ran up and down. The throbbing of her stepson's prick was transmitted to the sensitive lips of her cunt, shooting like flames throughout her slender body. Her clitoris scraped the shaft of his hard-on with each wild plunge.

Alice sucked her bottom lip between her teeth, biting down on it, her ecstasy overwhelming her. Her ass shook and plunged, twisted and writhed. She was taking her stepson's cock very deep into her greedy pussy, all the way into her stomach. The hairy lips were stretched around his cock like a tight rubber band, her tits shaking from her increasingly violent motions. Matt clung to his stepmother's wiggling, bouncing ass almost desperately. It seemed to him that her cunt would leave his cock with each upward jerk, and he didn't want that to happen. But Alice's cunt was not about to pull from his prick. She rode from the base to the very head, fucking him with amazing speed and wetness and heat and ecstasy.

"Ohhh, fuck me, fuck me!" Alice wailed, her nails digging into his shoulders. "Fuck me! Fuck your stepmom! Fuck your stepmom's hot cunt! Fuck your stepmom's wet, hot, hairy cunt! Fuck... fuck... Oooo, fuck me!"

Matt squeezed into his stepmother's bouncing, naked ass with strong fingers, arching his hips up as his balls became tight at the base of his throbbing cock. His eyes focused upon her jiggling titties as he gritted his teeth in ecstasy.

"Oh, God! I'm coming!" Alice screamed. "Your cock... you're making stepmother come, darling! Ohhhh... oooo, I'm coming so good, so fucking good!"

The orgasms whipping about her cunt created even more tightness around his cock. The waving sensation of her hairy cunt lips created the feeling of being sucked. It seemed to Matt that with each upward motion of her cunt, it sucked hard on his cock, causing his balls to draw up as tight as possible at her shaking ass.

"Ahhhh, fuck! Fuck!" Alice wailed in mindless pleasure. "I'm coming! My cunt... my pussy is on fire! Oooo, baby... darling! Your stepmom's cunt is coming, really coming!"

Suddenly, with an intense scream, Alice slammed her cunt down hard on her stepson, his cock buried as deep as it could be. The action of her hairy pussy lips at the base, sucking and flexing and squeezing, pulled the come juice up from his tender balls, making it roar through his cock and splash into her satiny cunt. The rapid spurtings of his come juice striking the walls of her convulsing cunt made Alice scream again, and a final orgasm went off in her pussy.

Her body shook violently as she screamed, her cunt being filled and flooded by his precious come juice. She sat upright on him, her hips jerking back and forth as he came, darting her hand behind her ass to grasp his balls. She pulled hard on her stepson's balls, pressing them into the crack of her ass, making them tight on her puckering asshole.

Unable to remain upright as her orgasm ended, Alice slumped forward onto her gasping stepson. Her tits seemed to close about his young face as she trembled, his cock still inside her gently pulsating cunt. She felt Matt running his hands up and down her flesh, from the base of her spine down over her smooth ass cheeks and then up again. The way he caressed her ass gave Alice a very pleasant feeling along with the glowing delight of orgasm.

After what seemed like hours, she sat upright again, his cock still inside her cunt. She wiggled playfully, grinning down at him. Matt's expression was one of wonderful satisfaction. He grinned up at her, then lowered his eyes to the bush of her cunt again.

"God, what a fuck!" she whispered.

"Yeah, Alice," Matt murmured, feeling about her pussy hair with gentle, stroking fingers. "You're great!"

"As good as Sam?" she teased, smoothing his hair back over his forehead. "Am I as good a fuck as Sam, baby?"

"Better, Alice," he replied. "She's good, but you're the best."

"Bullshit!" she laughed, lifting off him. "You never had a piece of ass until tonight. How would you know what a good fuck was?"

"I know what feels good," he said.

Her skirt fell over her hips as she stood. "You know, you're some kind of lucky kid."

"I know," Matt grinned.

"You just got fucked twice in one night, and by two different girls," Alice said. "For someone who never fucked before, I'd say that was damned lucky, wouldn't you?" She grinned at him and, affecting a deep Texas drawl, exclaimed in mock-cowboy style, "I'd say yur so durn'd lucky yur ridin' a gravy train with biscuit wheels and yur prolly feelin' happy as a hog in slops."

He nodded, grinning back wearily, acknowledging what she said.

Alice knelt and pulled his pants from his feet, then took her stepson's hand. She walked with him to the bathroom, where she used a cloth to wipe his cock and balls, thinking it was a shame to waste that sweet juice this way. She would have enjoyed licking him clean, but she was almost exhausted as he was.

"I gotta pee," he mumbled.

"Let stepmom help," she whispered, standing behind him and taking his cock in her fingers.

Alice looked over his shoulder as he pissed, watching the golden stream splashing into the toilet. She moved her fingers back and forth on his cock as he pissed, halfway jacking him. She was surprised to find how nice it was to see her stepson pissing, to hold his cock and feel the slight vibrations the stream caused as it flowed urgently from him. With her thumb and forefinger, she ran her hand up and down his cock, her eyes starting to become hot again, a tingle growing between her thighs. The pleasure of watching her stepson piss was new to her, and maybe even a little perverse, but Alice refused to deny it. It felt much too good.

She shook his cock for him, and then they went to her bedroom. Alice snuggled her stepson under the sheets, then climbed in beside him, leaving her skirt on the floor. She wrapped her arms about him, holding him close to her big naked tits, one of her warm thighs resting over his hip. She could feel the tip of his cock touching the curls of her cunt.

"Good night, baby," she whispered, kissing his cheek lightly. "I love you."

"Love you, too, Alice," he mumbled, snuggling against her tits and resting an arm on her waist.

Alice shoved his arm down, curling his fingers about one naked ass cheek, then moved her hand to his ass, holding it tenderly, listening to her stepson's breathing as he drifted off to a well earned sleep.

Chapter 18

Alice woke up with her stepson's cock prodding against her.

She was on her back, her legs open. The sheet had been tossed to the foot of the bed, and Matt was between her legs, trying to push his cock into her cunt.

"Mmmmm, what do you want, baby?" she smiled up at him.

"Pussy, Alice," Matt laughed.

"Don't let me stop you, lover," she gurgled,

wrapping her arms around him. She spread her legs more and lifted her ass up, giving him access to her cunt. "Don't ever let me stop you from getting pussy."

She moved her hands to his ass, finding it light and small in her palms. Drawing her knees up, keeping them wide, she arched her cunt to him, and sighed happily as the swollen head of his cock slipped into her.

"Ooooh, *so* nice!" she whispered, digging into his ass and pulling his cock deep. "I love to wake up with a cock in my cunt."

She pulled his face to her titties, holding the back of his head in one hand, the other still gripping his flexing ass. They both heard the liquid, sluicing sounds that her juices made as his cock plunged in and out of her.

"You're so wet and hot already, Alice," he gasped as her pussy closed tightly on his cock.

"I always am," she laughed, twisting her hips and grinding against his cock and balls. "Especially for *your* cock, honey."

She closed her thighs around his hips as he started thrusting into her. She squeezed his hips, scissoring her legs up and down, meeting his down-thrusts with upward motions of her hips. Drawing her long legs up, she locked her ankles just below his ass, humping from the waist down, fucking at him with short, quick thrusts. The sensations she enjoyed the night before returned again this morning, in full force.

Alice threw her naked ass up and down, grunting from the strength of his fucking cock. Her clitoris, as before, was being scraped by the throbbing shaft of his hard-on, creating an intense heat in her pussy. As he fucked her, Matt began to kiss and lick at her swollen, upstanding nipples, taking a one between his lips, his tongue swirling hotly and wetly. The sliding of his hips along her squeezing thigh felt so very good to her, almost as good as his sweet, hard cock felt inside her cunt. She made soft, choking sounds of pleasure, enjoying the way he sucked on her tits as they fucked.

She moaned in pleasure as she felt his hands slide down her body, then underneath to cup her ass, lifting it up to his cock. She squealed happily when he squeezed her ass, banging his cock powerfully into her pussy. She drew her knees up his sides, bringing them to his shoulders and lifting her cunt into the air. Matt was almost on his knees fucking her now, his cock beating rapidly upon her puffy, fiery cunt lips, driving deep. His balls began to slap against the spreading cheeks of her ass, as though teasing her puckered asshole. Wrapping her arms behind her knees, she pulled them as far back as she could, her crotch spread out for him.

"Mmmmm, ram it to me, Matt!" she gurgled hotly. "Ohhhh, baby, fuck it good! *Ahhhh!* I love it... so *fucking much!* Fuck your stepmom... fuck her wet cunt, darling!"

"Hot pussy," Matt groaned, slamming his cock in and out of her hairy cunt swiftly. "Your cunt is so fucking hot, Alice! You're really wet, too! I love to fuck you, Alice!"

"Then do it, baby!" she urged huskily, thrusting her cunt up and down in rhythm to his cock. "Fuck my hot cunt! Fuck my wet, hairy pussy! Fuck my snatch, my twat! Oooooh, my cunt loves your stiff, hard cock, darling!"

Matt was still clutching the spreading cheeks of her uplifted ass. Twisting frantically as he fucked her, Alice felt his fingers near her asshole, and began to swing her ass around in an effort to get a finger against it.

"Touch my asshole!" she yelped. "Matt, do my asshole... fuck me and rub my asshole!"

Without missing a beat, Matt slipped a finger to the heat of his stepmother's asshole, rubbing the puckered ridges of rubbery flesh swiftly as his cock stabbed in and out of her cunt.

With his finger massaging her asshole and his cock delving so deeply in her cunt, Alice began to hiss and whimper, almost choking with ecstasy. She shook her raised ass wildly, holding her knees far back, looking up with glazed eyes into her stepson's contorted face. She sucked on her bottom lip, moaning as the liquid heat inside her cunt began to boil.

"Ooohhh! Ahhhh, ram it, ram it!" she croaked. "Such a good way to wake up! Mmmm, give me that sweet, hard cock! I want your hard cock, darling! My wet, hairy cunt wants your cock all the time, forever and ever! Oh yes, fuck me hard! Fuck me *real* hard!"

Matt was looking down, watching his cock plunge into his stepmother's cunt. It was easy to see with her ass so high and knees drawn back. He could see the pink wetness of her cunt holding his cock, the shine of her juices on his prick and her fat, proud clitoris as it rubbed its way along the shaft of his cock. He stroked her tight asshole faster, grunting with ecstasy.

Alice began to murmur and whimper as her passion soared, her pussy clutching his prick, sucking at it greedily. She held her ass up, crotch fully exposed to his pounding cock. He rammed into her so hard, her breath was driven from her lungs in great gasps. With each of his plunges, her generous tits would jiggle. She tried to draw her knees back even more, but they were as far as they would go now. With her burning eyes, she watched the wiry hair at the base of his cock mingle with her own thick black cunt hair as he came down hard.

"You're going to make me come, Matt!" she whimpered. "I'm so close now... so close! Oh, God! I'm going to explode! Harder, harder! Fuck me harder, darling! Pound my cunt! Pound me, pound me, fuck me!"

A loud wail came from Alice when her orgasm started, becoming a scream of sheer ecstasy as the power grew. The throbbing waves of her orgasm set up that sucking sensation in her cunt, and once more it seemed as if she was sucking him off with her hairy-lipped cunt.

Matt's finger began pressing into the slick, rubbery tightness of his stepmother's asshole. The sensations there increased the power of her orgasms, and Alice yelped and wailed and gasped as a series of steaming convulsions shook her naked body. He felt his own cum boiling in his balls, ready to explode and spurt deep inside his stepmother's cunt.

"Now!" Alice screamed. "Now!"

Matt rammed deep into her spasming cunt, his body going stiff, his head thrown back and his eyes squeezed shut. With a loud grunt, he discharged into her pussy. Streams of gushing come juice flooded her hungry pussy, squirting inside the contracting, velvety walls. Alice screamed once more as she felt her stepson's come juice filling her cunt, and a final orgasm burned through her body like an exploding fire.

As she finished coming, a weakness came over her. She slowly lowered her legs to the bed, her stepson's cock pulling from her clutching cunt with a wet sound. Matt rolled to his side, breathing hard. Alice lay on her back, legs spread wide and her arms at her sides. Her naked tits rose and fell in her effort to suck air into her lungs.

A few minutes later she lifted herself up on an elbow, grinning at her stepson. "Now, that's what I call a real nice way to wake up. I wonder if you could wake me up every morning that way."

Matt grinned up at his stepmother, cupping one of her tits and giving it a squeeze. "I could sure try," he said.

Alice looked down at his cock and balls. His prick was slick and glistening. She caressed her hand around his young, tender balls, and quickly darted her face downward. She kissed his wet cock with hot lips, then his balls, relishing the strong, musky odour of their combined juices.

"That's enough of this," she said gaily, swinging her legs over the bed and getting up. "Want to shower with me?"

"Hell, yeah!"

"Then move your lazy ass," she laughed, twisting her naked ass into the bathroom.

Alice set the stream of water to a nice

comfortable temperature, then stepped under it, soaking her hair and moaning softly with the good feelings still inside her. By the time she had shampoo on her hair, Matt was in the stall with her. She shivered as he soaped her back, scratching it deliciously. She wiggled her ass while she washed her hair, and Matt began washing his stepmother's shapely ass, soaping her up good. He worked his hand into the crack, and Alice gave a lewd giggle, arching her ass back into his hand, wiggling it saucily.

Suddenly Alice yelped.

"Hey, watch that shit, guy!" she said. "You're supposed to wash my ass, not stick your finger up it."

Matt laughed playfully, goosing his stepmother again. Alice squealed and tucked her hips forward, turning around to face him. As the water washed the shampoo from her hair, she grabbed his cock in one hand, his balls with the other.

"I'll show you!" she said. "Think you can stick your fucking finger up my asshole, do you?"

She pulled her stepson close to her by his cock, tucking it between her thighs. Running her hand behind him, she quickly darted her soapy finger into his asshole.

Matt yelled and jerked away, grabbing his ass with both hands. Then, with a laugh she hugged him against her soapy tits.

"I can do that, too," she said.

"That's not fair, Alice," Matt replied.

"Oh, it's not? And why not?"

"You're a girl," he said. "Girls are supposed to like that, not guys."

"Is that right? And where did you get this bit of wisdom, darling?"

"I heard it, that's all."

"Then you heard wrong."

They finished washing each other, then stepped from the stall and dried one another off. Alice tickled his balls, causing Matt to dance about and try to get away, laughing gleefully.

"You're gonna make me piss if you don't stop, Alice."

"So piss," she giggled, tickling his balls again.

Matt let loose a stream of piss.

"Hey, you little fart!" she giggled, jerking him to the toilet. "Who do you think has to clean up around here? You piss in the fucking toilet! I thought I raised you with better manners than that."

Matt laughed up at her as she held his cock, seeing his stepmother's glassy eyes as she watched him pissing. Her mouth was open, and she seemed to be breathing fast, her tits rising and failing, her nipples swelling.

"That looks beautiful," Alice whispered.

"I like to watch you piss, honey."

She moved his cock, trying to make the stream wavy, but when she did that, he pissed on the floor more than in the toilet. When he finished, Alice kept holding his cock, not shaking it the way she had last night. There was a glazed expression in her eyes as she slowly went to her knees. Pushing at his hip, she turned her stepson around so that her eyes were on a level with his cock. A golden drop of piss clung to his piss-hole, and with a low sobbing sound, Alice snaked her tongue out and used the tip to flick the drop of piss from him. Closing her fist about his cock, she looked up at her stepson, her beautiful face contorted with a perverse expression of erotic desire.

Another golden drop of piss formed on his piss-hole, and she looked at it for a long, breathless moment, then her tongue sneaked out again. She ran her tongue over the head of her stepson's cock, circling his piss-hole. Then, with a soft moan, flicked her tongue at the drop of piss and drew it into her mouth.

Running her tongue about inside her mouth and tasting his piss, a shudder went through her. With a cry of pleasure, she buried her face against his cock and balls, wrapping her arms around his hips and clutching his young ass with tight hands.

"Oooo, you're so fucking sweet, Matt!"

She moaned against his cock and balls. Twisting her face about, she rubbed his sweetness about her cheeks and nose and chin, then began to kiss at his cock and balls hungrily.

"You feel so good against my face," she murmured, caressing her cheek along his cock. "I love the feel of your cock against my face."

Feeling his cock swell, Alice drew back and stared at it, her eyes very hot, moist and wide open. She sat on her heels, knees wide, holding his balls with one hand now, her other still clutching his tight ass cheek. Moving her ass, she pressed one heel against her cunt, feeling the pressure grow into a wet heat there. Releasing his balls, she closed her fist about his cock and looked up at him, jerking her fist slowly as his prick turned into that beautiful, desirable hardness.

Matt looked down at his stepmother, neither of them speaking, their breathing loud in the small bathroom. Still gazing up at her stepson, Alice pressed her lips to the tip of his cock, kissing it. The tip of her tongue came out and she began to make hot, wet circles about the swollen head, flicking the tip gently and caressing his flaring piss-hole. She placed her lips just over the piss-hole, kissing it as her tongue swiped slowly. She felt her stepson's body shake and she closed her fingers tighter into his ass cheek.

With a soft growl, Alice released his cock and moved her lips up and down the shaft, her tongue barely touching it. The hard meat of his prick against her mouth felt wonderful to her. There was a delicious sensation about running her burning lips up and down her stepson's throbbing cock. She swirled her tongue into the wiry hair, then flicked his balls. She used the flat surface of her tongue now, licking at his cock from base to piss-hole, slowly, the way a small child would savour an ice cream cone.

Matt's cock started seeping juices now, and as the juice beaded at his piss-hole, Alice licked them away. She kept her tongue out of her mouth, running it up and down the hard shaft and circling the swollen head, beginning to pant with hungry desire. The urge to suck her stepson's cock was strong, much stronger than she had ever felt before. She had enjoyed the feel of a hard cock throbbing between her lips often, yet somehow those urges to suck her stepson's cock off were especially strong.

Holding his cock at the base again, she ran her tongue about the deliciously smooth head, letting the heat sear into her mouth. Each bubble of fluid that seeped from his piss-hole was quickly licked away by her darting tongue. The taste of those juices created a hungry storm inside her naked body. They were more delicious than ever because that slippery wetness came from her stepson's cock.

Matt stood looking down with anxious eyes, his hips arched outward. He rested one hand on top of his stepmother's head. The heat of her wet tongue running up and down his cock gave him many thrills that were different than fucking Sam or his stepmother. Each of them had felt good, but this was different. His stepmother's mouth and tongue gave him an entirely different kind of ecstasy.

Alice could no longer keep teasing herself this way.

With a moan of passion, she closed her lips around her stepson's cockhead, her tongue fluttering. She grasped the cheeks of his ass again, her fingers digging into his flesh, and jerked him forward, driving his cock into the back of her throat. She gurgled as the swollen head of his prick prodded the burning entrance of her throat, sliding over her tongue and the roof of her mouth. Her lips spread tightly on his hard cock, stretching so sweetly. She sucked the full length into her mouth, feeling the wiry hairs at the base tickle them and her nose. Holding his cock deeply, she writhed her lips at the base and squeezed his ass cheeks, her eyes blazing up at his surprised face.

Pressing her tongue against the underside of his cock, she made her mouth a wet, hot tightness for him, sucking her lips back along it until she was just barely pressing them over his piss-hole. She sucked hard on his piss-hole, drawing juices from it, her tongue flicking them away. Then she jerked his ass forward again, taking his cock as deeply as it would go, sobbing with perverse hunger.

She bobbed her lovely face back and forth a few times, sucking hot and hard on his cock. Then she slowed down, sucking from his prick and smacking her lips. She held his ass tightly and whispered to him.

"I'm going to suck you, darling. I have to suck your cock! I need to suck your cock, Matt!"

Again she swallowed her stepson's cock in her wet mouth and jerked her lips back and forth, her tongue flying in greed. "Ohhhhh, you're so fucking sweet!" she wailed as her tongue flicked the piss-hole. "You're so sucking sweet! Cock-sucking sweet! Your cock is delicious in my mouth, darling! Ooo, I love the way it feels between my lips! So hard and hot... and I want to suck it off!"

"You want me to come in your mouth, Alice?" Matt panted, his naked body shaking with pleasure.

"God, yes!" she squealed.

She swallowed his prick again, pulling at his ass until her lips were pressing into the wiry cockhair. With her lips as tight as she could make them, Alice started sucking on her stepson's cock like a starved woman. Her tongue was in constant motion, fluttering along the shaft and flicking about his pisshole. The way his young cock stuffed her mouth was a delight she had never known before. As her face plunged forward, she pulled at his ass. Sounds of intense ecstasy bubbled from her with a wet, muffled sound, her eyes still blazing up at him.

She turned loose of his ass long enough to bring his hands to her cheeks, pressing them there to let him know what she wanted. Again she clutched his tight ass cheeks, squeezing them as she jerked his cock in and out of her scalding wet mouth.

Once Matt understood, she stopped jerking at his ass. He was now fucking her face the way he fucked her cunt. Alice's eyes rolled about in pleasure, thrilled that he fucked her mouth eagerly. Her lips tingled as he beat the base of his cock against them, sending excitement down her naked body to her cunt. Alice pressed her heel tighter yet into her wet pussy as Matt fucked her mouth, her moans an indication of her wild ecstasy. Her cunt seemed to be drawing inward, steaming with impending orgasm. Holding his ass in her palms, she felt as if her mouth was her cunt that somehow her mouth and cunt had switched places. She had never felt this way before.

The sounds of her stepson's grunts broke through her mesmerized brain, and she felt his prick throbbing against her sucking lips. She focused her eyes on his twisting face. He plunged his cock in and out of her mouth with frantic desperation now, and Alice knew it would not be long before she had a mouthful of come juice.

She dug her fingers into his ass, urging him not to hold back, telling him that she wanted him to come off inside her mouth, to spurt the thick sweetness down her burning throat. Matt, much too involved in his own ecstasy to pull his cock out, fucked in a frenzy, watching his cock plunge into his stepmother's mouth all the way, his balls banging against her chin.

"I gotta come, Alice!" he yelled. "I just gotta come!"

Alice gurgled and sucked hard, her tongue flying at his cock stabbed into her gripping lips, and at her burning throat.

As the come juice boiled out of his cock, she was gripping him hard. With the hot taste of his sugary-tasting come juice, she jerked at his ass, driving his cock into her throat. She gurgled wetly as the thick come juice spewed into her mouth. Alice gulped in wet delight, her tongue licking hard. Her mouth filled with the creamy sweetness from his balls time and again. She swallowed, making dainty choking sounds. The rumbling explosion of an orgasm seared her cunt, and she moaned around his gushing cock as her eyes closed in ecstasy. Swift squirts came out of his piss-hole, like a never-ending stream. Alice sucked and swallowed hungrily as she came, the fuzzy lips of her cunt contracting against her heel.

Feeling her stepson's body slowly shake with pleasure, she ran her hands up and down his ass, holding his cock in her mouth after he had stopped coming. She sucked from it slowly, then giggled lewdly as she licked her lips.

"Oh, you taste so fucking good, Matt!" she squealed, grasping his cock and drawing a bubbling bead of frothy come juice to his piss-hole. She flicked it up with her tongue, then kissed his cock.

Getting to her feet, she found she was weak. Leaning her naked ass against the sink, she laughed. "I came so damned hard when you did, Matt." She looked down at his cock. "God, you really come when you come, don't you?"

"You said to cum in your mouth, Alice," he reminded her.

"Hey, I'm not complaining," she laughed huskily, licking her puffy lips. "I'm glad you come so fucking much. I don't think I'll ever get enough of it. Mmmmm, you're one guy who can shoot off in my cock-sucking mouth anytime you want!"

Matt flung his arms around her, hugging his stepmother tightly as they stood laughing with pleasure.

Chapter 19

After lunch, Alice saw Billy Jo was lying on her rubber mattress, slowly drifting on the still turquoise water of the pool. The sight was unbearably tempting.

"Why don't we join Sam, Matt?" she said. "I've got this new bikini I'd love to wear for you."

Matt changed into his trunks, watching his stepmother wiggle her shapely ass into the tight bikini bottom. The bikini was white, with tiny red hearts on her right hip. The top, almost too small to hold her straining tits, also had tiny hearts, two positioned right on her left nipple. The bottom of her bikini was very small, and if she wasn't careful, curling pussy hair would peek over the top. As it was, the material was quite thin, and the faint shadow of her cunt hair could be seen.

Alice was pleased to see the way her stepson looked at her. She twitched her ass, taking his hand and leading him from the apartment. They skipped onto the decking of the pool like two happy children.

"Hi, there!" Alice waved to Billy Jo, who waved back.

Billy Jo was wearing a bright-red bikini today, and Alice noticed the lovely bulge of the girl's cunt as the float turned lazily in the sparkling blue water. Glancing at her stepson, she saw that he noticed it, too.

"Stop staring with your tongue hanging out," she hissed, goosing him in the ass.

Matt yelped and jerked his hips forward, losing his balance and falling into the pool.

"What was that all about?" Billy Jo asked.

"I goosed him," Alice laughed, sitting in a poolside lawn chair and crossing her legs at the ankles.

"In the ass?"

"Where else do you goose a guy?" Alice countered.

Matt surfaced, blowing water and laughing. "You better keep your hands to yourself, Alice!" he yelled up at her.

"Oh? What are you going to do about it?" Alice retorted playfully. "Goose me back?"

"You never know, do you?" Matt said, swimming to the edge of the pool and sitting there, dangling his feet in the water. "I just might do that."

Billy Jo looked from one to the other, her

blue eyes quizzical. She bent one leg up, but keeping it wide. Alice gazed openly between those slender, golden thighs, remembering what Billy Jo's cunt tasted like and the tightness of those blonde-haired cunt lips around her tongue.

She was surprised at how easily and quickly she and Billy Jo had sucked each other. They had licked cunts as if it were the most natural thing for them to do, as if they had been tongue-fucking each other for some time.

Billy Jo, seeing that Alice was gazing between her legs, made a very slight upward motion of her hips, then licked her tongue about her lips, a slight leering smile on her beautiful face. Alice grinned at the girl, stuck her tongue out, and wiggled it suggestively. Matt watched them, wondering what was going on. Whatever it was, he was pleased at how friendly they were.

For the first time since coming out to the pool, Alice noticed that Billy Jo's bikini was undone at her rounded hips. Her cunt was covered only by the front flap, and it looked as if a small breeze would blow it away and expose her sugary cunt.

"Is the water cold?" Alice asked, her voice husky with emotion.

"It's perfect, Alice," Billy Jo replied.

Getting out of the chair, Alice dove in,

swimming a few fast lengths, then climbed from the pool. With her back to Matt and Billy Jo, she used her towel to half-dry her shoulder-length hair, and heard the youngsters giggle. "Something funny?" Alice asked, looking over her shoulder.

"You can see through your bikini," Billy Jo answered.

Alice twisted to look at her ass. Sure enough, the material had become transparent! For just a moment, she felt her face grow warm with embarrassment, then realized she had nothing to be embarrassed about. She had fucked her stepson and sucked cunts with Billy Jo – what did she have to hide?

She wiggled her ass at them, then dropped the towel and, nonchalantly, faced them, one hand at the back of her neck, wringing the water from her still-wet hair and the other one on her jutting hip. "Take a good look, then," she said.

The dark triangle of her cunt hair stood out boldly, dark behind the white of her bikini. Even her nipples could be seen. Billy Jo darted her eyes at Matt and saw him grinning from ear to ear, then back at Alice. She got the picture, and she laughed softly, a musical sound of delight.

"So, that's how it is, huh?"

"Whatever that means," Alice said, sitting down in the chair. "I guess that's how it is."

She spread her legs without concern.

"Well, well," Billy Jo said in a throaty voice. "I can't say I blame you, Alice."

Alice looked at Billy Jo, daring her to make a nasty remark. But Billy Jo wasn't going to say anything nasty. She grinned lewdly at Alice, then at Matt. Billy Jo and Matt both looked between Alice's knees, seeing the shape of her cunt hair through the wet bikini.

"You know there isn't anyone else home in this hotel, don't you, Alice?" Billy Jo said in a husky voice. "No one can see you – us."

Billy Jo removed her top, her firm titties capped with those succulent pink nipples that stood up to the sun. Matt giggled as he looked at them.

"You sent Matt to me last night," Billy Jo said, making it a statement. "That's what he told me. You sent him to me for a fuck, right?"

Alice nodded. "That's right. You told me to."

"Does he know?" Billy Jo asked. "About us?"

"Not yet," Alice said. "You can tell him if you want. I don't mind."

"Tell me what?" Matt asked.

"Your stepmother and I..." Billy Jo ran her tongue over her lips, "we sort of, you know, kissed each other."

Alice snorted. "What Sam is trying to say, honey, is we sucked cunts. We tonguefucked each other."

"Really?" Matt asked, awed, the delight obvious in his young voice. "You two really sucked each other?"

Billy Jo realized there was nothing to be shy about now, and laughed gleefully, rubbing her naked tits. "Did we! We sucked each other dry, Matt!"

Alice saw her stepson's cock bulging in his trunks and that was all she needed to know. The straining of his young cock was enough evidence to her that he was excited about what was happening.

"Anyone want to skinny dip?" Billy Jo said, lifting her ass on the air mattress and tossing her scarlet bikini bottom into the water. Alice and Matt watched as the beautiful young blonde split her legs for a brief, teasing moment, then flipped over the side of the mattress, a flash of her white ass showing before she went under the water.

Matt removed his trunks quickly, his cock standing out very hard. Alice sucked in a gasp of pleasure as he dived into the water, watching him dart after the naked Billy Jo.

As they surfaced, Billy Jo yelled, "Come on, don't be a fraidy cat, Alice. Take your bikini off, show us those goodies!"

"You can see all my goodies through this fucking suit!"

Alice laughed, pulling her top off, then standing up to remove the bottom. She posed for a moment at the edge of the pool, letting Billy Jo and Matt look at her lovely nakedness, then she jumped in feet first.

When Alice came up sputtering, Billy Jo had Matt pressed up against the pool deck in the shallow end. Her springy tits were rubbing back and forth across Matt's chest, and his eyes glowed with delight. Moving toward them, Alice saw the flashing whiteness of Billy Jo's ass below the water, her stepson's hands feeling it. Billy Jo was moving her ass, twisting and pressing it against Matt.

Now beside them, Alice grinned at her stepson, shoving her hand between the two naked bodies. She gripped her stepson's cock tightly as Billy Jo pressed her stomach against it. "Now you're what I would call a happy boy."

"Gosh, Alice," Matt laughed in delight. "I think this skinny dipping is great."

"You would," she snorted, tugging at his balls hard enough to bring a yelp from him. "Horny shit."

"Mmmm, he can be as horny as he likes with me," Billy Jo mewled huskily, parting her legs as Alice pressed Matt's cock between them. "Anytime you're horny, honey, you know where to find me."

Alice squeezed Billy Jo's pretty naked ass when the girl slipped her hot thighs back and forth. Running her hand down over the shapely cheeks of Billy Jo's ass, Alice felt the head of her stepson's cock pressing through. Erotic pleasure shot through Alice, and her other hand lifted to close about a beautifully shaped tit.

"Ohhh, God!" Alice moaned, squeezing Billy Jo's tit and trying to cup the head of her stepson's cock as it came through those sleek thighs. "Ohhhh, this is nice!"

Alice pressed her bushy cunt against Billy Jo's hip, rubbing back and forth. Matt, holding one of Billy Jo's tits, slipped his other hand to his stepmother's. Billy Jo watched the delicate teenager's hand caress and fondle Alice's tit, his fingers twisting her hard nipple. Her hand moved off Matt's shoulder, rushed down under the water, and stroked Alice's bubbling cunt.

Billy Jo giggled, pulling from them and climbing up to sit on the pool deck, her feet dangling in the water. She spread her knees wide, balanced there precariously on her sweet ass. Her blonde-haired cunt gleamed in the hot sunlight, her clitoris visibly throbbing. The blond cunt hair made an erotic enhancement of her delectably pink cunt.

"Eat me, Matt," she murmured in a hot voice. "Eat my pussy, honey!"

Alice looked at her stepson, then up at the passion-laden eyes of Billy Jo. This beautiful girl, thought Alice; so totally wanton in her desires, and gives in to them eagerly; why hadn't she been more like this when she was her age? Matt was gazing between Billy Jo's slim thighs, already licking at his lips.

"If you don't suck that hot cunt," Alice said to her stepson, "then I'm going to."

Matt glanced at his stepmother, then moved between Billy Jo's spreading knees. Alice sucked in a breath of delight as she watched his lips kissing the smoothness of Billy Jo's thighs, working his young face upward. His tongue came out and licked at the sensitive inner flesh, making the blonde girl squeal happily.

Alice, standing at her stepson's side, leaned over and ran her tongue about Billy Jo's thigh, too. She ran her hand along the girl's thigh, caressing it as her lips kissed the girl's hip.

Alice watched, her eyes glazing over when her stepson flicked his tongue about Billy Jo's inflamed clitoris. She cooed softly and leaned back, facing the sun with an ecstatic smile on her young, beautiful face. Running her hand past Billy Jo's ass from below, her other hand scooting through the silken cunt hair, Alice parted the wet lips of the fiery cunt. Matt looked upon the sweetness for a moment, then opened his mouth and pressed it against the other teenager's sex. Billy Jo squealed, her body trembling as she arched her hips up, grinding her hairy pussy into Matt's mouth.

Alice watched her stepson's lips being surrounded by the blonde fuzz, hearing the soft, wet sucking sounds he made. The hand under Billy Jo's ass moved downward quickly, grasping her stepson's cock and pumping hard on it.

"Oh, eat her, Matt!" Alice moaned with passion. "Eat her cunt, baby! Suck her sweet pussy! Shove your tongue up her hot cunt and fuck it!"

With her mind reeling with wanton desire, Alice dipped below the water, holding her breath. She closed her lips about her stepson's cock, sucking on it hard and fast. When she had to breathe again, she surfaced, running her tongue about Billy Jo's shaking stomach, as if trying to taste the succulent cunt, too. Matt had pulled back a bit, and she saw his tongue licking those puffy, juicy lips hungrily. Alice lifted her body to the deck of the pool, leaning over and drawing one of Billy Jo's creamy nipples into her mouth, sucking at it.

Matt, licking around Billy Jo's pussy, shoved his hand over his stepmother's shapely ass, running his fingers into the crack, brushing them over her asshole and between her legs. He probed his stepmother's cunt with two fingers. Alice wiggled her ass for him, then slipped back into the water. She jerked on his throbbing cock some more, watching him suck Billy Jo's cunt. Once more she ducked beneath the surface and pulled his cock into her hungry mouth. Sucking hard, she twisted his young balls. It was difficult to suck cock under water. She couldn't breathe at all, and had to surface more often than she liked.

"Oh, that looks good, Matt," she mewled. "Seeing your face buried in Billy Jo's pussy! Suck her good, honey! Tongue-fuck her tight, hot cunt!" Alice was beating as hard as she could on her stepson's cock. "Let me!" she said suddenly. "Let me have a taste of her cunt, baby! Your stepmom wants to suck Billy Jo now!"

Matt pulled back, his cheeks wet with the boiling juices of Billy Jo's cunt. Quickly, Alice kissed her stepson's wet lips, and then thrust her tongue past Billy Jo's swollen, tender labia, and then hard and deep into her vaginal tunnel, fucking it in and out rapidly. She kept beating on Matt's cock. She felt Matt nudge her shoulder, and moved her face. Matt immediately shoved his mouth into the blond pussy again, licking and sucking greedily, one of his hands clutching the girl's firm, rubbery tit.

Billy Jo churned her naked hips about, grinding her cunt into Matt's mouth vigorously, whimpering her ecstasy loudly. "Oooo, suck me, suck me!" she wailed. "Tongue my hot cunt, Matt! Ahh, your tongue feels like a cock... fucking me! Eat my wet cunt, suck my pussy, lick my fucking hot cunt!"

Alice pressed her face downward, licking her tongue about her stepson's cheek, trying to reach his open lips as they sucked and pressed into Billy Jo's sugar-sweet cunt. Her fist squeezed and jerked at his prick in short strokes. Now and then, as her stepson sucked, Alice found the tip of her tongue could run about a puffy lip, too. When her stepson dipped his head lower, stabbing his tongue into the fiery, wet, tightness, Alice managed to lick the young blonde's distended clitoris. To an observer, it would appear that stepmother and stepson were fighting each other to suck Billy Jo's boiling pussy. In fact, Alice was not interfering at all with him. Alice's tongue licked about the swirl of blonde cunt hair, streaking up to lap at the girl's dimpled belly button, then over her hip and down her smooth thigh. While jacking on her stepson's cock, she was fondling and squeezing one of Billy Jo's saucy ass cheeks, scraping her fingers into the crack to rub hotly at the pucker of her asshole.

Again Alice went under water, gulping her stepson's cock deep into her mouth. With her eyes open, she gazed up to look at the fuzzy outline of Billy Jo's sweet ass. She sucked strongly on Matt's prick, her tongue swirling wetly. The swollen head was hot and smooth, and Alice tried to pull it into her throat. Her lungs were bursting for air again, and reluctantly she released his cock and went to the surface again. Hauling in a deep breath of air, Alice ducked back down, this time with her face at her stepson's ass. She licked the cheeks of his ass and darted her tongue into the crack, pulling at his balls and pumping on his cock. The tip of her tongue probed Matt's tight little asshole, and as she tried to penetrate him up the ass with her tongue, but she found herself out of air once more.

She came up to hear the squeals of Billy Jo. She was gurgling with ecstasy, twisting her cunt into Matt's mouth, humping up and down as if she were fucking him, fucking his face, holding his head tight against her crotch; Matt was licking and sucking wetly, slurping at the teenager's steamy pussy hungrily.

With her own cunt twitching in voyeuristic pleasure, Alice dipped again. Once more she shoved her face against her stepson's ass, and this time she darted the tip upon his asshole hard, penetrating the hot tightness. She felt Matt clamp his asshole as her tongue entered, but it was too late. Holding his hips as she squatted underneath the water, Alice darted her tongue back and forth, tongue-fucking her stepson up his asshole. She could imagine his grunts and groans of surprise when her tongue shoved up his ass.

She clawed his cheeks apart, trying to press her tongue in deep. She was thrilled to feel his asshole gripping at her tongue, tightening and loosening around it. Matt seemed to be relaxing his asshole when she shoved it into him. Apparently he had decided he liked this and arched his ass into his stepmother's face.

Alice plunged her tongue far up his hot asshole, again taking his cock in a fist and jerking it vigorously beneath the water. She could feel his cock throbbing, the hardness more pronounced than before. She knew he was getting ready to come.

She surfaced again, blowing the slightly chlorinated water from her nose.

"Ohhh, Matt, Matt!" she heard Billy Jo wailing. "You're going to make me come! Ohhh, baby, suck it hard! Ahhh, ram your fucking tongue in me! Suck my cunt... I'm about to come!"

As much as Alice wanted to watch Billy Jo's lovely body while Matt brought her cunt to an explosive orgasm, she wanted to make him come more. Sucking in more air, she went below the water again, her black hair fanning out around her head like a dark cloud, and drew his throbbing hard-on into her mouth. She began to suck in a frenzy, wanting to feel his come juice bursting into her mouth before she needed more air. She clutched at the cheeks of his ass, jerking his cock in and out of her mouth. She felt Billy Jo's feet resting on her shoulders, and even that excited Alice. She was starting to need air badly, but kept sucking frantically at her stepson's cock.

As she bobbed and darted her mouth onto his prick, she felt a wild, burning kind of orgasm about to shatter her bubbling pussy. Alice was aware that she made a noise when she came, often screaming her ecstasy. She tried to prevent her cunt from coming, sucking furiously on her stepson's cock, wanting him to gush his come juice into her mouth before her own orgasm burst.

Matt rammed his cock hard into his stepmother's mouth, and she felt his prick pulse. A sweet squirt of come juice splashed about her tongue, and Alice's mind reeled in delight. She caught one more spurt of come juice, and her lungs were on fire. Unable to stay under water any longer, she pulled her come-filled mouth from his cock, and watched two gushing streams of come juice boil from his piss-hole into the water before she shoved herself swiftly to the surface.

Swallowing her stepson's come juice, she was just in time to see Billy Jo bucking her hips up and down, grinding her cunt into Matt's face, yelling out her orgasmic ecstasy.

Alice began to whip her hand between her thighs, a finger darting in and out of her cunt, then up to smash her clitoris. She yelped as she made herself come, her eyes becoming dazed in her delight as she watched her stepson tongue-fuck Billy Jo to that shattering climax.

"Ohhh, you're good, Matt!" Billy Jo mewled when he pulled his smeared face from between her thighs. "I know men three times your age who can't suck cunt as well as you do."

"I wouldn't know," Alice said with a frown. "He's never sucked my pussy."

"Yet," Billy Jo giggled.

"That's what I mean, he hasn't sucked my cunt – yet," Alice laughed. "But that's going to be corrected very soon."

Matt stroked his hand between his mother's thighs under the water, rubbing at her gently pulsating cunt with his palm, grinning at her.

"The quicker the better," he replied.

"I learned one thing," Alice said. "It's damned hard to suck a cock under water."

"I can imagine," Billy Jo laughed, the sound low and throaty. "But I'm going to give that a try myself. It sounds like a lot of fun to me."

"It is," Matt grinned.

"Of course you'd think so," Alice said, stroking his wet cheek. "It's your cock getting sucked."

A noise startled the trio, and they looked round to see the hotel pool attendant approaching. Quickly, they made themselves more or less decent, giggling conspiratorially together.

Chapter 20

"Did you enjoy the day, darling?" Alice asked Matt.

He was rubbing at his eyes, his young face sleepy. He nodded at his stepmother, smiling widely.

"Sam is really something, isn't she?" Alice said, feeling that now was as good a time as any to tell her stepson the truth. "I've never known anyone as ready to fuck as she is, man or woman." "Except you and me, that is."

She paused, then giggled.

"And you know something?"

"No," her stepson answered, "what?"

"Sam isn't really called Sam. She's called Billy Jo. Billy Jo McCluskie. And she's married to Danny, your older brother."

Waiting for this bombshell to sink in, she looked a little nervously at Matt.

"Why? I mean, why didn't you tell me sooner?" he asked after a while, a slightly peevish note in his voice.

"Honey, I would have, if I'd known sooner. But I only found out when she told me. You see it's a long story…"

Later, they sat together on the couch. Matt had occasionally asked his stepmother a question, but otherwise he had remained silent until she had finished talking.

He yawned. "Wow. I didn't really know life could be so complicated. But what happens when I go back to *Los Altos*?"

"Matt, I just don't know. We'll have to wait and see on that one. I'm facing a lot of hard decisions too just now. We'll talk some more tomorrow, but don't worry, sweetheart, we'll work something out."

Matt sat at the end of the couch, his feet up on the cushions, facing Alice. She turned toward him, drawing her knees up and pulling her skirt over her thighs. Matt gazed at the crotch of her panties, seeing the bulge her cunt made inside the tight band. He was sitting in his shorts, showered and ready for bed. His hair was still damp, his eyes looking very sleepy.

Alice, however, was wide-awake, still excited over what she and Matt had done at the pool with Billy Jo. It had been excitingly dangerous there in the open. Anyone could have come upon them. She laughed silently, thinking of the shock they would have had. Seeing three people, all naked, in the pool, sucking cunt and cock. It was an experience she wouldn't mind repeating, she told herself. The very idea of being watched with her stepson's cock either in her cunt or her mouth sent shivers of sweet pleasure through her flesh.

She and Matt still peeked on people with his telescopes at night, but nothing much changed. Billy Jo knew that Matt had been watching her for some time. "That's the reason I've never closed my curtains," she had laughed.

The guest across the way, with his next-door neighbor, wasn't much fun to watch since they seldom varied the things they did, usually fucking only with the woman on the bottom. The janitor who had been jacking off on the desk top wasn't seen anymore. He had either quit his job or been caught at what he was doing. Even Billy Jo wasn't all that exciting to watch since they were fucking with her.

Alice needed more excitement, she knew. She needed something even more perverse than fucking and sucking at the pool in the hot sunlight, with discovery possible at any second. She wasn't sure what she wanted, needed, yet Alice knew her body and her cunt were craving more stimulation. At first she thought it had begun with Billy Jo, watching the way the beautiful young girl teased her stepson, but Alice knew now that it had been inside her all the time, waiting to be released. If it had not been there, surely she would have not sucked Billy Jo's cunt so readily.

She watched her stepson gazing sleepily at her crotch. He may be sleepy, she thought, but he was still interested in what she was showing him. His cock looked almost hard inside his shorts. She ran her tongue over her lips and shoved a hand along the back of her thigh, starting to tease her pussy with a fingertip. Pressing a finger under her panties, she rubbed up and down the slit, her eyes half-closed. She was not in the least bit sleepy and she knew she could finger-fuck herself, but that was not nearly as satisfactory as having her stepson fuck her – or sucking his cock or licking Billy Jo's cunt.

If only Matt wasn't so sleepy! She gazed at the front of his shorts, her eyes burning there. Perhaps if he pulled his cock from his shorts so she could see it, she could finger-fuck herself to a nice orgasm. The outline of his lovely prick was stimulating, but not as much as she wanted. Matt wouldn't object if she sucked on his cock, sleepy as he was. Still it was his cooperation that made it good, too. The idea of sucking her stepson's cock as he lay still wasn't appealing. She liked it when he thrashed about, humping into her mouth as her tongue swirled wetly. His enthusiasm was all part of it.

She swung her legs over the edge of the couch and stood up. Walking to the window, she saw Billy Jo had a light on in her living room. The girl was still awake, maybe as wide awake as Alice was. She thought of calling Billy Jo and, asking her to come up, but she didn't want to disturb the girl if she was getting ready for bed. Gazing into the night, she lifted her dress in back, caressing her ass through her flimsy panties, knowing her stepson was watching her even if he was about to go to sleep. She flexed the cheeks of her ass as she fondled them, stroking the backs of her long, smooth thighs. Looking over her shoulder at her stepson, she saw his cock was still the same, but he was gazing at her thighs and pantied ass.

"Poor baby," she whispered. "Today was too much for you, wasn't it? All that swimming and sucking had exhausted you."

Matt nodded, rubbing his eyes again Letting her dress fall back down over her ass, she went to him and pulled him to his feet. "Come on, you're going to bed before you fall over."

"I gotta piss, Alice," he mumbled.

There was an instant reaction inside Alice's body. A powerful jolt seemed to ripple through her and to her cunt. Holding both his hands, facing him, her eyes turned hot, smoldering as the thought burned inside her mind. She remembered what had happened to her when she had licked the drops of piss from his cock.

"Come on," she said breathlessly, leading him to the bathroom.

As Matt stood near the toilet, Alice sank to her knees at his side, pulling his shorts down to his knees. She held his cock at the base, aiming it into the toilet, her eyes blazing as she waited to see him piss. She licked at his hip, her eyes remaining on his cock.

"Go ahead and piss, darling," she murmured throatily. "Let me see you piss."

Matt shoved his hips forward, one hand on top of his stepmother's head. The stream spurted from his piss-hole, splashing into the water. Alice mewled softly as she watched, holding his cock with a thumb and forefinger. Unable to resist him now, she darted her tongue out, licking it along the shaft of his cock as he pissed. She probed the head of his cock with her tongue, almost pushing it into the stream.

Again she licked her tongue along his prick, then moved it slowly on the top of his cockhead, a fraction of an inch from the stream. Her cunt started boiling and she felt as if she might come.

Her hot tongue ran back and forth along the shaft of his cock, getting very close to tasting the piss with the tip.

Then Alice knew what she wanted, what that extra stimulation was she had needed. She turned her stepson toward her face, and he stopped pissing.

"Oh, don't stop!" she moaned. "Piss, baby! Don't stop. Keeping pissing!"

The warm, golden piss came out and splashed along the front of her blouse, soaking it. Alice turned his cock, making him piss upon her nipples. Her eyes glazed as a beautiful feeling flowed through her body. She lifted his cock, feeling the piss splatter along her neck, and finally against her lips. She moaned with unexpected ecstasy.

Slowly, she let her lips open slightly. Piss came through them and crashed against her teeth. The sensation searing her cunt grew stronger than ever. Feeling his piss splash against the tip of her tongue caused Alice's mind to erupt with perverse, erotic pleasure. She shoved her tongue farther into the stream, tasting his piss, and with a groan, opened her mouth wide, lifting his cock so he was pissing directly into her mouth. It filled her mouth and flowed over her lips and tongue. Her clitoris burned as if someone had put a flame to it.

She swallowed.

"Oh, God!" she wailed, and closed her lips about the head of her stepson's cock, letting him piss down her gulping throat. Alice sucked and swallowed greedily as he pissed, her cunt boiling over into a wild orgasm.

Matt was no longer sleepy. He was staring down at his stepmother with excited eyes. She had her lips over his piss-hole and was drinking his piss. He placed both his hands on top of her head, trying to work his cock deeper as he kept pissing. But Alice wouldn't let him. She wanted to hold only the head of his cock with her lips, tasting his piss spewing over her tongue and down her gulping throat.

Alice was coming as she'd never came before. Her cunt was convulsing tightly, her clitoris pulsating hard enough to actually make her body shake. Her eyes closed in rapture as her lips held the head of his cock just past his piss hole, the warm taste of her stepson's piss flowing into her mouth and down her throat. She held his cock with her forefinger and thumb, her other hand stroking his balls lightly, her ass twisting as her orgasms increased with power. She was moaning in blissful orgasm, one after the other.

She moved her lips only when he'd finished, running her tongue over them and smiling in ecstasy up at her surprised stepson. She caressed the tip of his cock back and forth on her lips, then patted his ass.

"Take your shorts off and climb into bed, baby. You're out on your feet."

Matt's eyes had turned sleepy again and she watched him stumble into her bedroom.

Alice went back to the living room, enjoying the feel of her piss-wet blouse clinging to her tits, her face glistening with it. She walked around, rubbing her hands about her titties, the wetness exciting to her. She gazed down at Billy Jo's still-lighted living room, wishing her curtains were still open.

Then a knock on the door startled her. It was after ten at night, and she wasn't expecting anyone.

"I was just thinking about you," Alice smiled happily as she took Billy Jo's hand and pulled her into the room. "You're what I need right now, I think."

"Strange coincidence," Billy Jo said. "I was down there thinking about you and Matt. When I saw your light still on, I knew you'd be up."

"Matt's in bed," Alice said. "I think we exhausted him today."

Billy Jo laughed. "You must be taking extra good care of him then," she said. "We didn't do all that much."

She eyed Alice's soaking blouse and a sly grin spread over her face. She leaned toward Alice and licked her tongue about Alice's chin. "Ah-ha! I know what that is, honey."

"If you know that, then you're not a stranger to it," Alice said, leering at the beautiful young girl.

"I'm not a stranger to very much," Billy Jo admitted, and licked Alice's lips. "It seems we're more like each other all the time, I'd say."

Billy Jo wore a robe, belted at the waist. Alice untied it and smiled when she saw the girl was naked beneath it. "Mmmmmmmm, nice," she murmured.

"And going to get nicer," Billy Jo whispered. Holding Alice's hands, Billy Jo dipped her head and began to suck on one of Alice's nipples through her piss-wet blouse. "Much, much nicer."

Alice was elated. She had nothing to be ashamed of because she'd loved it when her stepson had pissed into her mouth. Billy Jo, too, it seemed, was turned on by piss. She cupped Billy Jo's naked, sweet and shapely tits while the girl sucked from nipple to nipple, tasting Matt's piss on her blouse. Squeezing Billy Jo's tits, Alice felt her cunt start boiling again, as hot as before.

"Let me," she whispered.

Billy Jo lifted her head, her lips wet. Alice kissed them, running her tongue back and forth and tasting the piss on them. She removed Billy Jo's robe, letting it fall to the floor. Cupping the tight, shapely ass in her palms, Alice thrust her tongue into Billy Jo's mouth. She moaned softly as Billy Jo sucked

Ranchers' Dirty Wives ★ 327

it, her eager hands on Alice's ass now, lifting her skirt to her waist.

But Alice wanted her mouth against Billy Jo's sugary cunt.

She went to her knees, holding Billy Jo by the naked ass and burying her face into the blonde bush. She stroked her tongue about Billy Jo's inflamed clitoris, sucking it with her lips as the girl spread her slender legs wide, stepping forward to straddle Alice's face.

"Oooo, suck my cunt, Alice!" Billy Jo whimpered, grinding her pussy upon Alice's lips, bumping back and forth. "Suck me, suck me! Ahhhh, lick my pussy! I had to come here for this... I got so hot, all alone down there! Mmmmm, suck me... fuck me with your tongue, Alice!"

Alice, with her face pressed into Billy Jo's cunt, leaned back. Billy Jo followed her until Alice was on her back and she was squatting above her face, looking down at Alice with glowing eyes.

With one hand cupping Billy Jo's ass, Alice was whipping her other hand between her thighs, rubbing at her pulsating cunt swiftly, her hips twisting. She thrust her tongue deep into Billy Jo's seeping cunt, lapping the fiery juices hungrily, the blonde hair covering her mouth.

With a hot moan, Alice slipped her tongue from Billy Jo's cunt and darted it back towards Billy Jo's ass. She drew it across Billy Jo's asshole, bringing a squeal of delight from the squatting, trembling girl. Alice flicked her tongue about Billy Jo's flexing asshole then drew it back to the succulent cunt, delving deeply. Again she licked the fiery asshole, exerting more pressure. Billy Jo gurgled as Alice's tongue penetrated her tight ass.

"Let me suck, too!" Billy Jo groaned. "I've got to get my mouth on something hot and hairy, too, honey!"

Billy Jo twisted about, facing Alice's feet, and the women rolled onto their sides. Billy Jo clawed and tore at Alice's panties, shoving her skirt about her waist. When she laid her head on one of Alice's hot thighs, her face buried into Alice's cunt, Alice gave a moan and wrapped her arms about Billy Jo's hips, smashing her mouth back to that blondehaired, sugary cunt. She pulled at the tight, swelling cheeks of Billy Jo's ass, pressing her nose upon the small asshole, her tongue thrusting in and out of the hair-lined cunt swiftly.

Both women moaned in hot passion, their slurping tongues moist as they flew about each other's cunt. Being of the same mind, when Alice lapped her tongue about Billy Jo's asshole, Billy Jo would do the same with hers. When Alice penetrated Billy Jo's asshole and fucked it with her tongue, Billy Jo tongue-fucked Alice in the asshole. Their tongues darted from cunt to asshole, breathing hotly against smooth, delicious thigh flesh and ass cheeks.

Alice licked about the steamy inner cheeks of Billy Jo's ass, circling her sweet asshole and squeezing the smooth cheeks against her face, darting her tongue into the slippery pussy and then racing it back to Billy Jo's asshole. She twisted her cunt hard into Billy Jo's mouth, whimpering softly. The way Billy Jo's tongue took turns fucking her cunt and asshole was creating an enormous lust in Alice, her pussy throbbing with impending orgasm. The way Billy Jo's tight cunt sucked and squeezed her tongue, she knew Billy Jo was close to coming off, too.

When Billy Jo started to come, Alice was tongue-fucking her in the ass and Billy Jo was sucking frantically at Alice's cunt. As the spasms came, Alice pulled her tongue out of Billy Jo's asshole and began to plunge it in and out of her dripping cunt in a frenzy. They banged their cunts into each other's mouth, both shaking with the force of orgasm.

Tiredly, they pulled apart. Alice sprawled on her back as Billy Jo remained on her side, caressing Alice's thighs, gently kissing them.

"God, we're good with each other," Alice whispered.

"I know," Billy Jo said. "I think we were

drawn to each other from the beginning."

"But I still love a hard cock," Alice said.

"Mmmm, so do I," Billy Jo said, running her tongue along the inside of Alice's thigh. "Especially Matt's cock. That boy was the most delicious cock ever!"

The shadow of an idea was starting to form inside Alice's mind, but it was only a gleam at the moment. She turned back onto her side, kissing Billy Jo's thigh near her cunt. She swirled her tongue through the silky blonde cunt hair and sat up. She stroked Billy Jo's tits and kissed them.

"I wonder if he could handle both of us all the time," Alice murmured.

"Have you got some ideas, Alice?"

"I'm not sure yet," she said. "I've got to think about it a bit more."

"Whatever it is," Billy Jo said, "it's going to be a good one, I'd bet."

"I'll let you know once it's formed," Alice replied.

Needing to make one more test of Billy Jo first, she threw her leg over Billy Jo's face as the girl rolled onto her back. Then Alice pulled her knees under her body and leaned forward, kissing at the wet, blonde-haired cunt. She lowered her open pussy into Billy Jo's face, and as the girl opened her lips and thrust her tongue about her clitoris, Alice spurted a drop of piss into Billy Jo's mouth.

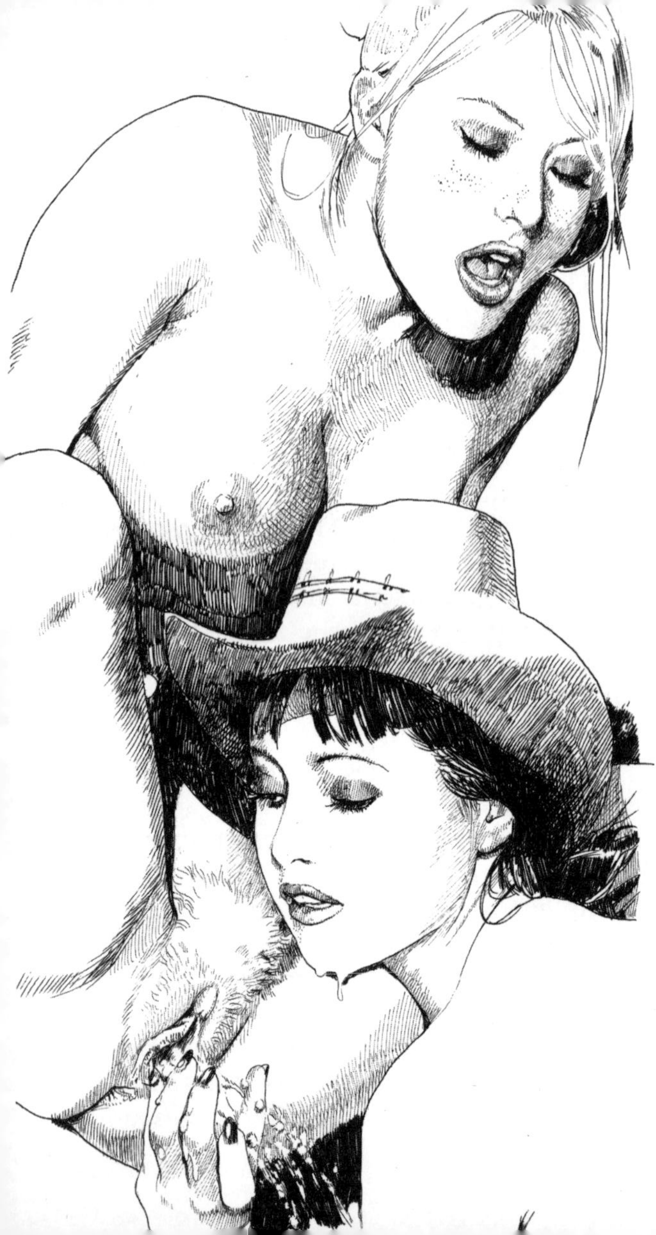

She heard Billy Jo squeal and then Billy Jo was clutching at Alice's ass cheeks, bringing her cunt down tight into her mouth, her lips wide around Alice's pussy. Alice squirted another drop of piss, letting it come out longer this time.

Billy Jo pulled her mouth away, saying in a thick, passion-filled voice, "Do it, Alice! Piss... piss in my mouth!"

A shudder of excitement went through Alice, and she began to piss quickly. As her piss flowed, she felt Billy Jo pressing her open mouth tightly into her cunt. She could hear the girl gulping and feel her tongue licking about her cunt lips. A shiver flowed through Alice's body, her eyes gazing into the girl's sugary pink cunt.

"Oooo, Billy Jo, Billy Jo," she moaned. "You, too! Please, Billy Jo, let me see you piss!"

A squeal of ecstasy bubbled from Alice when the golden stream began to spurt from Billy Jo's cunt. Alice shoved her face into it, moaning with pleasure. She opened her mouth and took the piss into it. While she kept pissing into Billy Jo's thirsty mouth, Alice smeared her face and lips into that blond-haired, pissing cunt. She wrapped her hands about Billy Jo's uplifted hips, clutching her sweet ass, drawing her face up to watch the streaming piss spurt from the lovely gash of the young girl's cunt lips, then she pressed her mouth down, gulping and swallowing as eagerly as Billy Jo was.

Holding each other tightly by the ass cheeks, Billy Jo and Alice sucked cunts, drinking each other's piss from those hairy pussies with mindless, perverse ecstasy.

Chapter 21

Matt stood in the little hall that was the entrance to their hotel suite, rubbing his balls with one hand and his eyes with the other. He was not surprised by what he saw.

Just around the corner, in the living room, his stepmother was sleeping on the floor, curled up next to Billy Jo. Both were naked. It was midmorning, and he felt great after his long night's sleep. He moved further into the living room and looked down at them. His stepmother was on her side, her creamy ass jutting back against Billy Jo's rounded hip. Alice had one leg drawn up, the other straight out. The hair around her cunt was revealed, and she was cupping one of her firm tits in the palm of her hand.

Billy Jo was sprawled on her back, one arm above her head and the other flung to one side. Her flawless titties stood up in firm roundness, tipped by pink nipples. Her chest was rising and falling evenly. Her flat stomach, with the dimple of her belly button, aroused Matt and his cock started expanding. The becoming triangle of her cunt hair looked like gleaming gold in the shaft of sunlight coming through the window. Her long, slim legs were parted, and the pink puffiness of her tight cunt sent a throb of desire about Matt's balls and lifted his cock to complete hardness.

Each woman was enticing to Matt in a different way. Both were beautiful, both had a fantastic body, both were amazing fucks, and each enjoyed sucking on his cock with vigorous enthusiasm. What more could a young boy want in the whole world? he thought. Most boys his age were still jacking off out behind the barn, but he had his choice of two really great cunts – Billy Jo and his stepmother.

Looking down at them, Matt began to pump his fist slowly back and forth on his cock. It was like waking up to live centrefolds, he thought with increasing excitement. His stepmother and Billy Jo were lovely enough to grace any magazine. In fact, both of them appeared even more beautiful to him than those unavailable centrefolds.

He scratched his balls again.

There would be no problem if he dropped down there and shoved his cock into either of those cunts. Both cunts were hot and always very wet, he knew. Neither his stepmother nor Billy Jo would complain if he fucked one – or both – of them right now.

His stepmother's clothing and Billy Jo's robe were scattered about the living room, and he knew he had missed out on some damned exciting activity the night before. Taking a lingering look at them, Matt turned and went into the bathroom. He showered and scrubbed his teeth, then pulled on a pair of jockey shorts and returned to gaze at the women once again. Finally he called room service and ordered hot coffee and cooked breakfasts for three.

The women were waking up. Billy Jo was struggling to sit already, looking at Matt as if she were disoriented for a moment. Looking down at Alice, she grinned. "My God, we fell asleep right on the fucking floor!"

There was a knock at the door. Matt went to sign for breakfast and returned, wheeling the trolley into the living room.

"Come on, wake up, sleepy head," she said softly. "Time to get up." She looked up at Matt. "Is that bacon and eggs I smell?"

He nodded proudly.

"You're a handy kid to have around, aren't you?" Billy Jo said, pleased.

"Who's handy?" Alice said, mumbling as she woke up.

Turning onto her back, she saw her stepson standing there in his jockey shorts, smiling at them. She grinned and stretched, arching her hips up. She held her arms out to her stepson, who dropped down and sprawled across his stepmother. Billy Jo sat and watched them hugging happily, grinning with pleasure. Finally she slapped Matt on his ass.

"Come on," she said. "None of that shit until after breakfast. Hey, you two! Those eggs are going to get cold... come and let's eat!"

"Oh, I suppose we better," Alice pouted, shoving her stepson off her. "But as much as I enjoy bacon and eggs in the morning, I can think of something much better to eat right now."

Billy Jo laughed. "That's because you're a cock-sucker, like me."

"And cunt-licker?" Matt offered, laughing.

"Yes, that, too," Alice replied, getting to her feet. "Do we have time to clean up a little, honey?"

"Sure, Alice," Matt said. "I can keep everything nice and warm."

His stepmother glanced at the outline of his cock inside his tight shorts. "Including that cock?"

Matt nodded. "You bet!"

Billy Jo, now standing, leaned behind Matt and pulled the shorts into the crack of his ass, making sure his cheeks showed. With a soft mewl, she kissed his ass quickly. "Now you look wonderful, Matt. Leave them that way, please."

They devoured the breakfast hungrily. While Alice and Billy Jo had second cups of coffee, Matt cleared the table. Alice and Billy Jo stared at his naked ass cheeks, his shorts still pulled into the crack. Alice realized that her stepson did, indeed, look very good that way. Seeing him so unconcerned and uninhibited caused her cunt to bubble with heat. She glanced at Billy Jo, and saw that the young girl, too, was experiencing a growing desire. Already Billy Jo's nipples were standing out and pointing almost to the ceiling. Matt's cock was straining inside those white shorts, too. It was elongated, arching upward, beautifully outlined his balls making a mouth-watering bulge below.

"Are we thinking the same thing, Billy Jo?" Alice asked, her voice becoming husky.

"I would say so, Alice."

Matt turned at the sink, his cock standing firmly against his shorts. He grinned at them, knowing very well what they were talking about. To tease them he tossed his hips forward.

"Why, he thinks his cock is indestructible!" Alice laughed.

"It damn near is," Billy Jo replied.

"Let's do something about it, Billy Jo," Alice murmured, running her hand between her inner thighs to rub her now burning cunt. "Let's take him on."

"Let's!" Billy Jo exclaimed.

"I won't fight, I promise," Matt laughed eagerly.

"You'd be a fool if you did," Billy Jo told him as she and Alice went to him.

They hugged his excited body between them. Feeling their tits rubbing at his flesh and two hairy cunts at his hips, sent Matt's cock into a roaring hardness. He wrapped his arms about them, fondling each rounded, smooth ass when they began kissing about his face. He opened his mouth wide and felt them both press their wet tongues into his mouth. The sensation of having two tongues into his mouth. The sensation of having two tongues in his mouth sent excitement racing about his young body. Hands shoved his shorts down and one of them was playing with his balls while the other caressed his cock. Each woman had a handful of his ass, too.

"Front or back?" Alice asked Billy Jo in a throaty voice.

"Either," Billy Jo replied, her voice equally husky. "It makes no difference to me."

"What are you two talking about?" Matt wanted to know.

"Oh, hush up and enjoy this," his stepmother murmured, licking her tongue across his lips. "This morning is all for you, honey."

Ranchers' Dirty Wives ★ 339

Matt's foot was placed on a kitchen chair, his other on the floor. They shoved his knee wide, and Billy Jo dropped to her knees in front of him, her tongue flicking against his thigh like liquid heat. His stepmother dropped behind him, and Matt trembled when he felt her wet, hot lips sucking at the cheeks of his ass.

Alice clutched her stepson's hips, drawing his ass backwards, her tongue fluttering up and down the crack of his ass, licking at his cheeks and delving between them. Looking down, he watched Billy Jo's wicked tongue moving along his thigh toward his balls. A ripple of pleasure shot through him when Billy Jo bounced his balls with her tongue, her blue eyes boiling up at him as she squeezed his cock in her hot hand. The tip of Billy Jo's tongue darted from her moist lips, licking up the seeping juices on his piss hole, then her hot mouth engulfed his cock.

Matt placed his hand on Billy Jo's head, more to steady himself than anything else. Billy Jo, holding the head of his cock with her lips, traced a fiery pattern about the sensitive head, flapping against his piss hole. Behind him, his stepmother was spreading the cheeks of his ass, her tongue running about the hot inner surfaces. He was feeling much too good to speak, but his breath was coming out in ecstatic gasps.

He gritted his teeth as Billy Jo slowly sucked his throbbing cock into her mouth, her hot lips sliding along the shaft in almost excruciating, teasing wetness, her eyes still sparkling with steamy pleasure up at him. Billy Jo's mouth was as hot and wet and tight as his stepmother's, drawing on his cock with her tongue and cheeks and lips. He groaned when he felt the tip of his stepmother's tongue probing at his tight asshole, wet and hot enough to scorch his flesh. Billy Jo had every inch of his cock inside her mouth now, and he could feel her throat working about his head of it, her tongue pressing it against the roof of her mouth.

Behind him, Alice was clutching her stepson's hips and pressing her mouth into his asshole, her tongue licking and fluttering against the tightly puckered hole. She was moaning softly in her perverse pleasure, her breath hot on his ass. Alice, tasting the ring of her stepson's asshole, felt her cunt pulsating in that delicious wet heat. She could hear the hungry sounds Billy Jo made as she sucked on Matt's cock, the sounds exciting her as much as what they were doing to and for him. She fluttered the tip of her hot tongue about his asshole, pressing it against the resisting tightness, her lips closed about it and sucking at the same time. Matt was arching his ass into his stepmother's face, but not so far that

Billy Jo would have any problem sucking his cock.

Billy Jo shoved her hands between Matt's legs and pulled at the cheeks of his ass, holding them spread for Alice. At the same time, Alice had shoved one hand underneath to fondle and twist tenderly on her stepson's balls while Billy Jo sucked his cock. Billy Jo's lips glided back and forth, her tongue in a constant, wet and hot, action. Her chin brushed Alice's fingers when she went forward, and as she held Matt's cock deep inside her burning, hungry mouth, Alice rubbed his balls about her chin.

As good as their mouths and tongues felt, Matt realized he would fall if they had not been pressing their faces against him this way. As it was, they were practically holding him up between them.

Billy Jo began twisting her lips as she sucked back on his cock, then gulping him into her mouth again. The wet heat of her mouth created beautiful ecstasy on his prick and in his balls. She made moist sounds as she sucked, moist and greedy sounds. Behind, his stepmother was straining to shove her tongue into his asshole. When her tongue penetrated his asshole, Matt nearly came into Billy Jo's mouth.

A grunt of pleasure exploded from his mouth and his expression of youthful pleasure was almost comical.

Alice thrust her tongue deep into her stepson's gripping asshole, then, with her lips closed hotly around it, she began to fuck him this way, her hand pulling at his balls. Below, Billy Jo kept holding the cheeks of his ass wide for Alice, her lips starting to suck faster and with more heat. He began to shake, both hands on top of Billy Jo's head. The sensations of his stepmother's tongue fucking into his asshole and Billy Jo sucking so hotly on his cock was almost too much for Matt. The whole expanse of his crotch, from his cock to his asshole, seemed to have been set on fire but with such a delicious fire.

"Suck me!" he groaned. "Oh, suck my cock, Billy Jo! Oh, you're gonna get a fucking mouthful! Alice... Alice, don't stop! Your tongue is so fucking good in my ass! Eat my asshole, Alice!"

The rumbling of his discharge boiled about inside his tightening balls, and his hips jerked to-and-fro. How his stepmother kept tongue-fucking him up the ass and Billy Jo retained her hungry lip grip on his cock, Matt didn't know. His hips jerked between them, his cock delving into Billy Jo's burning throat, then his ass pressing into his stepmother's face.

Billy Jo's tongue and mouth sucked with a fiery greed and his stepmother's tongue seemed to penetrate his asshole to his stomach.

It was something Matt had never felt before, but the sensations were so exquisite, he hoped they would do this again, and often.

His cock was about to burst, to send stream after stream of cum juice bubbling into Billy Jo's mouth. He was gritting his teeth and his eyes seemed vacant. Billy Jo drew powerfully on his cock, and his stepmother rammed her tongue in and out of his asshole. He was shaking from head to toe with ecstasy.

Both Billy Jo and Alice knew Matt was about to come, and they went at him with vigorous movements. Alice sucked at her stepson's anal ring while her tongue fucked in and out, clutching his balls in a hot hand. Billy Jo, feeling his cock throb and increase in size, gobbled him in a frenzy, her fingers squeezing the cheeks of his ass, keeping them wide for Alice's mouth. Matt began to groan, the sound rising and failing. He gave an ecstatic yelp when the come juice roared out of his balls and up his hard cock.

The come juice blasted from his piss-hole, the first spurt hitting the back of Billy Jo's mouth with some force, the next six coming in rapid succession, flooding it, almost making her choke. Moaning with hunger, Billy Jo sucked as hard as she possibly could, her throat burning with the sweetness boiling up from his precious balls. The convulsions that tore through Matt's body caused his asshole to squeeze around his stepmother's tongue, and Alice had a bit of a problem in fucking his ass with it. Billy Jo made wet gulping sounds as she swallowed the thick, delicious come juice, her tongue running about his cock furiously, her lips as tight as possible halfway down his prick.

Alice stabbed her tongue swiftly into her stepson's gripping anal sphincter, feeling a little jealous that Billy Jo was getting his cum juice. Her own cunt erupted shortly after Matt's asshole started squeezing her tongue, and she came in shuddering waves of pleasure. Billy Jo, moaning hungrily at Matt's gushing cock, shivered violently as her cunt convulsed.

Billy Jo's orgasm was so strong, she became weak, and with a wail, fell backwards, her lips coming off Matt's cock with a moist plopping sound. A final spurt of come juice burst from Matt's piss-hole, splashing upon Billy Jo's chin.

As Billy Jo's mouth left his cock, Matt was thrown off balance, and he went forward to his hands and knees, his stepmother's tongue leaving his asshole abruptly. He was on his hands and knees, panting heavily, his cock now dangling toward the floor.

"Ohhh, shit!" he moaned.

Billy Jo, sprawled on her back, writhing and twisting her ass against the floor of the kitchen, clutching her flawless tits with both hands. Behind Matt, his stepmother was sitting on her heels, her head down as she gasped for air, her eyes somewhat glazed.

"Oh, shit is right," Alice moaned.

"You bet!" Billy Jo echoed.

"I'll never be the same again," Matt said, rolling to his side weakly.

"Want to bet on that?" Alice laughed, feeling her strength returning. "Between Billy Jo and I, your cock won't be getting much rest, I promise that."

"Me, too," Billy Jo giggled, opening and closing her slim thighs, her cunt twitching.

Chapter 22

They spent what was left of the morning by the pool. Matt swam while Alice and Billy Jo talked over what the next plan should be. They would never prove that Rex had been involved in the Sanchez's deaths, but at least Alice could get rid of him as ranch manager. That was the first step. Then she should have a talk with Gus. She loved the old rancher and had been shocked, and just a tad jealous, to hear that he had been fucking Billy Jo. But that was why she had left him – their meagre sex life had become stale and routine. Billy Jo urged Alice to give it another try – there had been a lot of changes at *Los Altos*, and it was time for some plain talking. She and Alice knew what everyone wanted, and how little it would take to plan things so that everyone could win.

Later Matt joined them for a light lunch on the terrace of their suite. By then the two women had formulated a plan; there were going to be some big changes, and if the men didn't like it, too bad! Once Reed had gone and she had mended bridges with Gus, Alice would suggest they merged the two ranches; she had often heard that both would benefit from this. On the domestic side, she and Billy Jo would share the men between them. This would take a little tact and diplomacy, but nothing they couldn't handle. They both had enough sexual appetite to take on twice that number.

"It's sort of like a fantasy I once had coming true," grinned Alice. "In fact I've had it for years: I'm still in high school, and I watch a football game. I'm sitting in the bleachers, and every time one of those hunks look at me, I open my legs and give him a peek at my cunt. Before the game is over, the whole fucking team has a hard-on. I'm waiting in the showers when they come from game, naked and ready for them. I imagine how it would feel to fuck them all, one after the other. When they've fucked me, filling my cunt full of come juice, they make me suck them off, every last cock on the team."

"Mmmm, sounds like a great idea to me," Billy Jo said, hugging herself. "I'd love to do that."

"Wait, that's not all," Alice grinned lewdly. "After they make me suck them off and swallow all that delicious come juice, those guys stand in a circle around me and piss all over my body, on my cunt and tits and face and even my asshole."

"Hey, we don't need any more guys around here!" Matt said quickly. "I can take care of you two."

"You sure brag for a little shit," Alice said, caressing his face lovingly.

Billy Jo was gazing at Matt's cock. "You know, he just might be right at that. I've never seen a guy who could keep a hard-on so fucking much and for so long."

"Want to start right now?" Alice asked. "Let's go inside. We'll see if you can handle all this hot cunt, baby."

Billy Jo slipped to the floor, jerking her dress to her waist and shoving her panties down. She leaned over on her hands and knees, waggling her shapely ass sweetly, lewdly.

"You can start with me, Matt!" she cooed.

"And me," Alice gurgled, dropping to her hands and knees beside Billy Jo. When she pulled her dress to her waist, she didn't have to jerk any panties down – she was already naked! Matt looked excitedly at the two rounded asses being offered to him, his cock lurching with readiness.

Balancing themselves, Matt watched as they opened each other's blouse, and two fantastic pairs of tits came free. He saw his stepmother dip her head and close her mouth around Billy Jo's tit, sucking on it. When Alice drew back, Billy Jo did the same thing with Alice's tit.

Behind them, Matt watched as his stepmother and Billy Jo arched their backs, their cunts pooching from their slender thighs, one dark-haired and the other a golden blonde. He gazed at their twinkling assholes, seeing that Billy Jo's asshole was a pinker colour than his stepmother's. Each looked very appetizing to him.

Going to his knees, Matt leaned his face into his stepmother's cunt, licking up the wet slit and over her asshole. Alice mewled and shoved her ass into his face. Matt probed his stepmother's asshole and caressed his hand about Billy Jo's. Working a finger into Billy Jo's ass, he fucked back and forth, sliding his tongue up his stepmother's asshole.

"Oooo, fuck my ass, baby!" Alice yelped. "Fuck your stepmother up the asshole with your tongue!"

"Finger-fuck my asshole, Matt!" Billy Jo gurgled.

Matt shoved his face between the cheeks of his stepmother's hot ass, his tongue delving. At the same time he fucked Billy Jo in her young, tight ass with his finger. But then he pulled his mouth away, sliding his finger from Billy Jo's ass, and changed places. The boy tongue-fucked Billy Jo in her tight asshole and used his finger up his stepmother's ass. Alice and Billy Jo were squealing in pleasure, their shoulders on the floor now, kissing each other hungrily and squeezing tits.

Matt went from one asshole to the other for a while, sucking and licking and fingering. After a bit he stood on his knees, gazing down at the round, smooth ass of his stepmother and the equally beautiful ass of Billy Jo. He stroked his cock as he looked at them, licking his lips. Billy Jo and Alice kept kissing and sucking each other's tongue, their sweet asses high in the air with their juicy cunts pooching out invitingly to Matt.

"Fuck us!" Matt heard his stepmother sob with eagerness. "Fuck us both, baby! Take turns fucking us!"

Matt plunged his cock into his stepmother's cunt. He rammed hard, his balls slapping. Alice grunted in delight. "Oooo, that's how I need your cock, darling... real hard and deep! Oh, fuck me, Matt! Fuck my wet cunt hard!"

Thrusting his cock into his stepmother's cunt, Matt ran two of his fingers into Billy Jo's slippery, clinging pussy. Billy Jo and Alice both twisted their uplifted ass, sucking on each other's tongues again, their hands digging into naked tits.

"Me!" Billy Jo groaned. "Now fuck me, honey!"

"Fuck her, Matt!" Alice wailed.

Matt's cock pulled out of his stepmother's gripping cunt and he rammed it into Billy Jo's. Billy Jo groaned in delight and shoved her ass back to him. As he plunged his throbbing cock in and out of Billy Jo's tight pussy, he started running his finger in and out of his stepmother's cunt, then bringing it to her asshole, alternating quickly.

Within a short time, Matt began to fuck both his stepmother and Billy Jo, going from one to the other, his cock glistening with the juices of their cunts. Both pussies seemed to feel the same to him. Both were hot and juicy, both were tight, slippery. The only real difference that Matt could tell was in the colour of cunt hair, nothing else. Both his stepmother and Billy Jo wiggled and twisted their asses deliciously for him.

The very thought of her stepson shoving his cock into her cunt after it had been inside Billy Jo's, slippery with the young cunt juices, created enormous ecstasy inside Alice.

"Oooo, you're so fucking good, Matt!" she wailed loudly, licking at Billy Jo's lips. "God, your cock is so hard... so long! Fuck my hot cunt, baby! Oh, God... ram it to my hairy, wet pussy!"

"Fuck me!" Billy Jo screamed. "Fuck me, too!"

The wet, scalding heat of his stepmother's cunt seared the throbbing flesh of his prick. He was working a finger into Billy Jo's gripping asshole as he fucked his stepmother. Alice didn't have to scream for Matt to know she was coming. Her hairy cunt squeezed at his prick with convulsive tightness as she started screaming her ecstasy. The waving, rippling sensations of her cunt was like a mouth sucking his cock off. He rammed swiftly, hard and almost brutally into his stepmother's orgasming cunt his finger buried up Billy Jo's asshole, but not moving. Matt could see his stepmother's asshole flexing above his cock, see it tighten and become loose again.

He continued fucking his stepmother as she came, and slowly pulled his achingly hard cock free when she finished. He then quickly rushed his cock into Billy Jo's cunt, stabbing frantically as his stepmother moaned with the glow of her bubbling orgasm, her ass still high and writhing erotically. Billy Jo started yipping, twisting her shapely ass frantically as her orgasms steamed through her. She slammed her ass back against Matt, his cock buried to the very hilt. As her cunt went into spasms of orgasms, Matt watched as Billy Jo's asshole closed and opened.

Since his cock was still as hard as ever, his young eyes took on a mischievous gleam.

While Billy Jo was still coming, he yanked his cock from her blonde-haired cunt and, without warning, plunged it into her asshole.

"Ooohhhh!" Billy Jo screamed.

Matt grabbed Billy Jo's ass and started fucking her swiftly, his balls beating at her quivering cunt.

"That's my fucking asshole, Matt!" Billy Jo screamed as if he didn't know where his cock was. "You've got your fucking cock in my fucking asshole!"

"Yeah!" Matt laughed hoarsely.

"Ohhh, God! Ohhhh, God!"

Billy Jo wailed, but she didn't try to pull her ass off his cock. The sudden, unexpected filling of her asshole was creating a storm of lewd, erotic ecstasy inside her slender, shaking body. She lifted her head and screamed out her pleasure.

"Fuck me, fuck me! Fuck me up the ass, baby! Ohhhh, God… you're stretching my asshole… burning in my fucking ass! Ohhh, I love it! Fuck me in the ass, Matt! Oooo, shit… you're going to make me come again! Ram it to me, fuck me in my fucking asshole!"

Hearing Billy Jo scream, Alice sat back on her heels to see her stepson's cock flying in and out of Billy Jo's asshole. Her eyes glazed over and a rumbling heat went through her. She could see the stretching, pink asshole grip her stepson's cock as it went in and out from his balls to the swollen head.

"Oh, beautiful!" she gurgled. "Fuck her up the hot ass, Matt! Ahhh, give it to her fucking hot asshole!"

Billy Jo began screeching in ecstasy, tossing her saucy ass back and forth, riding his cock with her asshole, trying to twist and grind all the same time. She screamed over and over, throwing her head back, her beautiful blonde hair flying around her passion-contorted face.

"Oh, God! Give it to me, baby! Ahhhhhh, that sweet, sweet cock... fucking my hot, tight asshole! I'm coming! Ohhhhh, am I ever coming!"

The puckering tightness of Billy Jo's delightful asshole clutched at Matt's cock, making him groan with ecstasy, yet he managed to keep from coming off himself.

"I can't take any more!" Billy Jo wailed, sliding forward on the floor, her ass leaving his cock as she sprawled face down, those sweet, lovable and deliciously rounded cheeks quivering with continuous orgasms, lifting and pressing down as if she were fucking the floor with her bushy cunt.

Alice was crying eagerly. "Now me! Fuck me up the ass, Matt! Come on, I want to feel your cock up my asshole, too!"

She twisted about hurriedly, her creamy ass high in the air, her shoulders on the floor and her hands pulling at the rounded cheeks, exposing her twinkling asshole.

Matt rammed his throbbing cock hard into his stepmother's asshole. Alice gave a loud scream of surprised ecstasy as his cock stretched her asshole, thrusting all the way to his balls. The scream tearing from his stepmother's mouth increased, as did the shaking of her rounded ass.

Almost as soon as Matt rammed his cock up her asshole, Alice started cumming. He had not made a complete thrust and withdrawal before her cunt boiled into an amazing orgasm. She felt the heat and the hard throbbing sliding along the ring of her tight ass, the friction fast and hot enough to burst into flame.

"Oh, Matt!" Alice screamed in passion. "Matt, Matt… God, Baby! So good! Mmmm, baby, give it to me! Hump my naked ass, darling! Ahhh, ram that sweet cock… bang my ass… fuck my asshole!"

Alice's words were incoherent, tumbling from her mindlessly. Her body was flooded with sensational ecstasy, the sheer perversity of being fucked in her ass by her stepson making her feel so lewd, so deliciously lewd! She could not believe the strength of her orgasms, nor the searing heat. The only thing she knew was ecstasy. Her asshole felt stretched like never before, the tight elastic ring gripping her stepson's hard, pounding cock like a scalding vise of flesh. It felt to her as if her cunt would melt from her body, that her muscles would snap and her bones shatter. The slapping of her stepson's stomach against her naked ass seemed loud in the room, creating waves of shivering pleasure to race about her creamy flesh.

Through it all, Alice felt her stepson's cock increasing in size, throbbing beautifully deep inside her burning asshole. She could even feel his balls beating upon the hairy lips of her spasming cunt and extremely inflamed clitoris.

The orgasms steaming through her caused her asshole to tighten and grip Matt's cock. It seemed to be sucking his cock, flexing with fiery heat. It couldn't be possible, her raging mind said. Her asshole couldn't suck a cock! There was no way a person's asshole sucked... yet hers was sucking frantically on Matt's cock!

Matt was fucking in a frenzy, on his knees, gripping his stepmother's sweet hips with his fingers, his eyes enormous as he watched his cock being devoured by her asshole. His balls were so tight, they felt painful. His come juice was boiling, ready to spurt, yet for some reason it didn't. He kept fucking into his stepmother's clutching asshole with short, powerful strokes, driving in to his balls then pulling back with just the tip of his cock inside her fiery asshole.

Alice was thrusting her naked ass back at him with desperate motion. She wanted him to cum off inside her ass, wanted to feel his sweet cum juice bursting deep up her asshole.

Billy Jo had rolled onto her back now, watching with still burning eyes, her legs apart, cunt showing.

Suddenly Matt yelled.

But it was too late.

His stepmother had become too weak, and she flopped forward when he drove hard into her asshole. She sprawled on the floor, and her stepson, still on his knees, grasped his cock frantically, jerking on it swiftly, moaning with disappointment.

Alice turned around, stretched out beside Billy Jo, her eyes still hot and showing that she, too, was disappointed.

Come juice started flying from Matt's cock, his fist pounding it in a frenzy. The come juice gushed from his piss-hole and splashed upon the thick hair of his stepmother's cunt, getting on her pulsating pussy lips. He even came on Billy Jo's cunt, but it was due more to the wild way he was jerking off than by any plan.

Alice and Billy Jo stared at his cock, feeling the come juice splatter upon their cunts. They both spread their legs wide, arching up to get as much come juice as they could on their hairy cunts.

As the spurting ended, Matt sank back on his heels, panting heavily, still clinging to his cock. "Oh, shit!" he snorted in disappointment. "I wanted to come in your asshole, Alice!"

"I know you did, honey," Alice said.

She saw the glistening come juice on the golden hair of Billy Jo's cunt, her tongue running over her lips. Billy Jo and Alice had the same idea at the same time.

"Let's do it!" Billy Jo said, eagerly.

With squeals, Alice and Billy Jo turned and faced each other, their long tongues licking through cunt hair and at the wet slit of each other's cunt.

Matt watched them licking up his come juice, their faces becoming smeared with it. He kept watching until they had licked it all away, and then begin to tongue-fuck each other, lying on their sides.

With a giggle, he got to his feet and arched his hips forward. And then, without warning them, he began to piss.

Moans came from Billy Jo and his stepmother as he pissed all over them. As their naked bodies were drenched with his piss, they sucked at each other's cunt with a fury of hunger, of once again mindless passion.

Matt aimed the golden stream upon his stepmother's cunt and Billy Jo's face. Billy Jo turned her face up into it, opening her mouth to let him piss into it, then going back to Alice's cunt with a squeal of ecstasy. He ran his pissing stream up the two writhing bodies to his stepmother's face. Matt pissed into his stepmother's mouth and then onto Billy Jo's cunt. She laughed happily when his stepmother rammed her face back into that honey-blonde pussy, sucking and licking at his piss.

By the time it was over, Alice and Billy Jo had sucked each other to an orgasm again, their bodies drenched in Matt's piss, their hair matted to their skulls. They pulled apart, both of them gazing up at Matt, their eyes smouldering in the perversity of wanton lust.

Alice lifted her arms to her stepson. "Come down here with us, baby," she whispered softly. "You belong between Billy Jo and me."

Matt snuggled between the naked bodies of his stepmother and his new sister-in-law. Alice and Billy Jo turned to face him, kissing his cheeks and fondling his cock and balls.

"You'll come up my asshole next time,"

his stepmother murmured against his ear, her tongue probing it.

"And mine," Billy Jo said, tickling his other ear with her tongue.

Matt wiggled happily between their smooth bodies, his cock starting to swell again under the stroking fingers of his stepmother and lovely little Billy Jo.

Chapter 22

"Honey... lover!" Danny exclaimed as his young bride eagerly licked his cock.

He had been out of his cast for less than a day, and this was the first chance he'd had to fuck her since his accident. But she seemed happy to go on doing what she had done for him when he was laid up in bed.

Danny couldn't complain – his bride's oral lovemaking was very good. But his prick ached with the need to burrow into her warm, wet flesh.

"Baby, get on top of me!" he said, trying to wrench her head away from his upthrust, waggling dong. "Now that we've got the chance, let's screw."

"I want to screw this sweet thing!" Billy Jo said passionately as she rubbed his moist, hard pecker against her cheek. "But I've got to talk to you first."

"Talk at a time like this?" Danny rasped unbelievingly.

"Yes! Right now."

"Well, what the hell is it?" he demanded, clutching her by the chin and forcing her to look at him.

Billy Jo scrambled forward to lie beside him on the bed. She gripped his hard prick and stroked it gently.

"Darling, I have to confess," she began. "While you were in that awful cast, I did something that maybe you won't like."

"What, for Christ's sake?" he asked anxiously. He just wanted to get the talk over with, so he could sink his throbbing hardness into her sweet, tight cunt.

"I... well, I wasn't exactly true to you."

"What?"

"Please, darling – now don't be upset." She stroked his prick a bit harder. "I... had sex with Seth."

"No," Danny moaned. But he couldn't seem to get angry – not while Billy Jo was diddling him so well.

"And with Hank," she added.

"Sonofabitch!" he exclaimed. But he didn't move to get away from her or to stop her hand from gliding up and down on his blissfully pulsating rod.

"And... with your father," Billy Jo continued.

"And with… your little brother Matt and your stepmother, too. Both at once."

"Dad, Matt and Alice too?" the young man gasped. "*Jeez-us Kerr-rist*, Billy Jo!"

"Hush now. Don't blame them. It was all my fault. I wanted to do it with all of them."

"*God damn!*" he panted. "I reckon I'm… married to a… shit, baby, that feels good!"

"I'll bet it does," Billy Jo said, still stroking – but not hard enough to make him come. "Just like it felt good to me when I fucked your brothers and father. And they liked it, too. But we were all so worried that you'd find out."

"So now you… went and told me!" Danny writhed as he panted.

"Because you have a right to know," Billy Jo said. "You're my husband, and I love you."

"Still? After being with… my whole fuckin' family?"

"Yes! You're my man, Danny, and I won't look at anybody else, ever again, unless you tell me it's all right."

Billy Jo quickly slithered atop him and encompassed his hot pecker in her wet, clutching hole.

"Ah!" he exclaimed. "Oh, that feels great!"

His bride began to fuck him slowly, grinding and pumping. Her silken cunt seemed to suck at his hard, thrusting manhood.

"But I was thinking," Billy Jo said, "How nice it would be... for everyone..." She punctuated her phrases with skillful thrusts of her pussy, swallowing Danny's hard cock all the way to his balls. "If we could all... live and love together... like one big, happy family. I'd enjoy it and... it wouldn't mean I... loved you any less."

"But Jesus, I... oh God damn, baby, just screw me!"

Billy Jo smiled down, her blue eyes shining, her blonde hair framing her lovely face. "You mean it's all right? You don't object?"

"Well, it'll take some... getting used to. But if that's what you... want..."

"Lover!" Billy Jo exclaimed. "Oh, my wonderful, big, sweet husband!"

She lay forward, squashing her full tits against his manly chest, and screwed him with a fervor which surpassed even her performance with any of her brothers. Groaning blissfully, Danny bucked upward in her tight clutches. His balls swirled. His head grew light.

When he came, it was like the burst of a geyser in Billy Jo's belly. She screamed with delight and ground down around him, vibrating from head to toes in the most sublime orgasm she had yet known.

"Darling, we're going to have such good times!" she said afterward, petting him as their loins remained locked in a warm, wet embrace. "It'll be wonderful!"

"Well, like I said, it'll take some getting used to."

But the more Danny thought about it, the easier the proposed adjustment seemed. He could hold his own against Hank, Seth and Matt, he believed – certainly against his old man. And he would be king of the castle, because Billy Jo was his! And then there was Alice. He'd always had the hots for his stepmother. He assumed that if it was open season for his wife and kid brother, then there was another benefit of the arrangement. That is, as long as Billy Jo always remembered who was boss.

"You've got to promise," he said, "that if I decide to put a stop to the sharing, that's it! You'll be mine and nobody else's."

Billy Jo hugged him and kissed his neck. "Oh, yes. I promise, darling! Whatever you say goes… always."

Danny grinned. An interesting future seemed to lie ahead – for Billy Jo, him, and the whole McCluskie clan.

Epilogue

Nowadays, the old bunkhouse at the McCluskie ranch was more often used for family parties and social events than anything else. The cots were still there; ready for when the hired hands would come for the annual roundup of the cattle and to drive them into Mulberry. Now the cowboys would spend only a couple of nights a year, maybe, no more.

This Thanksgiving, Alice had laid on a superb dinner for the reunited family. The bunkhouse's interior appeared lovely in the soft light of oil lamps and candles. Rosita, who had helped prepare the food and lay the table, would join the table later, when she had finished serving them. And, to everyone's surprise, Viv Lanier, looking simply ravishing, had joined them – at Alice's request. After his sacking, she had been left high and dry by Rex and had thrown herself upon Alice's mercy. Feeling sorry for her, and thinking that the brothers might well do with another attractive woman around the place, she had promised to give the pretty redhead a few days' trial as her secretary next week. Alice liked the way she looked, too, and at her insistence, Hank and Seth had apologised to Viv for the way they had treated her, apologies which she had accepted with good grace.

With Alice and Gus at either end, they all sat down to a long trestle table that positively groaned with food; the older McCluskie couple now shared a bed just as before, but with a newfound happiness. Billy Jo had joined them one evening and the three of them had made wild, uninhibited love far into the night. Danny, Seth and Hank had also enjoyed their stepmother's body both singly and all together. When she told Gus this, he first looked surprised, then amused.

"Heck, Gus," said Alice a little defensively, "next to Billy Jo seems I had a lot of catching up to do."

Gus's weather beaten features cracked into a lopsided grin.

"Well, I guess we McCluskie boys never minded sharing a good thing, after all."

The wine flowed and the conversation was lively, full of extravagant boasts and challenges; the air fairly crackled with sexual innuendo. The women giggled and the men guffawed. At one point Hank took a wager with Seth as to who would show her tits first, Viv or Billy Jo. Alice overheard and, laughing, reached behind to undo her brassiere. Then she unbuttoned her blouse and treated everyone to a lingering show of her magnificent breasts, tweaking the nipples until they hardened.

At the end of the meal, Gus banged his spoon on the table and cleared his throat. The room fell silent.

"As you know, I ain't much for long speeches so, hell, I'll just say 'let the party begin'!"

Cowboy whoops greeted this announcement and in no time the two McCluskie wives had stripped to the buff, with their husbands and brothers-in-law quickly following suite. Viv, a little bashful at first, was soon down to her panties as she took first one, then another of the McCluskie males' hard cocks in her mouth. Even Rosita, the buxom little Mexican maid, wore only her white frilly apron and started to suck the youngest brother's cock as if her life depended on it, while he in turn started to lick delve his agile young tongue into his stepmother's cunt.

"Jest look at that boy, why he's at that pussy faster'n a duck on a June bug," laughed an admiring Hank to Billy Jo as he slipped into her from behind.

"Hell, this ain't my first rodeo," Matt protested, grinning at his elder brother.

"Had a good teacher in Billy Jo, too, s'far as I recall," gasped Alice as she neared her first orgasm under her stepson's skilful, but merciless, tongue.

Soon the orgy was in full swing, with all

four women enjoying the varied attentions of the five males: Seth fucking Billy Jo from behind while she thrust back energetically, grinning at him over her shoulder as she saw his face begin to contort with his first climax.

"Have to do better'n that, Seth honey," she laughed as, gripping her hips and lettting out a deep groan of satisfaction, the lean cowboy spurted his seed in several strong jets deep into the squeezing, velvety tunnel of her vagina.

"Don't you fret, Billy Jo, I got plenty more of that, any time you want it!" boasted Seth; his place was instantly taken by his father. Gus first dipped his thick, stiff penis into Billy Jo's dripping cunt and then, suitably lubricated, positioned the head at the brown pucker of her anal sphincter and started to press in.

"Oh, *Daddy!*" squealed his blonde, lissom daughter-in-law as the handsome older rancher gently pushed his pecker deep into her bowels. "That's right, fill me up, Daddy, fill your dirty daughter-in-law right up to your big, heavy balls," she groaned, "then shoot me full of your thick, creamy cum!"

But Gus McCluskie had more ambitious plans. Holding Billy Jo tightly around her midriff, he flipped them both into a prone position on the floor that was strewn with bright, decorative Navajo rugs. The sexy young

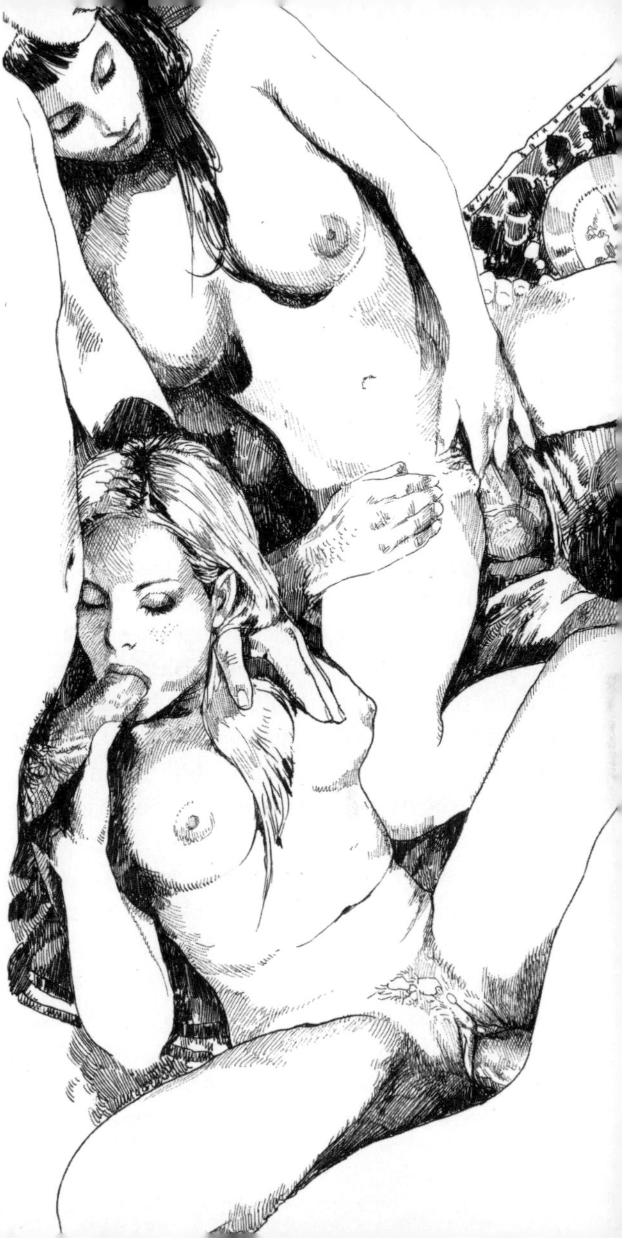

bride sat, impaled, on his hard, skewering cock, her legs hanging limply outside his own. Gus started to drive his stiff meat fluidly up into her tight, clutching anus as she groaned with a strange mixture of pain and sensual delight.

Through half-closed eyes she could see Hank push his way through the twisting bodies before them and kneel between their splayed legs; he gripped his large, erect manhood in his right hand and then parted her swollen pussy lips in order to introduce his cock into her cunt more easily. Billy Jo prepared herself for the ordeal of this double impalement as Hank slid his cock into the molten interior of her already well-fucked, sperm-drenched cunt; only a thin membrane separated father and son's plunging poles of flesh. She sighed with pleasure as she was buffeted between the two men, a quiver of excitement starting between her spastically twitching legs and building into waves of pleasure that swept over her with greater and greater intensity. She sensed someone above her and looked up, a little surprised to see that Alice was straddling the churning, bucking trio.

"I have a little gift for you, dear," she smiled and with that Alice bent her legs in a half-squat so that her big, hair-fringed cunt was no more than a couple of inches above Billy

Jo's upturned face. Billy Jo saw that Alice, too, had been recently fucked and that one or more males had deposited an impressive load of viscous sperm in her vagina, for a thick, white liquid was now seeping out between her hairy labia and falling like heavy, warm drops of rain on her nose, mouth and forehead.

"Open your mouth, Billy Jo – it's your husband's cum. Open your mouth, darlin' and swallow it all…"

The young blonde wife did more. She glued her parted lips to the older woman's fleshy, swollen cunt and tongued and sucked the delicious mixture of juices, swallowing repeatedly until Alice started to buck and twitch her cunt on Billy Jo's mouth like the rider of a skittish bronco at a rodeo.

Ohhhh… fuck, *fuck* yes, that's it honey, yes, darlin', I'm cummmmming… now… *now, NOW!*"

Me too, thought Billy Jo happily, as the bunk house filled with the happy grunts, groans, moans and whimpers of the extended McCluskie family. Me too…

THE END

Just a few of our many titles for sale...

Lazonby's Heiress
Little does Alison realise her duties as secretary of Lazonby Hall include being a sexual 'play-doll' for the lascivious desires of all in the house. Mrs. Simpson is Mistress of the Hall in name, but now it's Alison's luscious young body that holds the title!
£7.50

Helen's Southern Comfort
In the heat of the night Danny watches as his innocent wife is treated to pleasures she has never experienced before by his well-endowed neighbour. So begins a journey of sexual discovery for the Nielson's that takes them to the very edges of extreme sexual practices.
£7.50

Highland Seduction
Amanda's visit to the Scottish Highlands becomes a nightmare as increasingly bizarre sexual ordeals are heaped upon her by the predatory residents of Sandaid Manor. Even her handsome husband cannot save her from the degrading ordeal to which she is subjected.
£7.50

The Education of Catherine Peterson
Bored, beautiful Catherine wants a job with her husband's firm. She gets one only to discover her husband's infidelity. Soon, the couple are sucked into a vortex of lust from which they cannot escape – even if they wanted to. Office sexual politics were never quite like this.
£7.50

Los Angeles Girl & Punishment for Claudia
Special double edition. Model and virgin, Della, finds herself giving more than she wants to on her photo-shoots in Los Angeles Girl. Claudia is a Nazi spy in wartime USA with a penchant for spanking, being spanked and submissive sex in Punishment for Claudia.
£12.50

Orderline: 0871 7110 134
Customer Service: 0800 026 25 24
Email: eros@eroticprints.org

WWW.EROTICPRINTS.ORG